# King of the Jungle

### KS Silkwood

UNTHANK

First published in 2013
By Unthank Books
www.unthankbooks.com

Printed in England by Lightning Source, Milton Keynes

A CIP record for this book is available from the British Library

Any resemblance to persons fictional or real who are living, dead or undead is purely coincidental.

ISBN 978-0-9572897-1-0

Cover artwork & design by Tommy Collin

# Part One

# 1

Yeah, I see you, baby. Come walk this way, don't be shy. Yeah, throw me a quick look. I'm here every day and you know it. Every day you come in and sit on the grass. And every day I'm here, reading a book, sitting in a deck chair under the tree, an Indian Horse Chestnut. You walk that way in and this way out, just so I notice. Well, I have. I notice all of you walking that way in, walking this way out. I'll never acknowledge you. I'll never say hello, never say good-bye. Do you know what would happen if I started being nice to you? Do you? We'd get married. There, is that what you want? Because that's what would happen. We'd go out, have fahhhhhn-tastic sex, fall in love, get married and live happily ever after. Amen.

Think I'll stop reading now and go and sit in my mess room.

Oh, thank God. Twenty more minutes and I can close those doors and it's unofficial lunchtime. I'm exhausted. 'I can only give you four weeks work.' Those were my boss's exact words exactly four years ago. Thanks, that's all I need, I said. Four weeks. And four years later I'm sitting with my legs up against the dirty fridge, skiving, waiting for one o'clock so I can have my official lunch. If big, bad Mr. Council came round now and caught me? Well, fuck you, Charlie! I don't care about the new contract or about working hand in hand with my local community; no, not at all. And you know what else? I've shortened the sleeves of my polo shirt. I don't

3

care if that falls under personalising uniform, long baggy sleeves are just not flattering.

I based my look on David Byrne of Talking Heads performing *Psycho Killer* on *The Old Grey Whistle Test* from January 1978. The colour combination is similar enough, and what with the dirty cloud grey combats, and the cheap polo shirt faded from washing it on 50 degrees instead of thirty, the yellow is now mellow thankyouverymuch. Oh, I'm a real live wire all right.

I love lunchtime. All the girls from the surrounding offices come in and lounge about on the grass; right outside my mess room! Office types, but pretty. And some are clearly from some sort of magazine publishing house or something - they have a kind of *fashion* look; or perhaps they actually are followers of fashion. I'm not sure I'd thought of that before. You see, I'm a snob. Yes, I work in a garden. Yes, you could call me a Park Keeper. But I'm not your orthodox Park Keeper. For starters, I'm not an alcoholic, and I don't drink White Lightning or Special Brew in a mug to make it look like I'm only drinking tea. So, I'm not an alcoholic, although I do drink. Like last night, I was out, but only socially, only with friends; and I'm not talking about the homeless-tramps-smackheads-prostitutes and the crack whores. Not those friends. No.

Here comes Frenchie. She's not French but I thought she looked it. Then one day I heard her on her mobile, and she's English, with a nice southern English accent. Like where this public garden is. Anyway, messy dark haired Frenchie, always lies down after a salad, pulling her top up to just beneath her pleasantly small breasts, exposing her belly to the summer sunshine. She tries. She has started to try. And by that I mean she walks that way in, but walks this way out and past me. Last week, I saw the beginning of a smile as she went by, but my work colleague was in the way, and I couldn't see through his head while he was telling me (again!) about his old job as a litter picker in Hyde Park. So she smiled at the back of his head instead. I would have caught that smile if I could've seen through his head. I might have smiled back, and then we would have gone out, had fahhhhhntastic sex, fallen in love, got married and lived happily ever after. Amen. See how this works? See how I have to occupy myself to get through the day? See how because of an inherent capacity to sabotage, I am sitting here, have been sitting here, for four years? Yeah, it's funny. It's hilarious, isn't it?

Fourteen more minutes. Official lunch is fourteen minutes away and then I'm safe. For one whole official lunch hour I can sit outside under the Indian Horse Chestnut and read my book, occasionally glancing up to see if the girls are in. There's more than just Frenchie. There are quite a few who play the game. That way in, this way out. Some look over just to check, to see if I'm sitting there. Or maybe not. That has crossed my mind you know. I'm a sabotager, not an idiot. A sabotager, not a saboteur. Surely a sabotager is someone who sabotages himself, while a saboteur sabotages others? Right? Right? Come on . . . humour me.

Anyway, you see, I'm inconspicuous under this tree, it's actually out of the way. So how do they know I'm here? Because they do. Because I don't look like an orthodox Park Keeper. I don't look like a tramp for a start. And I didn't used to be a tramp, which seems to be part of the previously required application criteria. But things are changing. When I joined, tramps were working the parks and gardens. And other tramps were their friends. I mean it! A pack of tramps set up, like, a Tramp Sanctuary in a wildlife area of one of the larger gardens, with the full support and blessing of the Park Keeper. He used to drink with some of them before he dried out. He's like a dead man walking now. I think that groundhog day scenario keeps them alive. Without it, with a renewed and conscious everyday ability to engage, they grow old quickly. It's a realisation that time does exist beyond the bottle and the daily sedation that comes with it.

Oh, and sadly, Mr Fuck You Charlie Council discovered the Sanctuary one day and called in the pigs to kick them out.

# 2

Another day, another . . . day. Yep, it's 07:32 and I'm back. Empty the bins, bury the tramp shit; it's a beautiful Thursday summer morning! Just the start I like. I'm on the long week, which means working the morning shift, with Saturday, Wednesday and Thursday being fourteen hour days. Sunday's a lie in, just a thirteen hour day. Day of rest? Monday and Tuesday and Friday are half days, just 07:30 to 15:00. Short days. Only seven and a half hours, with my work colleague arriving at one o'clock so I can have official lunch. Then I'm off from 15:00 Friday until 13:00 Monday. In on Tuesday, off Wednesday and Thursday, back 13:00 Friday and the long shift. Love the summer shift. I know, it sounds complicated, but it really isn't. You get used to it.

07:52 and I'm bored already. I never used to get bored, this is a relatively new feeling. I used to have something to do, something to keep my mind occupied. If we keep going I may tell you, but don't hold your breath because that side of this story is none of your business. What's it got to do with you? Nothing. There, it must be serious because I hate the word 'got'. It's like 'rot' or 'gut', isn't it?

Anyway, the first of the drunks have arrived. They're waiting for me to open the gates. GATES OPEN AT 8 O'CLOCK, IDIOTS. But then, they are drunks and tramps and homeless and smackheads and and and. See? No wonder I'm bored already, there's no respite, a daily fucking grind of the same bullshit. Oh, yeah, I've heard this one before: I'm jus' two weeks, two weeks from goin' into rehab, guv', honestly I am. Yeah, me too, I'm always just weeks away from rehabilitation myself, but more of that another time because now that I've opened the gates it's time for my breakfast: coffee and an organic croissant. Fucking tramps are drinking Super already. 08:03. That's what I like to see! Dedication! I hope Ronald Polio shits himself today. I hope his alcoholic diarrhoea soaked jeans dry in the 28 degree heat and he staggers about, shitting and pissing himself all day and to death. One day he surely will.

This is not a good sign. I must be nice, I must be nice, I must be nice.

# 3

They're all gardeners. They're all fucking gardeners. Everyone I meet's a fucking gardener. It's amazing. I know I work in a garden, but I must be the only person who's not a fucking gardener! Imagine that. So who's place am I taking? Answers in good time; if ever at all. I'm not being deliberately awkward, well, yes, I am, but you'll see, you'll find that I am quite difficult and awkward, one might say unnecessarily awkward, in fact. But contrast that with how nice I am as well, and can you see, can you see it? A picture is forming. Yeah, like a Ro . . .

Ahhh . . . Nearly, yeah? Nearly had me then. The confession of it all. We're so confessional now, aren't we? Does no one treasure anonymity any more? You know what I'm saying. What makes you think you're so important? Good-bye person. I won't even call you a friend because we've only just met and I'm not that nice.

Sorry. Let me apologise. Please. I'm sorry. End of shift irritation. You see, this geezer comes up to me and says, 'What is this tree called?' And I said, 'Jonathan.' And he said, 'Sorry?' And I said, 'Shhh, don't mind him, Jonathan, he doesn't know.' The geezer blinked and said, 'Is it a Horse Chestnut of some kind?' And I said, 'I don't know, but if you'd like to discuss Tarkovsky's debt to Bergman then' . . . And he says, 'Why the interest in classical music?' And I said, 'If I meant Tchaikovsky I would have said Tchaikovsky's debt to Balakirev' . . . It was at this point, the geezer, a tourist of Australian extraction, said: *I'm a gardener too . . .* '

So I told him it was an Indian Horse Chestnut.

Because everyone's a gardener . . .

# 4

Where is my favourite ever work colleague? Where is Graham? Or Smeagol, as I call him - because that's what he looks like. Northern Irish, sixty in September, and a lifetime of modest low maintenance, low intelligence jobs, in the rubbish and litter industry. A short, bald man of Smeagolesque aesthetic, the litter is truly precious to him.

He refused to bury a tramp shit once. Point blank refused, even though it was done on his shift. Oh, I wasn't pleased when I saw it. It was like a cow pat. A cow pat tramp shit. Perfect. Anyway, after some slightly awkward debate, I took the pain, dug a hole, and slid it (well, more sort of scooped really) into the hole with a stick . . . See? Dreams can come true!

It's Friday, he's late. It's 12:42 and he's late. He starts at 13:00. But despite me telling him I don't want him here until 12:55, he always comes in early, sometimes half an hour early. I've given up. He doesn't want to be late for a job that on that shift it doesn't matter if he's late so long as he's here before I need to leave. That's dedication for you. He's late today. I hope he hasn't fallen off his bike because I want to go at 14:00. Yeah, I know that's an hour early, but so what? I need to leave early, get a start on the weekend and . . . That's none of your business. What's it got to do with you? Nothing. That's what.

# 5

Oh, my head. Graham's gone. I sent him away. I staggered in to work today, and dear God, it's hot, I'm sweating, and yes, I'm hungover. Severely. My head is hurting. I have to put it like that because if I really described it, I might actually accept that I feel that bad. It's psychology. A state of mind. When I woke up this morning I felt okay, drained, but I felt quite reasonable. Then, on the way in, I don't know what happened. I suddenly felt like shit. Absolute shit. Panadol Acti-fast, where are you? Come on. Go away, Frenchie. I don't want you to see me like this, as this dehydrated husk that the sun shrivelled up like a Hammer Horror; and it hurts, my head really, really hurts.

King Kong. Much better now. A little sleep and a lot of water, plus three Acti-fasts, and I have managed to initiate some sort of recovery; it's past the worst. Oh, I know I won't sleep tonight. The alcoholic sweats and the racing mind desperately attempting to remember just how it was that I happened to get into that wretched, spiteful condition in which I found myself.

But what a weekend. What a . . . Oh yeah? What's it got to do with you? What. Does it have. To do. With you? Zero, my hero. I'm going to empty the bins. Find that interesting if you can. Come on, come with me. I'll show you how interesting emptying bins is. Brace yourself, it's a fucking roller coaster.

This is what I mean. Look at this. Fuckers are sitting right next to the bin, and yet . . . Rubbish everywhere. Some teen gangsters were sitting here, so it's cans of Red Bull and pools of flob all over the place. Oh, and some new graffiti. Edgware Road Posse. At least that's what it looks like. No simple generic type used here. No Helvetica or something nicer, something like Futura Extra Bold. I think I read somewhere that Stanley Kubrick liked using Futura Extra Bold, even for his **STAY OUT, PRIVATE PROPERTY** signs. And, of course, the titles for *Eyes Wide Shut*.

Let's see, shall I empty this bin or just squash the contents down? What do you think? Squash of course! I'll be fucked if I'm going to empty it just for this lousy amount of litter. I will recycle the cans though. Hmmm, Special Brew, K cider, and Super. Nice. That's good to see. My Tramp Posse have been in, and good boys that they are, they've put their cans in the bin. See how well I've trained them? It's all about mutual respect. We respect each other. They even know not to ask me for money; isn't that good?

Bollocks. I hate getting caught sorting the bins. And it's more full than I thought. Ummm, okay, I'll have to do this one, but that's it. And I'll walk this way, rather than that way round to the black wheelie bin, because I don't want to be seen doing my duty in front of Office Girl. She's looking over . . . *Jesus!* Not now! Not while I'm doing this! Why's she do it? The one time I'm emptying the bin and she comes in and sees me. It's a trauma all right.

Now, luckily, I'm quite adept at making it seem like it's a chore, but one that I'm nonchalant about, sort of like aloof, a reinvention of the actual act to the point where it doesn't seem like I'm emptying a bin at all. Like I'm looking down on you because I don't care that I have to do this. That's how I think I justify it - come on, humour me, just a little bit. *Fine.* And now look. Office Girl is only walking towards me, nice legs, baby, and see, she's smiling at me as she walks past and sits on the bench. Well, look, I'll let you into a secret. I returned that smile, but coy-like, not like a greeting but like a private glance, a signal that could lead to more on another day. Hah! If only she knew. Did I mention the falling in love, having fahhhhhntastic sex, followed by getting married and living happily ever after? Not for a while. That gag must be fading . . .

She's quite pretty, although possibly more well-groomed than pretty. And it would be unfair of me to lead her on with nice smiles and flirty looks; because I don't mean it, any of it. I'm not that nice. And it's dangerous for me to be nice. I don't think I've mentioned that, have I? Yeah, it's a danger for all concerned, my being actually nice, believe me.

Because, you see, here I empty bins and bury tramp shit. Here, I wear a uniform, albeit modified, a breach of Council and company rules; a sackable offence in fact. Here, I wear this uniform. But the main thing is that to these people, to Frenchie and Office Girl, to the Irish Fairy, to the homeless-tramps-smackheads-prostitutes and the crack whores, to the police, to my bosses, to *these* people I am someone else, someone *good* . . . HAH! If only they knew what we know, yeah? I'm nice in a certain way, but really that's me being horrible. It'll all make sense in the end. Or sooner than that; I can't decide which. Time to sit down and read a book.

# 6

Oh God, those mid-week days off just fly by and before you know it it's Friday and you're back at work. If you can call this work. You may be wondering what it is I actually do. Yeah, I know, it had to come up at some point, in more detail, to provide some sort of clarity. Well, the truth is I'm not really sure any more. You see, I've been rebranded, (remember: Talking Heads, *Old Grey Whistle Test*, circa 1978) and now I don't really do anything. Thank you, Mr Charlie Council, I come on your face.

Basically, because there's now a gardening team that does all the work, I only have to open the gates, empty the bins, bury the tramp shit, wait many hours, and then lock the gates. Before the brain wave rebranding, I did all the gardening (I AM NOT A GAR-DENER). I mowed the lawns, pruned the bushes, dead headed the roses, *et cetera, et cetera, et cetera*. For the same money. The same actual money. Oh, this is a low paid job all right, but it's also low maintenance; even more so, now that all I have to do is walk about a bit. Genius.

This may lead you to ask the question: *So, come on then, what is it you actually do all day?* I've tried telling you - nothing. *Nothing.* Or walking sometimes. Walk. About. A high visibility deterrent for the drunks, the tramps, the smackheads, the crack whores, the degenerates and the mentals. Am I repeating myself? It's a repetitive job. What else? Sit under the Indian Horse Chestnut re-reading *The*

14

*Magus*, or dreaming of another life . . .

My other life.

Yeah, perhaps. That might be what I do. It's difficult to say because there's a chance I'm avoiding thinking about that too much. Wow, that was almost reflective without disguising my feelings with deflection, sarcasm, or explicit use of language . . .

# 7

Well, I'm early for a Sunday, 08:24. Think I'll get the paper. The Sunday Times. I like the Culture, don't I? And the Sport section. Style mag's not too bad, but sometimes it's predictably generic on gender politics and articles. The food bit's good though. I used to like that mental, the geezer who makes food out of frozen molecules and intravenous bacteria. That's what it seems like anyway.

Oh, perfect. This is brilliant. Look at this. It's a Sunday and it's 08:30. A member of the public is looking at the opening times on the board which, incidentally, I have colour coded for easy understanding. You'd be surprised how confused people get by GREEN STICKER = OPEN, RED STICKER = CLOSED. He's squinting, Subway and the Sunday Mirror under his arm. Look at those shorts. He's probably five years younger than me but looks ten years older. Excuse me a minute, I'm going to put him out of his misery.

'Garden opens at nine o'clock.'

'Oh, right. Okay.'

I unlock the gate, open the gate, close the gate. Lock the gate. I'm about to go to my mess room when:

'Can't I come in anyway?'

'Garden opens at nine o'clock.'

'Can't I come in now?'

'If I let you in I'd have to let everyone in. And the garden opens at nine o'clock.'

'Yeah, look. Everyone.'

'You'd be surprised how quickly . . .'

'Cunt.'

'You have a nice day.'

'Fuck you.'

Then he walks off. It's Sunday and it's only 08:33.

Once, I went to a Danger At Work, no, wait, *Violence* At Work seminar. My work colleagues, suffering various degrees of hang-over dehydration, alcohol withdrawal, and general social degeneracy, were twitching and hee-hawing, occasionally scuffling and wrestling each other; but not in a gay way. It was like watching a pack of ungroomed baboons. I wonder what that makes me? King Baboon?

King of the baboons.

Anyway, at this seminar, the fat dude, with his pleasantly authoritative voice and a cheerful manner, gave us the low down on how to deal with Violence and the Public. The conflict side, the aggressive confrontational side. Apparently, we just walk away. Yeah, we just walk away. That's it. Approach. Aggravate. Walk away. Because that's what happens. That is how it works. Someone does something wrong. You walk over (with weary resignation). They get angry. And then you walk away. Who wins? Do I win? Moral high ground? I said this, the Approach, Aggravate, Walk Away line, and the fat dude laughed. Everyone laughed. I'm so funny. Did he think I was joking or did he know I was right? Maybe it sounded like a joke, so everyone laughed because they thought that was what they were supposed to do.

Jimmy, who I used to work with the summer before last in a pretty little garden near Abbey Road, started to mumble and cough his way through a sentence, which began with Kids and ended with tik droogsn yucanntte razin widroogadd ixx . . . Which means: Kids take drugs and you can't reason with drug addicts. Like I said, I worked with him for a summer. He was sitting on his own because he hadn't washed his uniform since the sixties. And teenagers bothered him. He became all agitated at the sight of a pack of teen shits wandering into the garden to smoke some low grade ganja. Is it worth it? I was more agitated by Jimmy, his smell. I'd step away and he'd step closer. I'd turn my head and he'd step round to face me. I looked at his overgrown beard once. Fuck, it needed pruning. And whatever it was it was quick, the thing crawling between the bristles and yesterday's or last year's dinner. A maggot or something. Poor fucker. Like most Park Keepers he was unmarried, single, old, stinky. Where's the time for love in a job like this? Where's the time for a bath? Or to wash your uniform? Why should you care what you look and smell like in a job like this? I care. Only just, but I do care a bit. I just think of Frenchie or Office Girl or WHOEVER.

Did you notice I said was. Was unmarried. Yeah, Jimmy the Stink died in January. That's three from that garden in the last few years. I had to get out. I had a trauma of my own but at least it wasn't fatal. The geezer whose shoes I filled died in the hut. IN THE CHAIR! A member of the public was out walking her dog and noticed the garden was still open. She wandered in - her lucky day I bet she thought; not so lucky for Barry. He'd died in his chair, rolling a fag. I only met him the once before he died. He wasn't much of a conversationalist, but he was nice in his own surly way. And so, that's Barry Surly and Jimmy the Stink. I didn't know the other one who carked it. It was before my time.

# 8

Kenny's dead. Special Brew killed Kenny. Last summer, I was locking up and Kenny was asleep on a bench. So I said, 'Garden's closing now, mate.' NOthing. 'Excuse me, garden's closing now, mate.' I shook him a bit. 'Garden's closing now, mate.' Finally, he stirred, dazed and confused, and said, in Scottish, 'Kin yu rid ma meind?' And I said, 'Yeah, it says: Garden's closing, I need to leave.' 'Oh, okey,' he muttered. Then he goes, 'Haff yu git a cigarette, pal?' And I said, 'Nah, that stuff'll kill ya, mate,' and he laughs and shakes his can of Special Brew at me and says, 'Naw, *this* stuff'll kill ya.'

The other drunks, tramps, homeless, smackheads and prostitutes, have like a code of silence about DEATH. They all seem to disengage their brains with the information. The fact that someone they were sharing cans or needles or bottles with yesterday, is dead today. It's like they think it won't happen to them. What do they think Kenny thought ten years ago? Five minutes before? When you live day to day, I suppose you wouldn't think about anything, except whether you wake up and whether you can get your next fix or beer. Or who owes you. Oh yeah, I've witnessed sheer apocoholic
outrage at someone fucking off without repaying their drink obligation. Murder, pure redrum all right. 'HE OWES ME, MAN! HE OWES ME! HE OWES CONRAN BEER! IT'S NOT DONE, MAN! IT'S AGAINST THE RULES!' 'Where did you last see him?' 'EDGWARE ROAD, MAN! HE SAID HE'D BE

HERE 10 O'CLOCK! HE OWES ME! WHERE IS HE?' 'There he is.'

And lo and behold, skinny, and I mean skag skinny Skinny Stuart strolled towards us, and fat, Welsh, rotten teethed Conran runs up to him, and laughs and heehaws and acts all chummy, eyes on the blue off-licence bag. In fact, never taking his eyes off the blue heaven Skinny Stuart had in his skagorexic fingers. I was surprised he could even carry that bag with two whole cans of nuclear water in it. Skinny Stuart's dead now. Arse Injected Death Sentence got him. Not via his arse, as Conran suggested, but through sharing needles. No one flinched. And the next day someone new strolled through the garden, sat down, and opened a can . . .

# 9

Just had a Bukowski weekend. That's all I can say. All I can re-member. That isn't strictly true, because I can remember much too much. Stupid id or superego or whatever. YOU'RE SUPPOSED TO SUPPRESS BAD MEMORIES, AREN'T YOU? What's the point, what a disaster. I mean, I had a fantastic weekend. If devas-tation, trauma, conflict, love, loss, sex, rock and roll, feeling alive through regret, and *really* feeling alive because of turmoil, is a fan-tastic weekend. What do you think? Aha, you know, I might tell you this story one day. Sooner than you think if I can forgive my-self. If I can redirect the sheer filthy humiliating degeneracy of it all. And the best thing is the only person it's really affected has been me. Yeah, ME! Why? Why did I do it? Penance probably . . .

That's not true. I think some other people have been involved, and therefore affected; it stands to reason. You see, I met this girl. And Christ, I'm close, I'm so close to telling you what happened. I'm a grown man by the way. I don't look my age, and I'm taken for twenty eight, but I am older, in my thirties. Get over the shock. So anyway, I'm a grown man . . . Thirty four years old, and, hang on, this is not for your ears! I nearly tricked my own self then!

What the hell. It is related to this world, and after all, that's where I met this bird. Don't get too carried away, she cost me at least ten Euros and I didn't even get my fingers wet! Yeah, I know, ten Euros! In texts! The addiction to the reply! Jesus would have wept for certain at our pathetic sense of self importance that technology has brought us. Demanded of us. What a sad bunch we have become.

Anyway, I met this bird and she was okay, nice, funny and quite interesting; almost my type. Except that we had nothing in common. But I ignored that, and for three days I joined the human race, expected, no, *demanded* my fix; the cheerful bing bong that my phone makes, that signal of interaction with another human being. And guess what? I can't remember what she actually looked like. Nothing. Blank. Like a plain English cheese or something equally dairy based. Funny, yeah? Hilarious. I'm not that fussed by aesthetics to be honest; I make a good couple with almost anyone . . . Does that sound mean of me? Does it? Come on, bear with me, *humour me*, I'm still drunkenly fragile; it was a long weekend, and I deserve a little sympathy, don't I? In my condition? Maybe not . . . Stupid id or superego or whatever . . .

Fuck, I'm rambling. I can't remember what I was going to say, what was it? . . . Ah, there you go, *clever* id, superego or whatever. Finally . . .

## 10

I'm having a bad day. Scratch that. A woeful day. Nothing changes for people like me. Nothing. You, you're lucky. You're probably happy, content with mediocrity. Happy to just do the things that you do. You're not depressed. Not really, not like me. People always say things like: I wish I could play the piano or dance or play football or sing or paint or draw . . . Imagine you can. You can do one or more of those things and yet you don't do it. You can but won't, or don't. Nureyev wakes up at twenty and decides he's never going to dance again. Einstein says, 'I can't be bothered.' Picasso comes home from the studio and says, 'That's it! Pack your bags, it's poverty and horror for us from now on! I'm going to be a chimney sweep instead!' Hmmm, I think that's quite glamorous. See? There it is. The finding the mundane fantastic and the fantastic mundane. Don't ever bring this up again. NEVER! I don't want to talk about it. What's does it have to do with you? Nothing. That's right, you're getting it now, finally understanding something. Sorry? What's that? Not really? You don't really get it? What's not to get about nothing . . .

Let me apologise. This may happen quite often. We're not friends, I know that, so I shouldn't treat you this way. Why should you be on the end of an irrational and bitter verbal ejaculation? You shouldn't. I mean, you can if you like, because I'm sure by now you realise I don't mean it. I'm sure by now you realise *I'm trying to tell you something*. But it's a slow bleed, a trickle really.

# 11

Let me describe the garden to you. I know, it slipped my mind. Gardens are gardens, ain't they? No. They ain't. I'm feeling a bit colloquial today. Anyway, the garden I look after is long and thin - a bit like me (I'm more the sinewy type, actually). Anyhow, it's long and thin, with two lawns separated by a seated area and a pair of what we affectionately refer to as "The lungs", based on the fact the flower beds look like . . . And the garden is surrounded by huge brown towers with green armour. Fourteen of these towers protect me from all of life's dangers and fears. Trees, as they're more commonly known. And to be honest, they're not that good at protecting me, but they like it when I big them up.

Once, I was sitting under the protection of the Indian Horse Chestnut reading a book (*Money*, by what's his name), and this geezer, a workman or something, comes up to me and didn't even wait for me to finish my paragraph before interrupting.

'Excuse me, mate. Is this the garden for the prostitutes, like?'

'For the what?'

'The prozzies, like?'

'Is there a garden for the prozzies?'

'Ah was told, like, the prozzie park was in this direction.'

'I think you're a bit early, mate.'

'Oh, okay.'

'And I think the prozzie park is round the corner. ******
Gardens is what you're looking for.'

'Cheers, mate.'

'Take it easy. Mate.'

Now, the only reason I know about the prozzie park is because
someone else popped by once and asked the same question. There's
a sex shop across the road, but I hadn't been aware of any street
action around these parts, and couldn't help out on that occasion.
An hour later the happy chappy returned and told me it was ******
Gardens he'd been looking for, and I said, Thanks for the tourist
information, and he said, No problem.

Since then I've been a pillar of the sex community in terms of
my . . . *facilitation* relating to working hand in hand with my local
nightshift shaft brigade, liaising almost weekly with desperate souls
and the lonely sailors. I know one or two of the girls. Did I say
girls? They were girls a very long time ago but apparently still get
twenty quid for a blow job. Twenty quid! That's really expensive
now I think about it. And have you seen the teeth on these birds?
Gammy. Oh, yeah, this is the low end of the scale, the shit end of
the stick. I read somewhere that you could get a blow job for three
quid in Kings Cross. You just have to wait until they need their next
fix, apparently . . .

One day, I was walking back from the recycling bins round the corner, and having just dumped three tonnes of empties - the usual sus-
pects: Super, Special, SKOL Super, White Lightning, K Cider . . . I
passed by a girl in a white rain coat. Now, this happened really quickly,
a blur of sorts. But I'm not joking, despite the fact I think she was a
prostitute, she was the most beautiful prostitute I ever saw. I haven't
seen that many it's true, not compared to some, but she dazzled me in
that split second; the white rain coat, short dark hair, sharp features,
red lips. Just beautiful. Maybe she wasn't a prostitute. Perhaps she was
just walking down the street . . . I don't know. I'd made an assump-
tion, hadn't I? By the time I turned round to watch her walk away,
she had gone, POOF, thin air. I could've fallen in love right there
and then, it was possible, could've fallen in love with a prostitute.
That's just my luck if not my actual type . . . What would she have
made of me though? Did she even see me as we passed each other?

What if I'd stopped her, said, 'Hello,' looked into those eyes and saw her look back at me with trick, money, trick, money, flashing coldly at me? Would she have known I wasn't a trick, a punter. Would she have looked right through me and thought, 'Thanks, but this is what I do. This is who I am . . . You don't want this me. This me is for someone else. For money, a job.'

And she'd have been right.

# 12

It's hot today. It's so hot I can feel my heart sweating. Even my best attempts at not moving a single muscle are failing to stop the perspiration aggravation. These long, hot, weekend days are the true horror of this job, because the casually deranged are joined in the sunshine by the professional mentals. It's the weekend. It's Saturday. And it is hot.

So guess what happened. Mmm-hmm, that's right. I've had another moment in time, an event to expand my horizon. It was lunchtime, okay, it was unofficial lunchtime - 15:26. Or a late break if I'm playing by the rules. Anyway, I had just had my lunch, so for me it was lunchtime. I was resting, with my feet up and my sweating heart, when suddenly, at my door, a man lingered, middle aged and not unlike a sort of grey frog really. I noticed he was looking at the flower bed in front of the mess room, marvelling at it, but rubbing one of his flabby chins.

'Excuse me,' he said, in a high pitched voice. 'Can I ask you a question?'

'Of course.'

'Can you tell me about horticulture?'

'Not really. It's quite a big subject and I'm not a gardener.'

'But you work in a garden. Can you tell me about horticulture?'

'I can't. But if you're that interested, perhaps you should think about doing some sort of course or something?'

'Can you tell me the names of the flowers?'

'I don't know the names of the flowers.'

'Can you tell me about horticulture?'

'No.'

'I used to know about horticulture. I was doing half a City and Guilds in Northumberland and then THEY PUT ELECTRIC IN MY *HEAD*! Can you help me?'

Now, at the "and then" part he pointed to his head with both index fingers and started to cry. At the "Can you help me?" part he was calm again. *He* was calm. Me? I was less than calm by now.

'I'm not sure how . . .'

'I used to know about horticulture. I was doing half a City and Guilds in Northumberland and they said to me, "Timothy . . ." My name's Timothy by the way. What's yours?'

'. . . Jonathan.'

'Hello, Jonathan. My name's Timothy.'

'Hello, Timothy.'

'Hello, Jonathan. I was doing half a City and Guilds in Northumberland and one day they said to me, "Timothy . . . the pills (lip trembling) aren't working," and then (crying and pointing) 'THEY PUT ELECTRIC IN MY *HEAD*! Can you help me?'

'I'd like to but . . .'

'I can't remember the names of the flowers. I used to know the names of the flowers. Can you help me remember? I just want to be the way I was, the way I used to be before . . .' And he did the crying thing again, a sort of dry sobbing, in a frustrated, pleading way.

'I don't know the na . . .'

'Can you help me, Jonathan? You don't care about me! Can you help me?'

'I have to get on with something now,' I said, getting up and grabbing a half moon, you know, just in case.

'To do some work? Some gardening? Are you going to do some gardening now, Jonathan?'

'I am, Timothy, yes.'

I stepped out the mess room and locked my door. As I did, Timothy asked me again about the names of the flowers. Absentmindedly, I said, pointing at each, Cleome, Rudbeckia, Cosmos Sonata and Chrysanthemum Gold Plate. Yeah, you fucking heard me. Cleome, Rudbeckia, Cosmos Sonata and Chrysanthemum Gold Plate. I looked to the sky, to God actually, and didn't thank him. Not a chance in Hell I was going to thank him for that.

I turned slowly to Timothy, expecting a lambasting, a scathing psychotic assault on my character. But instead, Timothy was just smiling and repeating: Cleome, Rudbeckia, Cosmos Sonata and Chrysanthemum Gold Plate. He was smiling broadly. Happy.

'Thank you, Jonathan, thank you. You are a lovely man.'

'Thank you, Timothy. You are a lovely man too. Have a nice day, take it easy, okay?'

'I will, Jonathan. I'm going to go and lie down now, Jonathan. Thank you.'

And he did. He went and lay down. And I don't think I saw that smile leave his lips. Me, despite the searing heat and the pain in my heart, me, I went for a walk. I had to get out of the garden. For a whole thirty seven minutes I wandered the streets, desperate for anonymity, for relief. At that moment I decided I needed to leave this job. I'd had enough. Why should I have to deal with . . . Why me? God does know, doesn't He? Oh, how He knows how to get to me . . . Oh, how He knows how to punish me. Of course I knew the names. Of course I'd seen the delivery list; carried the trays of fifteen and twelves; laughed, as the gardening team melted as they strained to plant them last month in the boiling mid-May heat wave.

No one I know has to put up with this. No one outside of the job, that is. My friends, enemies, butchers, bakers, candlestick-makers - they don't have to deal with any of this. Oh, you should hear them when we're down the pub, with their new media new middle class ways; they're a fucking treat I can tell you, confess to you, actually. Yeah, there you go, some information at last. See? Not that surprising perhaps. Is that it? Is that all? Maybe. But don't count on it, not yet. It's only the beginning of the mediocrity. Live the dream, not this nightmare, this horrid day I've endured. God bless you, Timothy. You've taught me a lesson about humility, compassion, HUMANITY. Thank you, Timothy. You are a lovely mental man.

One of God's fools to another.

# 13

I've just been looking in the mirror. You may be under the impression I'm a vain man. I'm not. No, really, I'm not. It's probably the first time in months I've had a good look, a reappraisal I suppose.

I'm getting old. Not in an old man sort of way, more like a softening of the sharp features I had when I was in my teens and twenties. Angular features. You could argue I look better now, healthier. Yeah, that's it, healthy. My hair's okay too. Still dark, barely any grey, sorry, *silver* hairs. A little recession, but my short modish cut still works, it still suits me while I maintain this slim body shape. And despite the softening of my sharp features, I look all right. But Jesus, where has the time gone? Four years in a job like this . . . For what? Why did you stick it out? Does it sound as if I like my job? Do I seem like this is what I should be doing? You tell me. Mundane fantastic, fantastic mundane? But that was a trick. I hated the . . . It wasn't for me all that other stuff. I had no passion for it, and you need passion, ambition, and drive.

Drive. That's a good one, isn't it. There was no place for someone like me. No place at all. You see, in my other world I'm a problem. I'm not sure I would say a threat, but you know, you know what I mean. Here, I'm a pleb. Here, I'm a servant. The nice young fellow who looks after the garden, waters the flowers, talks to the trees, buries the tramp shit.

I don't know why I'm suddenly being reflective and confessional. We're close aren't we, you and I, to the transparency we've both been waiting for. I can't help but think you'll be disappointed. 'Is that it?' you'll say. 'It's just that?' And I suppose you'd be right. For me, and this is a rule I've made up specifically for myself, for me, there is only mediocrity or brilliance. No in-between. Think about it. There's no point believing in anything else. Quite good - not good enough. Pretty good - that's rubbish. Brilliant? That's better, much more like it! Why would you settle for less? Brilliant is best. Brilliant elevates. God knows there's enough celebrated mediocrity in the world; but why, why celebrate or commend the okay?

Because that's the majority.

Do you know what it takes to do something brilliant? Have you ever felt that feeling? Do you know the price you pay, the effort and the trauma, the friction and conflict necessary to be brilliant? Much safer to avoid that question than to be perplexed by it daily. Eradicate the problem, don't suffer. Be a big fish in a small pond. Or yeah, come on then, be the king of the jungle, a shitty everyday jungle, entertaining only yourself. The heartbreak comes when I think of the deception, the deceit and performance I act out every day of this miserable existence I put myself through. Every day. Come on, bear with me, be on my *side . . . someone* be on my side.

# 14

That was an interesting evening. I was out last night, won't tell you where. And despite the tiredness I felt, I managed to rouse myself enough to actually socialise; but not with the gypsies, the tramps or the thieves . . . No, not them. Anyway, the actual event itself wasn't particularly exciting, but sometimes you just have to show your face, don't you? And after recent events, I really needed a change of scene . . .

So I went to this thing and caught up with some people I know, friends I suppose you would call them. And I sat through a whole load of stuff I wasn't particularly interested in (no change there then), but did manage to fake enough apparent enthusiasm to hold a conversation about it afterwards. Just about.

Anyway, as I stood around in the foyer of the busy, derelict East End film theatre, with some cheap fizzy wine in hand, surrounded by what looked suspiciously like actual human beings, I spied, with my little eye, something beginning with E . . .

Have you ever had that thing, that look someone gives you, one that has DANGER! DANGER! written all over it? Well, usually I have to put up with the sleep encrusted unfocussed eye of Ronald Polio or CONRAN or whoever. But last night . . . Evil. Sheer sexual evil. It was one of those Peckinpah moments, an assault captured in slow motion, followed by an unnerving gut rush of attraction.

This slim blonde, with a sort of ungroomed no style haircut, really pale blue eyes, and thick, carved lips, stood there, giving me this nasty, nasty stare. So I matched it. And then I raised it. And then I looked her up and down, admiring her green baby doll dress, challenging her to challenge me.

Come on then . . .

It turned out my friends knew her friends, and that sheer sexual evil was conveniently camouflaged as the gang discussed the short films, that they, unlike me, hadn't just slept through. I didn't speak to her, I didn't need to, because there was a sort of *tactical ignoring* thing going on after the very *un*-tactical initial eye contact.

Every now and then she did that thing, you know, that looking across you thing so she could catch a glimpse. I know she was doing it, because so was I. When one of her new media new middle class friends spoke to me, she feigned disinterest and gazed into her empty plastic cup, posing and pouting, interrupting to tell us she was getting a refill. It was quite a show. Someone told me her name but I can't remember what it was. Something beginning with E . . . for EVIL.

As the evening wore on, I continued to ignore her, even when she was standing right next to me, her arm occasionally brushing against mine. If you didn't know it, you might have thought we were in that really early bit, when you're still hiding the fact that you like each other; and the heavy twinge from my perineum almost invited a confirmation.

So, in the end I made my excuses and left. Well, I had work today, didn't I? And anyway, I don't really have the time for romance . . .

# 15

Just kicked Ronald Polio. No, calm down, kicked him to see if he's alive. About three hours ago he limped in, drank three cans of nuclear water, collapsed where he stood, and so far as I could tell he went to sleep. Well, the problem was that every twenty minutes or so I decided I should check on him. Nothing special, just a look, just to be sure. Anyway, when I saw with my own eyes the wet patch spreading down the front of his trousers, well, I can tell you, initially I laughed. Pissed myself, in fact. But after another hour he hadn't moved, not a muscle.

It's a fear of mine - finding one of them dead one day. And the bizarre thing is I always think it'll be in the morning, when I get in; like one's climbed in overnight to drink and to die happy in this heavenly, sap green sanctuary. Like an elephant. Like when they make that weird trek to wherever it is they go to die . . .

Anyway, I imagine it would be like that, a private discovery. A dignified moment for an undignified life. I would know the minute I saw the body. An objective, clinical response would kick in (I've thought it through so many times over the last few years). I wouldn't go over immediately, I'd do the bins first; whoever it was could afford to wait a little bit longer. Then I'd phone the office to tell the supervisor I'm in and that there's a dead tramp in the park. No, not a tramp *shit* - a dead *tramp*. Then the garden would stay closed while we waited for all the pigs and the ambulances to eventually turn up. My gaffer would have to come down and (ahem) console me by giving me the rest of the day off . . . Yeah, I know, but at least allow me to dream.

So, I kicked Ronald on his good foot. Lightly. Tentatively. I didn't really want to get too close (the piss, remember). But after that loving tap, I heard him splutter and wheeze and snot, and I knew then that he was okay. He stunk. Dry piss, wet piss, a sliver of diarrhoea. The dribble of Special Brew vomit leaking from his nostrils. Ha! He's all right! He's okay, isn't he?

A few weeks ago, or was it last year, I was waiting for the No. 27 bus. I wasn't in uniform, I was in civvies, and Ronald approached some people in the queue, begging for money. This tiny spacker fizzed and coughed up a laboured request for other people's cash. When he came to me, he said, 'Can yu spare sum change, pliz?' And I said, 'Ronald, it's me, from the garden.' And he goes, slightly angry, 'Ah kno who y'are! Can yu spare sum change! Pliz!' And I said, 'No, you know I never carry any change exactly because of this. It's the same for all of you. You know the rules.' He looked sad, sighed, and said, 'Sorry for askin. And I said, 'It's okay, you take it easy, have a good night.' That made him laugh. And then he wandered off, a forlorn figure in search of a few pence to buy some drink to get through the night. God having blighted him with polio and all the added burdens that come with it.

He broke his collar bone a few months ago, or was it last year, and refused to stay in hospital to get it fixed because he wasn't allowed to drink. For him it was better to be in agony than to *be in agony*; can the grip of alcoholism really be so tight? It's not something I can relate to, to understand. It seems so stupid. And yet his collar bone was jutting out, it was anatomically *wrong*! He sat with Conran and Skag Skinny Stuart, and drank until it didn't hurt any more. Even funnier was the fact that he'd broken the opposite collar bone to his spacked up hand. He can't hold a can *and* drink with that hand, it doesn't reach. So he uses his left, but that side hurt because of the broken collar bone. Can you imagine?! The pain he had to sedate . . . The willpower he exercised to limp out of hospital and into the nearest off-licence.

He's my hero, a barely living god. And one day he will surely piss and shit himself to death.

# 16

All right, so you know that I get quite a lot of female attention, some of it good (like recently), and some of it not so good (like today). This bird comes up to me while I'm sweeping some leaves. Yeah, I know, I was actually caught doing something, don't worry, it won't happen again. Anyway, this bird comes up to me and apologises for interrupting.

'Sorry to bovver you.'

'Okay.'

'I'm the best dressed woman in Paddington.'

'I'm sure you are.'

'I *know* I'm the best dressed woman in Paddington.'

'I can see that,' I said, looking up from the little pile of leaves I'd gathered, and recognising her as the most recent recruit to our little circle of tramp, smack, crack and alcoholic f(r)iends.

Now wait, please allow me a moment, I want to get this absolutely right. Okay, this best dressed, mixed-race forty something, was wearing a peach, two piece, half zipped up, half zipped down hooded tracksuit, garnished with stilettos, and a nice low cut black basque. When exactly is London Fashion Week?

'I'm the best dressed woman in Paddington,' she repeated.

'You're not wrong.'

'My name's Elizabuff. What's yours?'

I slyly looked at the trees. '. . . Jonathan.'

'I'm free munfs pregnant, Jonafun.'

'It's a hot day. You should take the weight off and have a sit down in your condition.'

'I fink I will. After I've bought some drink. You don't mind, do you, Jonafun?'

'No. Of course not.'

She grinned, but I don't think it was at me. Her head was looking in my direction but her eyes were focused beyond. Then she wandered off. Slowly, in deliberate little steps, more like a shuffle really.

An hour later it was lunchtime and the garden was packed. So I'm in the mess room listening to the radio, just for a minute, when a girl comes running up to the hut and tells me that I have to call the police because someone's swearing and threatening to cut people's throats. Okay, I tell this scared young woman, Leave it to me. When I get outside, I spot Elizabuff sitting on a bench gesticulating and gobbing off. I assessed the risk and decided that it was worth approaching, aggravating and walking away. Phoning the pigs was unnecessary. After all, it was their lunchtime too.

Elizabeth was shouting: 'YOU FUCKING LAZY CUNTS. I DON'T PAY MY TAXES FOR YOU TO SIT AROUND ALL DAY DOIN' NUFFINK!'

The nice office workers were doing their best to eat their wraps and salads and mozzarella and cherry tomato ciabattas. I approached her (of course) with weary resignation.

'Hey, Elizabeth.'

'Oh, hello, Jonafun,' she smiled, suddenly girly-like. Flirty even.

'Hey, darlin'. You can't shout at people while they're having their lunch.'

'But it's not their lunchtime,' she said softly. 'They've bin in here for ages . . .'

'It's their lunch hour.'

'But they've bin in here all day, Jonafun. I don't pay my taxes . . . My Farva don't pay his taxes fuh . . . He's a nuclear physicist. I used to be a solicitor, Jonafun.'

'You used to solicit? How long's *your* lunch hour been?'

She leaned forward. 'Jonafun?'

'Yes, Elizabeth?'

'Will you come home with me?'

'No.'

'Will you make me feel nice?'

'No.'

'Will you have sex with me?'

'No.'

'Will you make *love* to me?'

'No.'

'WHY NOT?'

'I'm busy.'

'Have you got a girlfriend?'

'Are you trying to make a grown man cry?'

'Is it because you prefer skinny girls wiv no tits?'

'It's funny you should say. Just recently . . .'

'Not like these,' she giggled, pushing her breasts together.

'No, not like those.'

Let me describe these breasts to you. Imagine two Tesco carrier bags. Half filled. With water. In a basque. They were like that. Imagine it. Exactly. What a pin-up.

'What star sign are you, Jonafun?'

'Pisces.'

'I'm a Scorpio, Jonafun.'

'Ah, there you go, you remind me of my sister. She's a Scorpio too.'

'Is she free munfs pregnant?'

'No. You've been three months pregnant for about fourteen months, haven't you?'

'Yeah, I'm free munfs pregnant. And it's a little girl.'

Or a little elephant. 'I think babies prefer milk of magnesium, not Special Brew.'

'I am *cutting down, Jonafun,*' she said, earnestly.

At this point, a gentle looking lady and a young office girl sitting next to Elizabeth, giggled a bit, and looked at me like I was just so patient, so *good*.

'Listen,' I said, 'I need you to be quiet for me, Elizabeth.'

'Anyfin for you, Jonafun.'

I put my finger to my lips. 'I need you to be quiet for me, shhh, quiet like a mouse, quiet like a mouse in a mouse trap.'

'Anyfin for you, Jonafun.'

'Do you promise? Remember, quiet like a mouse, quiet like a mouse in a mouse trap?'

'I promise, Jonafun.'

So, having taken one for the team, having lost twenty minutes of my life sedating this wild, rabid beast, the fucking police only decide to turn up. As soon as she spotted them she shifted on the bench, spat on the path and shook her head.

'I AIN'T TALKING TO THEM! I AIN'T FUCKING TALK-ING TO THEM! AND YOU, YOU SKINNY CUNT! YOU'RE A FUCKING GRASS! I'M GONNA GET MY TWO HUSBANDS TO COME DOWN HERE AND BREAK YOUR FUCKING LEGS!'

'Elizabeth, I've been right here, talking to you, for the last twenty minutes. Someone must've . . .'

'YOU SKINNY CUNT! YOU'RE NOT ALWAYS AT WORK!'

'Well, if your husbands are going to find me, this'd be the best place to start. And actually, I'm not skinny. I'm just not fat.'

Then I left it to the plod. They approached, with weary resignation, and took my pain away. Lunch hour had passed, and only a few late comers were sitting on the lawn. The gentle lady and the young office girl had already gone, smiling at me as they left. Was it out of support or sympathy? Pity, probably.

About a week ago, or was it a month, I saw Elizabeth getting off with Ronald Polio. Mmm-hmm, that's right, sitting on a bench, tonguing him and stroking his trembling, piss soaked inner thigh. Poor, poor Ronald. Homeless, stricken with polio and alcoholism, and now the added bonus of almost certainly contracting an Elizabeth based sexually transmitted disease; will it ever end for him? With standards like that you may wonder how I could possibly resist her four stage advance? Did I mention the peach tracksuit? *Peach.* Exactly. Not really this season's colour, is it . . .

# 17

The Little Irish Fairy, sorry, please forgive me, the *vertically* challenged, Irish, homosexual pensioner, brought one of his boys by earlier. This foreign kid, early twenties, burly, with a tanned complexion, gelled hair, black sleeveless t-shirt and tight black jeans, strolled by the hut followed by the Irish Fairy. I know what you're thinking. That's a lot of detail I remembered. Well, there's a very good reason for that. But the easier explanation, for me, is that this isn't the first time the Irish Fairy has brought one of these boys by for an indiscreet exhibition of his self fabled pulling ability.

'What do you make of *him*?' he sing-songed.

'Very nice. If that's what you're into.'

'That *is* what I'm into.'

'I know. Hey, listen, I think it's buy one buy another one special offer on Special Brew at the off-licence today.'

'Oh, I had too much to drink *last* night,' he sang.

'Did you?' I said, unsurprised.

'Yes. In a minute I'm going to go and have a lie down and watch a blue movie.'

'Is it from the fifties?'

'*No*,' he squeaked, '*Amsterdam* . . . You can join me if you like?'

'Is there room for two in your bed?'

'There's room for three!'

'And what did the little one say? Roll over?'

Narrowing his eyes and pouting, he said, 'Do you know, you're a fucking baahstud!'

'Get my name right: I'm a fucking cunt bastard.'

Camply, he huffed, 'What is your name by the way?'

'Rumplestiltskin . . .'

'*Rumplewhat?*'

'I said . . . doesn't matter.'

The Irish Fairy, dressed in a Belarus football shirt, with beige knee length shorts, white socks, and an ever so fashionable pair of tanned sandals, paused before he next spoke. He was smiling to himself, probably thinking about something wonderful as he swayed ever so slightly in the barest of summer breezes. A distant memory perhaps, an existential reflection, a moment of happiness in his sixty three years. Or . . .

'You do have such a beautiful mouth. Look at those lips. No wonder you . . .'

'I think your boy's waiting.'

'He can wait. He knows I like to take my time.'

'Seems the impatient type to me.'

'He'll learn to control himself.'

'He's lucky to have such a highly motivated father figure to help him out.'

'Are you sure you wouldn't like to join us?'

'Do either of you have tits and a fanny?' I said, making a vaginal masturbatory gesture; even though he'd never know what that meant.

'Eeurgh! Don't say that! If my mother, God rest her soul, had heard what you just said!'

'If your mother had ever seen what you do . . .'

'Oh, she was a good woman! God fearing!'

'Do you fear God?'

'*Well . . .*'

'What do you say at confession? What do you tell your priest? What's the price these days for activities of an inverted nature?'

'I wouldn't know, I never say. There's somethings that're private.'

'*Selective* confession? In the eyes of God?'

'In anyone's, I suppose . . .'

I looked into the Irish Fairy's eyes and saw the best part of a six pack of Special Brew. And lust. The dirty little fucker had looked at me all through that exchange as though his cock was in my mouth. Yeah, I know, imagine how *I* felt. I think that's the first time I actually needed to take a skin-flayingly hot shower after talking to him. And if I hadn't redirected the conversation towards God, I think he might've tried to kiss me.

As it was, he scuttled off with his latest boy to the off-licence. He told me once, that when he first arrived in London he'd never heard that particular use of the word "gay" before. 'Are you gay?' they'd ask him. 'Yes, I'm very happy,' he'd reply. I think they all crack that joke, it's from the fifties, isn't it? Then he goes to me, 'I don't fancy you, you know, but . . . the things I could do.' And I said, 'Have you looked in a mirror in the last forty three years?' But he didn't hear me, his eyes were too gluey . . .

You may well wonder how or why it is that I can bring myself to indulge this lecherous innuendo on such a consistent basis? Well, it's simple. It keeps him *alive*, doesn't it? And on that day, when was it, last year, the year before, I reckon he ran off for an old man's wank, this vertically challenged, Irish, homosexual pensioner.

I think it's time for a cup of tea now, read a book, and wait the long wait to lock up.

# 18

It's very peaceful at the moment. It needs to be peaceful if I'm to make it through another staggering fourteen hour day. Roll on the first of August when the times start to come down by half an hour every two weeks. Saturday blues, isn't it? What, instead of the Sunday, Monday, Tuesday, everyday blues . . . Uh-oh. Wait a minute. Uh-oh, these guys are dangerous. Shhh, shhh, quiet like a mouse, quiet like a mouse in a mousetrap. Fuck. I've been seen.

'JOHN LE-NNON!'

'Hey, man, how are you?'

'JOHN LE-NNON! I had a fight with a squirrel!'

Okay, now these three guys are from Afica. No wait, I know it's Africa, but the other day I was walking into work and I saw some graffiti and it said: AMERICA 666, AFICA voodoo. The next day someone had corrected the spelling mistake, so it read: AMERICA 666, AFrICA voodoo. Anyway, these three guys were from various countries in AFICA, from Somalia or Rwanda or something. They like to preach, they like to shout, and they like to drink. White Cider Death - 59p a can or £1.49 a two litre bottle. I was slightly concerned when I first realised it was me they were calling JOHN LE-NNON! My hair was longer then, sort of Sergeant Pepper era. Not that I was going for that look, I just hadn't had my hair cut for a while. The association upset me a bit, until I realised it was just the hair, and not an indirect subconscious desire to assassinate me. In the end, I needn't have worried, because I am their brother.

'JOHN LE-NNON! I had a fight with a squirrel!'

'So I see. That was a big squirrel.'

'JOHN LE-NNON! You are a good man, JOHN LE-NNON!'

This one, the loudest, had eyes swollen like two crimson plums. That cat, he's been fighting again . . .

'Hey man, what happened?'

'John Le-nnon, it was a big squirrel . . .' he said, ruefully, swaying and shadow boxing. I doubt the squirrel had to be as fast as it was big, judging by this cat's slow-mo hand speed.

'You wanna look out for those squirrels, they'll have your nuts . . .'

'JOHN LE-NNON! You are a good man, JOHN LE-NNON . . .'

'We are good men,' I said, giving him the thumbs up as I started to walk away. The other two were oblivious, a frosty mist having descended over them hours ago - what sort of a combination *is* crack and White Lightning? That's some chaser!

Poor fuckers. Look at them. They're wasted. Do you know, people are scared of them. They seem intimidating, but I had to hug one last summer. Yes, it *was* last summer. They'd been winding him up and he was shouting and screaming. So I had no option but to go out and appeal to their better natures.

'Hey, guys? Hey, you guys have to keep the volume down. The hotels round here will call the fucking pigs, and we're all in the shit then.'

'Sorry, JOHN LE-NNON!'

'John LE-NNON!' The upset shouting one . . . shouted.

There was about eight of them sitting on a bench winding him up. I don't know what it was about, countries or something; village stuff, or the horrors they'd all witnessed; said they'd witnessed. As he came up to me I could see he'd been crying. He was definitely stressed out.

'Hey, man. What's up?' I said, softly.

'They don't understand. They are bastards!'

'I know, I know.'

'I try not to listen, but they are bastards, John Le-nnon. They do it because they know I am ill!'

'I know, I know.'

46

'Look what they make me do! Look at me! I am suicidal! I cut myself! I want to die! But I am a good man, John Le-nnon. I am a good man.'

'I know, I know.'

'You are a good man, I respect you. I didn't come over on a banana boat like these others . . .'

Behind him, one of them quipped, 'No, he came over on a BA-NANA PLANE!'

I ignored it because at this point he sobbed and showed me his arms. There were a lot of cuts on those arms. Long ones, short ones, thin ones, fat ones, noughts and crosses. I shook my head and gave him a hug. 'Come here,' I said. 'You just need to calm down, man. You need a break from these guys. Go for a walk or something, just get some distance, yeah? Come on, you have to look after yourself. These fuckers won't do it. Come on.'

He patted his heart and told me I was a good man with a good heart. That I was his brother. Then he said, 'These are my friends, John Le-nnon, but I want to kill myself. I am depressed, I am suicidal, John Le-nnon. You are a good man. I respect you so I will go home now. I have a flat the council give me. I will go home now. FUCK THEM! FUCK THEM!'

And he did. He went home, wherever that was. I don't think the others even noticed he'd gone. They'd started fighting, pushing each other about; and frankly, I left the cunts to it, because by then, I was too tired to care.

# 19

Oh, my fucking head.

I hate sleeping in the hut. My head hurts. The air that I'm breathing hurts. And so does my cock. Yeah, I was at a party last night. Uh-uh, don't need to tell you where. But by the time I left at 05:36, eventually managing to catch a night bus, it wasn't worth my going home; so I came straight to work instead, arriving at the keen as mustard hour of 06:44.

Hang on a second . . . I can't . . . seem to open . . . my eyes. It looks to me like what appears to be an unnecessarily bright Sunday morning. The sun is streaming right through the crack in the French doors of my hut, and straight onto my face. Typical. Fortunately, because it's Sunday, I only need to open at 09:00, but my head is paining me *so much*, that I'm currently wracked by a cocktail of fatigue, alcoholic agony, and an ever so *slight* anatomical disorientation. It's sort of like waking up from a hangover without actually having been asleep - a bizarre, spiteful, almost hyper-real state.

It serves me right really. I never know when to stop. I knew I should have left the party earlier. I did intend to, honestly I did, and I really should have, especially after what happened . . . I might tell you about it one day, but now at 08:51, laying prone on the hard wooden floor of my dusty hut, covered by my hi-vis work jacket, blinded by the sun, and frozen with the fear of my returning consciousness, I have to get up and stagger out to open the gates.

Oh God, I still feel really, really terrible. I've never been able to sleep properly in the hut. After I opened the gardens, I tried to sleep on the table, stretching my legs out over the fridge and the cooker, but it was impossible to settle. So instead, I've sat, in agony, waiting for closing time; occasionally retching, but always suffering. Hey, don't worry, it's only been a thirteen hour wait . . .

My phone's been going. Each horrid bing bong punishing me, shattering the fragile calm I'd been working so hard to establish. I don't know who the texts are from. I do know who they're from. It's to do with my cock hurting. Can you guess who it is yet? No? Oh well, never mind.

Okay, I'll let you into a secret. Do you remember that bird I met, well, not met exactly, more traded sheer sexual evil with? Yeah, well, that's the one. I bumped into her at the party. Bumped into her quite a few times actually . . . But only the once that really mattered. Weird thing is, I don't actually remember giving her my number. I'm not usually that careless . . .

. . . To be honest, I'm struggling to remember anything from last night. It's a fading memory, like smoke in the wind or something. I do remember she was funny and interesting; just my type, actually. But beyond that? Despite the physical evidence, alcohol has stolen much of the evening's activities from me, especially now that the day has passed and I've barely slept; that weird, almost hyper-real state returning, sedating me into the belief that it really all could have been just an illusion . . .

Fuck, I'm exhausted. That really is the last time I ever do this . . .

# 20

The gardeners are in. The five man team, which consists of two men, are in. It is Tuesday, after all. And having successfully recovered from my weekend, the gardens need a tidy up. Mowing, edging, a bit of pruning. I could do it, but it's no longer my responsibility, is it? Not since the *rebranding*. I have done a little bit of sweeping - before opening of course! As if I'm going to be seen by the public sweeping! Come on! Anyway, the gardeners are here, but I'm avoiding them by pretending that I have to do my own duty, that of patrolling. This consists of walking around with my headphones on, jiving and dancing about down the other two gardens. Yep, you heard me. The other two gardens. I look after THREE GARDENS! Have I not mentioned this before? That's because it was (a) unimportant, and (b) not any of your business until now.

The other two gardens are smaller but require slightly more cosmetic attention. They're my pretty little babies. Not like the main garden, which is decorated by the . . . You know what it's decorated by - FIENDS. These gardens are just round the corner, which means that I get to go off site. Basically, that translates as allowing me to go to the shops or wander about; eat ice creams; have a mocha in one of the local Greek caffs that I actually like; or pop to the pub to watch the football. Officially speaking, I'm not supposed to be "off site." Sackable offence, isn't it? Except that my unholy trinity represents a blind spot. Ah, the freedom. This is one

50

of only two sites where this occurs. The other poor fuckers have to spend all day stuck in their gardens; and believe me, some of those gardens are bad voodoo. Thousand yard Vietnam stare syndrome.

I'm in the middle of a busy tourist and office area. There are shops and restaurants, off-licences, pubs, hotels - you get the picture; and it's anonymous because of that. It's fabulous! It's glamorous! Everything I need is right on my door step. I want for nothing. It's like a home from home, a community. The Big Bus guy I nod to but never stop to chat. The Italian cafe I never go in despite the gardeners using it twice a week. The chip shop guys who call me boss and I call them gents. Oh, I'm a celebrity all right. Yeah, I am too. Even one of the prozzies said to me: 'Everywun knows you, dunt theh?' Do they? Okay, well, did you ever think that I hadn't been noticed around here? Hadn't been eyeballed by the waitresses and the hotel cleaners? Come on. The kebab shop owner asked last summer's work colleague, a Polish kid with a porn and gun obsession, why I never speak to any of them. A whole row of shit shop proprietors wondering why I never talk to them, why I'm *distant*. I think that hurt the Polish kid's feelings. He thought *he* was the king of the jungle! Sadly for him, he was just, and only, my monkey.

You see, and you have probably guessed this, that I like my anonymity. The casual interactions with the tramps and the mentals and the general public, are just that: casual and anonymous. This is what I do, but not who I am. Thanks, but they don't want to know the real me. That me is for someone else (perhaps someone I've met recently), and not for money, a job.

The gardeners are busy working the main station, but I'm hanging out at _____ Square. Shhh, shhh, it's quiet in here. A small garden enclosed in a cul-de-sac by a variety of hedges and shrubs, and surrounded by a couple of renovated Georgian hotels and some grotty flats. There are just the two gates to open and close. It's quite posh really. Elegant and solipsistic. Mostly the traffic wardens and builders use it for their frequent breaks, flicking their fag ends and coffee cups into the flower beds every . . . single . . . day. Imagine how pretty that makes it look. Yeah.

I like it in here because from one end of the lawn I'm sort of hidden, and I can sing and dance a bit. I used to go out with a dancer. She went to Rambert but should have gone to Studio. Fuck though, they even sit better than we do, stand better, lie better, bend to pick something up better . . . Dancers . . . Time to see if the five man gardening team of two are okay. I like to check on them, you know, just to make sure they're coping doing all that hard work I used to do all on my own.

They're fine. Graham's arrived, which means I'm almost ready to go home and . . . Hey, you know the rules! I'm weary now. Too much dancing in the gardens. I'm almost ready to go home and put my feet up, have a cup of tea, read a book, do nothing.

My home from home.

# 21

I hate this job. My boss just came round, and for fuck's sake, how fucking interested does he think I am? Okay, I was in the hut listening to some music, and the door's locked, so when he tries it he can't open it. Because of a little bolt lock. I put that little bolt lock on the door because otherwise the putrid members of the general public will just open it, just to see, regardless of whether the hut is any of their fucking business or not. Oh, the people I've scared by shouting at them as they've approached that handle.

One time, I nearly broke the door kicking it and shouting as I wrenched the handle up. I said, 'WHAT'S IT GOT TO DO WITH YOU!' I was FEEEEURIOUS! And the poor fucker stepped back quickly, as quickly as someone with a walking stick can, and said, 'Sorry, I just wanted to see . . .' To see what? I said, noting that I'd pulled the lock off and broken a panel in the door. Good morning, he said, his daily exercise regime from the local hospital having been galvanised by my vitriol. His recovery seemed to be going very well judging by the speed he was managing to hobble off at.

Anyway, my boss, he's like a Labrador. Have you ever seen an angry Labrador? Well, he knows about the door thing. So I jumped up and opened it, all pally and the like, 'Hi, nice to see you, how's it going? Oh look, we've new bags for putting rubbish in.' That sort of thing. Friendly. Then we spent the next twenty minutes talking about flowers and bins and benches and uniforms and collection points and the rota and Mr Charlie FUCK YOU Council and his FUCK YOU Council buddies getting upset about a work van being parked in the way of their BMW's and Rovers and how they were FEEEEEURIOUS and thought a major liberty had been taken and how much piss can you take and, well, that was about it. I get these moments sometimes, moments of *collusion*.

My boss is okay. I think he thinks that by discussing the garden issues with me like this that it includes me somehow, in a positive way, like it's fun or something. Remember, initially he could only give me four weeks work. Mmm-hmmm, that's right, I'll say it for you, 'How long ago was that? What are you doing here? What are you *still* doing here?' Well, when I was a . . . *Whoops*. Hey, I'm not ready for that yet. But days like today, or rather, twenty minutes out of one thousand, four hundred and forty, will bring that particular moment of collusion between us closer and closer.

# 22

What a great fucking day this is turning into. The pigs pitch up and ask me to back an ASBO to do with gypsy beggars. Then a prostitute turns up and tells us all about her tricks and her pipe. Yeah, pipe. I thought she said she really wanted a pie, and suggested lemon meringue. That wasn't what she wanted. I am a sponge for this stuff, it's true. I'm bombarded with information all the time.

The pigs arrived about 13:20, cheerfully and politely knocking on my door (because they know about the FEEEEURY it causes me). They asked me if I'd add my substantial weight to the gypsy ASBO process, which I reluctantly agreed to after a few jokes and attempts at deflection. We stood there, outside my hut, chatting about pegs and curses - of which I think I'm a victim of by the way. Don't believe me? I was in Victoria station about fifteen years ago when a gypsy asked me, Lucky heather, sir? Shocked by this I gave the old bag a pound. A pound for a bit of tin foil and a dead flower. Yeah. Fucking A1. It was a curse, wasn't it? Must have been, I mean, look at the evidence . . .

Where was I? Oh yeah. We stood there outside my hut when this local prostitute walked up to us. A mousey, scrawny blonde, she was all done up in her best outfit, fresh from Topshop. And she'd really made the effort for something called a Caravan Project. Gypsy related? No, something to do with the local hostels, a community initiative or something, for the smackheads, crack whores, prostitutes, tramps and thieves.

'Ouah, yous lot are ruining mah business. There's no punters round ere no more.'

'That's a good thing,' a plod said.

'Ah were out from eight furty last night and dint get me fust job till ten furty!'

'Are you still using?' the other plod asked.

'Noah, ah've bin clean for free munths now. Ah'm a good girl.'

'You've made an effort today. Special occasion?' I enquired.

'Ah knoah, ah look even more beautiful today, dunt ah?'

'You're certainly well groomed.'

'Ah knoah, ah look all beautiful and there ain't no punters. Yous lot ave scared em all off.'

She did look better than the last time I saw her, when she was slumped, dazed and confused, in a hotel delivery doorway. I think she needs to blend her orange foundation in a bit more next time, because today she'd done her roots as well . . . For the next twenty minutes she told us, probably for the first time ever, that she had just broken up with her boyfriend, that she were only twenty wun, had gone on the game at fifteen, scored her first pipe at seventeen (just because some black guy kept going on about it), missed her year old little boy - who lived with a cousin, and that what she really, really wanted that day, was a pipe. Like I said, I thought, okay, not really, but I pretended to think that she said Pie. You have to have a joke with a prozzie, don't you? What else is there to talk about? Anyway, she goes on about how two year ago she were earning two hundred and fifty quid a day round these parts. What was the tax return on money like that? Ah, cash in wet and sticky hand I reckon, don't you? Some geezers had asked her only the night before what they could get for a tenner: 'MAH little TOE! You can suck mah little toe while ah stuff it down ya throat and choke ya!' Oh, that did make her laugh. Street humour, obviously. As you might imagine, the two plod were being very conscientious about it all. Me, I wanted to know how much for what. It's interesting, isn't it? The price for this end of the scale. It turns out that if she was needing a fix that tenner would have bought quite a lot. Not confirmed, just hinted at, because I said, 'Blow job?' and she

56

kind of went, 'Ten to twenty for the cunt.' I think that's what she said. What with the accent it was difficult to hear clearly, and then with the police presence I didn't want to ask her again. She did confirm it was cheaper in Kings Cross though, *obviously*.

I don't know if it was just the sheer weight of social interaction, but later I had an almighty fucker of a headache. King Kong versus Godzilla. It hurt to laugh, that's how bad the headache was. All down the right side of my skull. I think it was probably psychosomatic, that headache, a symbol of my ever increasing circle of fiends; an average day, in an average way, with the pigs, my pain, and the prozzie.

# 23

I'm going to get the sack. It's true. In a job where you either die or, um, yeah, you just die, dead man's shoes style, I'm going to get sacked. No black bin bag for me. I've walked the line. I've danced along that line. And now today is the day I endure the ignominy of being the first non alcoholic or drug dealer to be removed from duty. You know why? You know what for? Ho ho, *I'm not in uniform.* I'm still in my civvies and I'm not getting changed. Yeah, it's Friday and I don't care. Come on one of you big, bad men, come round, for once, to my garden, and catch me not in my custard and dirty cloud grey uniform. I want you to catch me. I'm a bad boy. You must know how this makes you look? How your authority is being undermined, yeah? Come on, sack me. It's the end of my shift and I need to be released. I can't come back on Monday. I DON'T WANNA! I shouldn't be here anyway! Come on! Please! But it's not going to happen, is it? It's Friday, and the bosses and Mr I Come On Your Face Charlie Council and the bumfuck-browncocklove brigade are all down the Thai boy bride emporium, choosing their outfits and squeezing their fat feet into slim fit gents size nines!

There's no risk involved really. Do you know what would happen if my boss came round now? He'd just ask me to change. *Please change.* Yeah, fucking please! Ah, the council geezers might not be so polite, but I'd get round them. I'd get out of it somehow, because I love them and I love my job. I love everybody. Thank GOD for this life, thank ahhhh, just a few more minutes and I can go.

# 24

My lip hurts.

I had a fight last night. The Monday and Tuesday late shift passed by without incident. Unlike yesterday. It was my day off, and after having a shower and then a bite to eat, I made my way to this thing; another one of those things that I'm disinclined to talk about. And I ended up having a fight. That's not all. I'm a bit upset, actually. Yeah, it was a roller coaster evening of unfortunate revelation.

It all began quite well, with plenty of free drink and a whole load of people that I'm not that fond of, but, you know, don't mind seeing from time to time; small doses and all that. Anyway, after chatting with some people I knew, I just milled about, minding my own business (honestly I did); and I was being very successful at it too, avoiding what's her name, and evading that geezer - what's his face. Then, sadly, I bumped into someone I just knew I couldn't avoid.

Now I must confess (selectively), that I was engaged in polite conversation with a female at the drinks table. Nothing suspicious, just small talk, like: 'What's your favourite colour? What's your favourite smell? What side of the bed do you sleep on? Come and see me again in another five drinks.' That sort of thing.

Yeah? What? You *have* met me before . . . ?

Well, anyway, this bloke I knew from a variety of related events, caught me standing by that alcohol table, and my attention was suddenly drawn to the trendy Japanese beer just sitting there, teasing me. I really, really did try, honestly I did, to ignore this sharp

60

faced poser, decked out in his terribly fashionable new media new middle class East End chic.

But you see, the thing is, he always seems to want to *spar* with me. And so, unable to escape, I indulged him. We chatted about this and we chatted about that. Then, after a few drinks, can't remember how many it was, we strongly disagreed about something, and in a macho act of placebo bravado, had a reluctant, minimalist fight.

By this time we were outside in the street, and the wiry fucker caught me slightly by surprise. He was quicker and stronger than I thought, and he socked me right in the kisser, splitting my bottom lip. With the blood from my mouth on my fingers, I looked at him, startled at how serious he had suddenly become. The punch hadn't really hurt, but I was still stung by it. I mean, I'm a grown adult, and grown ups don't have fights, do they?

Then I twatted him back. A sweet right hander to his jaw. And I swear I heard his teeth gnash together, the kinetic energy shuddering through his gums, incisors clashing; his yelp shocking me as I realised he'd chipped his top left front tooth.

A whole load of people jumped in, separating us; which was funny because we were finished, our pain thresholds having quickly been broken. He was laughing though. It was a fake tooth, a cap or something. He was pushing people out of the way, refusing to phone the police or for an ambulance; calling everyone pussies. Then he gave me a coy, sly grin, nodding like he'd momentarily felt alive for the first time in ages; that fear and threat of violence having been faced. Not *that* much fear or threat, but then, when was the last time *you* hit someone? Took a punch back? Did anything other than what you usually do every . . . single . . . day?

Thought so.

Anyway, I cleaned myself up, had another drink, and then went home. I was upset. I don't like being injured, especially not the face. And that bird I was talking to before my newest, latest enemy interrupted? Well, she's lost now, gone forever. Never to be seen again.

. . . Probably.

61

# 25

Just found Ronald Polio buried in the shrubs. There I was, walking up to lock the far gate, when I heard a rustle in the Mahonias. Well, that was just a rat, but my attention was drawn to a dark shape further along, close to some Buddleia. Anyway, I spied, with my straining eye, Ronald Polio in the shrubs. From what I could see, using the window light from the hotels that was catching his dented and glistening head, he'd been bleeding and was definitely asleep (or some more likely form of apocoholic unconsciousness). At least he wasn't dead. Luckily for me, he's for ever blowing bubbles out of his nostrils; look at the green shit coming out of his nose. Yuck.

What a dilemma. It's locking up time, and I really should phone the police and wait for them to come and sort him out. However, I *could*, and I'm only saying this, it's not what I'm actually going to do, I could leave him there. The thing is, even if he wakes up he won't be able to climb out, will he? Polio, remember? What's he doing like that anyway? I've seen him fall in before, but this . . . ? It's like he's been laid there. His head's against the base of the Buddleia and his legs are crossed; it actually looks quite comfortable. Whoa! His hand just twitched! The spacker one! What a flipper. I really should lock the other gates before deciding what to do.

## 26

Well, I went home. I saw Conran on my way to the last gate, and he told me to leave Ronald there and he'd come back for him, or rather, 'CONRAN WILL COME BACK FOR HIM. CONRAN'LL GET HIM OUT.' 'Promise?' 'YEAH, MAN. CONRAN WOULDN'T LIE TO YOU' . . . Well, he did and he didn't. He did come back for him but decided he couldn't be bothered to help Ronald over the railings. And so instead, found the pigs, and told them Ronald was injured and bleeding and might be in a coma. So the pigs phoned the office, phoned the number on the bylaw boards, phoned the Operator, phoned everyone they could think of at the Friday night empty office hours of 22:06 to try to get a key. Mmm-hmm, all that just for a key. London's finest deciding to pool their resources to help a tramp in a locked garden, when CONRAN had promised that CONRAN would deal with it. Anyway, eventually, they found another local PC who had a spare key for one of the other gardens, and they let themselves and the ambulance geezers in to rescue poor Ronald Polio. By the time they got to him, he'd woken up, pissed *and* shit himself, been sick, and had an almighty crick in his neck from leaning against the Buddleia. Not only that, but as they all tried to help him to his spazzer feet, he angrily informed them he didn't need any help, asked if they had some spare change, and then limply stormed off in a huff to get a drink; his bloody and sticky forehead the least of his concerns. What a hero. What a barely living god . . . How awe inspiring. Better, even cooler than when he crawled out of that hospital bed. Can you hear them? Can you hear the screaming of the cans . . . ?

So, this morning I opened up, emptied the bins, checked the shrubs for tramps and almost immediately bumped into the plod and, shhh, shhhh, my official line was that I hadn't seen him. I bit my lip with the surprise; and it hurt, really, really hurt. The shock on my face, the disbelief! What? No! Really? He was *what*? Buried in the *shrubs*? How *did* I miss him? Oh, the questions. Oh, the sincerity. Oh, the woe . . . It was fine, the plod were laughing about it. It gave them something to do on their night shift. Or at least something different to do from irritating the prostitutes and talking about the internet or their cars or widescreen or downloads or minutes or whatever. But perhaps that's no different to talking about tramps or smackheads or prostitutes or shit kids or Irish Fairies or whatever. That's deflection, isn't it, the plod conversation? A deflection from dealing with social ills.

So if that's their deflection, what's mine, because I've just realised that I've been discussing my everyday for a long time now. Is that a deflection? What do you think? You can tell me if you like, I won't cry.

I'm tired now. I need to rest. I really need to bleed the sickness of complicity out of my damaged and rapidly crashing operating system.

# 27

I may quit.

Mmm-hmm, that's right, I've had enough. It's the end. You see, I think all this is having a detrimental effect on me. These, these social interactions I've been forced to swallow then spit out. I'm infected. Those *interactions* had been so bad, I pleaded with my stupid id, superego or whatever to save me. And do you know what happened? It didn't fucking work. Why would it? The trauma, friction and conflict I was battling against (every day it turns out), well, it stops today. I promise. Because it's time. Don't bother sitting down, because to be honest it's irrelevant, insignificant really. No, really, I'm not joking . . .

It all started so well. I opened the gardens and checked the bins. No tramp shit this morning, and no dead tramps. Ah, that fabulous Friday feeling, the end of the week. That's a Friday to Friday week in this job, and works out at eighty seven and a half official hours of work time. That's a lot of hours. Next week is like a week off by comparison. Just the Monday and Tuesday, starting one o'clock sharp! SIR, YES, SIR!

There's a reason I'm pointing this out.

So I opened the gardens and checked the bins. Then I had breakfast - a mug of Douwe Egberts and an organic croissant. Then I avoided the pigs by running down to _____ Square and hiding behind the hedges. I nearly emptied a bin there too. I did look at it, and for quite a while, but in the end, and after much deliberation, I decided against it. On my way back to the mess room I strolled provocatively past some office girls, smiled for a change, and said, 'See you later' . . . Uh-oh, no falling in love and getting married. Not to office girls anyway.

To my delight, that old slag Elizabeth was sitting on one of the benches, still wearing that peach outfit and still free munfs pregnant by the looks of it. Shhh, shhh, quiet like a mouse, quiet like a mouse in a mousetrap I crept ninja style towards my mess room - but stupid ninja stealth! I was spotted!

'Hello, Jonafun.'

'Hey, Elizabeth.'

'You don't mind me drinking here do you, Jonafun?' she said, pointing to a not too discreetly hidden little blue bag of nuclear water heaven.

'Nah, you knock yourself out, babe.'

'Jonafun?'

'Yes, Elizabeth?'

'Have you . . .'

'Have I what, Elizabeth?'

She seemed to change her mind. 'Have you seen Ronald today, Jonafun?'

'Not today. He'll be by later. Maybe he's at the Cabaret Project.'

'I met these two Russians last night, Jonafun. I've been a baaad girl, Jonafun. Do you like bad girls, Jonafun?'

'Sometimes.'

She rubbed her fanny area. 'I'm a bad girl.'

I sighed quietly. Ninja quietly. 'Well, they do say there's no rest for the wicked.'

'I never wanted to be a bad girl, Jonafun . . .'

'I know. See you later.'

It wasn't even ten o'clock.

I had my official ten o'clock break, extending it all the way to unofficial lunchtime. The office girls drifted by as I sat reading under the Indian Horse Chestnut (*One Day in the Life of Ivan Denisovich*, by Aleksandr Solzhenitsyn). For some reason I didn't take much notice of them. It was hot, but not punishingly hot, and it felt quiet; a stillness in the air; calm. I was oddly relaxed, the weekend within my grasp.

Graham arrived and told me (again) about when he worked in Hyde Park, and management gave them flasks of tea to cut down on the time it took them to walk back to the mess room for their breaks. Why did he tell me this story? Why did he tell me this story *again*? I don't know. Suddenly it didn't seem to matter; so I listened like he was telling me for the first time, and I nodded and laughed, and shook my head at the absurdity. What absurdity was that? Doesn't matter, does it? The weekend was within touching distance.

As it approached two o'clock, and having heard another of Graham's tales from the shitty, this time about finding a severed head in a bin in Bayswater, I decided to change out of my uniform - you know, in preparation for my unofficial leaving time. I squeezed into my wide bootcut jeans, put on my chocolate Adidas Italia 74s, washed under my armpits, and slipped into my tight-fit retro style navy polo t-shirt. Then I shoved my dirty uniform into the original early eighties Puma bag I bought two years ago on Sunset Boulevard, slung it over my shoulder, checked my hair, put my Aviators on, and stepped outside.

'Why aren't you in uniform?'

'Sorry?'

'Why aren't you in uniform?'

It was Mr Fuck You I Come On Your Face Charlie Council.

'Why aren't you in uniform?' he repeated, his thin moustache twitching, the sheen from his fat bald head close to blinding me. Meanwhile, the sweat patches from his admittedly expensive looking short sleeved shirt, rapidly increased as we spoke.

'Sorry?'

'The new contract dictates that all employees must be in uniform during the designated work hours. Anyone not in full uniform is sent home. Why aren't you in uniform?'

'Because I just changed . . .' I said, pointing to the mess room.

'I'm phoning your chargehand. I'm sending you home.'

'You're sending me home?'

'Yes.'

'Great.'

'Are you trying to be funny with me? What's your name?'

'. . . Jonathan.'

'Well, Jonathan, I'm telling you you're suspended for the rest of the day.'

Is this what's called aggravating? Perhaps I should have just walked away. Instead, I went, 'Fine.'

'I'm phoning the chargehand and we'll discuss further disciplinary actions. I won't be spoken to in this way. What are you looking at?'

'Your skin seems so soft. What moisturiser do you use?'

'I beg your pardon?'

'Your face. What moisturiser do you use?'

'Well, I . . . I don't use any moisturiser. I don't see what that's . . .'

'Apparently you can get this special *man moisturiser* now. For male grooming. I don't use it. Anyway, if I'm suspended for the rest of the day, which has about forty six minutes left, then I'd better go. Is that all right?'

'Do you want to lose your job, Jonathan?'

'. . . No.'

Mr Charlie Council frowned, then glared, then snorted, then said, sternly, 'You're suspended until further notice. Leave the garden now.'

'Right. Thank you.'

Then I said a quiet fond farewell to Graham, who shifted from his left to his right foot before nodding meekly. Poor Smeagol had been standing right there the whole time, and every so often he tried to interrupt. I'm not sure what he was going to say, but his attempts did make me laugh. Imagine it. What could he possibly have to say? That it was okay, that he was on duty now, that I had worked through my lunch? That they were given a flask of tea by management when he worked in Hyde Park? Would any of these reasons or excuses have made a difference? My favourite nightmare had come true. Mr Fuck You I Come On Your Face Charlie Council had come round, and caught me not in uniform.

You see, there's still this massive stink about the rebranded uniform protocol. Most of the others wear their uniform to and from work. But I'd rather be DEAD than be seen walking the streets in my blanched custard and dirty cloud grey outfit. Oh, *thank goodness* he didn't see the modified sleeves! We were warned about leaving early as well, but who doesn't on a Friday? Come on, one whole measly Greenwich Mean Time hour early? Bollocks.

It's only now I'm making my way home that I'm getting annoyed about it. He didn't even say hello! Straight in with the aggravation! Has *he* been to the Violence at Work seminar? It was aggravating, wasn't it? That tone? Then the reeling off of the contract specifications. I haven't even signed that contract! What the fuck do I care? Suspended? From what exactly? I'm off this weekend. I'm off on Wednesday and Thursday too. How is being suspended Monday and Tuesday anything other than a bonus? That gives me a whole week off. I should get suspended more often. I *should* have been suspended more often. The complaints I've encouraged, the lack of commitment I've shown; the sarcasm! That was the best one. Mr Council had received a complaint from a member of the public that I had a sarcastic air about me. Do you know what it was about? I have no idea. It could have been any one of a number of insignificant incidents. Why do I bother? What's the reward? It's certainly not the money. Poverty all round in this job; the shit end of the stick. Yeah, five squatters, two homeless, and a partridge in a pear tree. Two of our number live in the mess rooms! They can't even afford to pay rent! Five of our pack of scavengers live in a derelict squat in Harlesden or somewhere equally scenic! Another one sells drugs and sticks prozzie cards up in phone boxes! It's good money apparently - hundred quid for two three hour shifts. All this, and I'm going to be suspended for not being in uniform on a Friday afternoon! Had I been one minute quicker, or five minutes later, none of this would have happened! But once I was caught, what could I do? What could I have said that would have made any sense of the importance that Mr Fuck You Charlie Council was placing on that uniform issue? Come on. Tell me what I could have said. Anything you like . . .

I could have said "Fuck it." I could have told him to spin and stuff his idiot job. But I didn't. I couldn't. Because what else am I going to do? WHAT ELSE CAN I DO? You see, that's the question. It's the thing I don't do that's the biggest crime, the greatest tragedy of this wretched existence.

And so, finally, here's the pay off. The disappointment. Okay. Maybe you've guessed it already, I don't know. The truth is this, and it's not that spectacular. In fact, since I retired from that horror, I've done much, much better things with my time, and had great, great adventures. I've been a twenty nine year old checkout boy; a hospital A&E Rapid Response Team Member (basically, cleaning human shit and wank off cubicle walls); a plastic factory operative; a tinker, a tailor, a soldier, but not a sailor. I've begged, borrowed, stolen, murdered for money. Sort of. Okay, not really murdered. All this to avoid returning to the one thing God presumably put me on the earth to do. Blighting me with a curse greater than alcoholism. Worse than crack, smack, and fucking the gammy prostitutes on a Sunday afternoon. No, it's worse than all of that. The truth is almost upon us. Even I have to accept that it used to be true. The agony, the fearsome agony I'm feeling. RONALD! . . . Ronald? How did you do it? How did you crawl out of that hospital bed? The drink called you, didn't it? The screaming of the cans! Well, I silenced my lambs. I gave up and walked away. And was never happier than the day I closed the door to my studio and never returned.

Yes, hello everyone. My name is [not] Jonathan, and I am [not] an . . .

# Part Two

# 28

Shhh, shhhh . . . You don't have an invite but I think I can sneak you in. This is a Private View. No, no, shhhh, I know you probably don't know anything about art, but don't worry, you're in good company. Not *me*, all these others . . .

This used to be a trendy shoe shop, but these days it's been taken over by a local Design House, and then rented out on short lets to new and upwardly mobile East End artists. Or friends, obviously. Nothing like mutual congratulation to cement exposure and boost careers. I like the building more than I like the work.

Oh no. Here's a fucking enemy. Been reading some obscure American fashion magazine for your look have you? It's Simon Tabernacle. Look at his hair! Look at that pseudo army boy no style cut with a red and black two tone kiss curl. Fuck, I can't believe he's wearing a white Prada jacket with what looks like a white Chanel tennis dress. *Big mistake*. With his scrawny body and pasty puppy fat face, he really ought to wear more colour . . .

I was at art college with Simon and, generally speaking, during those three years, I hardly acknowledged this try hard's existence. Now look at him. A big fish in a big pond. He is so, so talented.

Oh, sorry. No. He's not.

Simon's pouting at me and waving his hand extravagantly in the air, or, more likely, wafting away the pompous stink from his filthy mouth-hole.

'Haven't seen any of your work about recently. What *have* you been doing?'

Quietly, I said, 'What's it got to do with you?'

'Oh!' he shrieked. 'I'm just interested in other artists' work, that's all! There's no need to be so defensive about it!'

'Poor little magpie. Looking to steal my silver?'

'What on *earth* are you talking about?'

'You know very well what I'm talking about. Your predilection for shiny things. Like ideas. Other people's ideas . . .'

Simon fluttered his eyelashes. 'Don't be like that. You *know* it's dog eat dog.'

'More like dog eats cock, Simon. Metaphorically speaking. In your case.'

Sucking in his cheeks, Simon composed himself. 'No really, what have you been up to? Tell me.'

I shrugged. 'Emptying bins and burying tramp shit.'

Looking as though he'd just swallowed a tramp shit, Simon spat, 'Well, fuck you if you want to keep it secret! I don't know why you have to be so difficult!'

I half smiled. 'What have you been doing? What you been up to?'

'0101 0101 0101, 0101 0101 01011111. 0101. 0101111111111. 111111111.'

It sort of sounded like that. I wasn't really listening or interested. At least the wine is free. I hate those Private Views where you have to buy the drinks from a temporary bar; like when they've obviously just been down the shops and bought a few crates of Grolsch. The tramps would laugh at the weedy impact that lager has on these horrors and wannabes.

Can't complain about the girls though. Look at them. Just my types. You remember - *funny and interesting* . . . Nice eyes too. Is that liquid eyeliner? You need a very steady hand. Uh-oh, I have a bad feeling about this. Erica is here. Listen, whatever happens, do not allow me to be isolated with Erica. Why am I saying that to you? Shhh, shhh, you're not really here. Nice legs, baby. *Someone* stop me.

. . . Hey, I tried to turn away but it was too late. Erica smiled at me, and even worse, gave me a slightly evil look *and* was wearing her hair up. Both my Achilles Heels. *Someone* should have stopped her . . .

Anyway, she poked me in the ribs and licked her lips; like how I imagine the wolf would in *Little Red Riding Hood*. Is it me or is the wolf the mother and it's all about the grandmother's fear of being replaced? Yes? No? Maybe . . .

'Haven't seen you for a while,' Erica salivated, *seductively* baring her teeth.

'No.'

'Not since Farley's party, wasn't it?'

'You know, it's strange, I don't remember Farley's party. Was I there?'

'I remember you being there.'

Sniffing, I said, 'I'm sure I had work the next day. Did I stay long?'

'Long enough,' she smiled, touching my arm.

'So we've met before? I think I do remember you now. Yeah, that's right. It wasn't Farley's party, it was Sophie's exhibition. A couple of months ago. We chatted briefly by the drinks.'

'I don't remember that. I just remember the party. I thought you said you were going to come by the studio and check out my little work of art again?'

'I don't like art.'

'You seemed quite interested in *my little work of art.*'

'Did I? Are we talking in code?'

Erica pouted. 'Seems that way. It's like a game you play.'

'If only I could remember the rules.'

'I thought someone like you just made them up as you went along?'

'Believe me,' I said, looking her straight in the eye, 'it's much more complicated than that.'

Erica bit her cheek. 'Well, if I remember it right, we only have the falling in love, getting married and living happily ever after left to do.'

'Stop being so provocative. Come and see me again after another five drinks.'

'Ha! That's the second time you've said that to me.'

'Repetition's good. Ask anyone showing tonight. And how's your husband?'

'Oblivious, and you know it.'

'Do I . . . ?'

Walking away, Erica said, 'I'll see you later. Maybe.'

'Mmm.'

That was close. See? See how it works? What. The. Fuck. Was she going on about? I've never slept with her. Have I? Farley's party? Come on stupid id or superego or whatever . . . You know, I think that fucking thing works better than I think; which is weird, isn't it? Considering it's all in my head . . .

I first met Erica (you remember when) at that screening for some really boring short films I was dragged along to. She was the friend of a friend's friend that I mentioned, and, well, I just knew she was trouble from the very first E for evil look she gave me. That really nasty one, a look up and down, the one that said: Who the fuck are you? Lick my clit. One of those looks. You know the type. *Come on.* No? What, *never?*

Anyway, *of course* I remember Farley's party. How could I forget? She was wearing a beige knitted playsuit and long leather boots . . . Hmmm. Bless you, Erica, that approaching thirty thing and the reassessment we all go through; funny, isn't it? As for her husband, that poor fucker's definitely, *definitely* in trouble.

Oh, and by the way, I was taken advantage of . . .

Just look at this. I really can't be bothered with the work on show. It's so nondescript and banal, it's merged with the white of the walls; and that's not a good thing, you know, not like Rauschenberg or something. Let's have a look at these lesbians instead. A noisy one and a pretty one. It's always a noisy one and a pretty one, isn't it? Look at the effort they've put in, the amount of mascara they're both wearing; the post art school vintage fashion and charity shop chic. I like the pretty one. That has to be liquid eyeliner. You need a very steady hand, don't you? I might ask her, you know, just to test, just to see. I'm inclined to enquire because I spotted her looking my way when I walked past earlier. She's quite young though. Early twenties I'd guess. Too young really, but her dark

76

messy beehive and red lips are enticing me. Can I? Should I? What harm would it do to just see . . .

Hah! Have you ever seen an angry lesbian? Territorial or what! I think Jenny is bi judging from the way her girlfriend swooped and dive bombed as little Jenny and I shared a joke and a few tactile  moments by the drinks. Don't worry, I backed off. I'm old enough to be her bad uncle, aren't I? However, one can't help but feel there's going to be a row later. About *love* and stuff. About commitment. About IT'S WHO I AM! And, BUT I LOVE YOU! . . . Fuck, Jenny's just a kid, and her girlfriend would be better off chilling out rather than push on these matters. It's just my opinion, that's all. None of my business really.

Yeah, I should take it easy tonight, what with being back at work tomorrow. Mmm-hmmm, suspension is over just in time for my long week. Thankyouverymuch. Ah, the trauma, friction and conflict I have to put up with. My boss phoned me on Monday  wondering where I was. I told him I thought I was suspended, and it turned out he'd forgotten all about it. So anyway, after some informal discussion, it was agreed to keep me out of the spotlight until Friday, and that way everyone wins. Mr Fuck You I Come On Your Face Charlie Council finally feels his cock grow hard for the first time in twenty years, and I get away from the tramps, prostitutes and smackheads for a suspended without pay week of bliss. Result.

So instead, on this Thursday night, I turn up here, at this Private View, where I'm, umm, surrounded by . . . That's not poetic, that's just an alternative penance. But I'm being silly. I love Private Views. I love seeing some art and all these artists and designers, the tinkers and the tailors. And I love seeing Erica cross my periphery from time to time. How many drinks did I say she should come and see me in? Five? What am I on now?

Here's my mate and his girlfriend. Listen, I'm not going to introduce you. You don't need to meet them. It's not that they're interesting or pedestrian or whatever - it's you. You don't need to meet them. You just stay where you are, because I'll let you know if there's something worth knowing about. Don't I (nearly) always? Come on, bear with me. Be the someone on my side.

# 29

Hmm, I'm not sure how to put this. Turns out I was on four drinks. By eight I was suffering mild ill judgement, and by nine . . . Erica. My moral radar completely shut down after ten, and well, it's not fair, is it? What is she doing attacking me when I'm weakened by proximity, familiarity, compromise and submission? It wasn't the drink. It didn't matter what the number was; it was that *look*, the look she gave me when I walked through the door. The eye of the tiger.

And now the tiger sleeps. Is asleep next to me. Any more of this and it'll become an affair; and I'm not ready for that sort of commitment. I have to get up for work in a bit. What time is it? Oh, that's all right, it's early, nearly ten. And that gives me enough time to get her up and out without exposing my secret. Yeah, did you ever think I'd told anyone what I do for a living? Even when I do they don't believe me. It's a real treat, I can tell you. Do you ever have that? That not being believed thing? It must be something to do with my face, I obviously don't have a believable face. Either that or it's unbelievable, the things I do . . . There we go, that's it, much more likely.

How am I going to explain this though - the tiger sleeps deeply, and her conscience appears clear. Me, I'm wondering about that husband. We're not talking about him, and that's a bonus, but this really can't happen again. A drunken liaison in a toilet at a party is one thing, but this? This is dangerous. I could get hurt. Sorry, if you just heard a weird hissing it was me laughing. Shhh, shhhh, tiger stirs. Am I going to be forced to cuddle her? Looks like it, and that's a disaster. It's so dangerous I feel like crying. How long until I can go to work . . . ?

# 30

King Kong. I feel much better now. I'm hungover, hungover all over in fact, but here I am, eating a lolly in the afternoon sunshine, sitting quietly under the Indian Horse Chestnut with my book, and things are looking up. Frenchie's in, Office Girl too, and there are some others, Sunburnt Girl and Wish I Was Ten Years Younger Girl. That's me wishing I was ten years younger, not her. But . . . look at that eyeliner . . . Bad uncle.

Wish I Was Ten Years Younger Girl asked me for a fork once. She'd forgotten to pick up one of those free plastic sets you get with salad bowls and was stuck having to use her fingers. Well, I obliged of course, washing my very own fork before handing it over. As I looked at her I remember thinking how pretty she was. Like a really pretty gypsy, all black hair and ungroomed, yet fashionable too. It was then I wished I was ten years younger. I really had to rein in the intense urge to move from proximity to familiarity. I sensed it, a mild kick in my guts, that I really was too old for her, even to chat. Have you ever looked in the mirror and seen what's actually staring back at you? We edit so much at those moments, we have to. But the truth only really comes out when you're face to face with the inescapable, the bitterly accepted and reluctant truth, that it just can't happen, you can't do it, can't continue. It hurt me realising this. I thought I was just looking tired, but that tired look never went away. Don't get me wrong, I can get away with looking younger. The obvious problem is that I'm not younger, I *am* old now. I don't look tired. I look *older*. So I gave Wish I Was Ten Years Younger Girl a polite, sterile smile, and sat back down to read my book while she ate her salad. When she returned with the fork, offering to wash it up, I cheerfully replied that I'd do it, and quietly, shyly, said to her, You have a nice afternoon. Cheerful. Polite. Sterile. Good uncle.

# 31

Look at this twat. Fantastic. As he's staggering past he's using the hut to keep his balance! Who? You may well ask, but then I'm surprised you don't recognise him. Look closely. No? Are you sure? Hmmm, okay. Well, I'm pissing myself at Alan Ashby. Yeah, that Alan Ashby. The one that owns seventeen hotels in the area and three bed and breakfasts. He's also a retired film producer, a childrens book author, a fashion photographer, and a former hairdresser to the stars! Oh yes he is! One time, a few days after it had been raining, this tiny, stumbling, sun reactive glasses wearing pillar of the community, came up to me while I was busy doing something really important. Can't remember what.

'Do you have a lot of puddles in this garden?' he slurred, a raking your posh gravel driveway slur.

'No.'

'I fell in a puddle in here the other day.'

'In here?'

'Yes, I just said. One can drown in a puddle, you know. Do you have a lot of puddles?'

'No.'

'I was soaked through. Are you sure you don't have dangerous puddles?'

'Yeah, I'm sure. Although I did see you last week as I was going home, lying flat on your back in Hyde Park after the rain.'

'Me? In Hyde Park?'

'It was you. You were flat on your back. In Hyde Park.'

'Oh.' He swayed, ever so slightly, processing that revelation. 'So you don't have big puddles in this garden then?'

'No.'

'I'm going to report it to the Council. I used to be on the Council, you know. I know a lot of those Councillors. Don't care much for them. Why I packed it in.'

'To become a fashion photographer?'

'Yes, how did you know tha . . . ? I packed that in too. Bailey. Do you know I used to cut his hair . . .'

'I'm busy actually.'

'Of course, of course,' he waved. 'Don't let me distract you.'

'Thanks. Bye.'

And off he eventually tottered. The two bottles of whisky clinking and swinging dangerously in a little thin blue bag, all the way back to his Hotel and Hairdressing and whatever else empire.

I remember last summer when he phoned the pigs because of all the drunks in the garden. Yeah, *he* phoned the police about the drunks! He was hammered when he did it, and a week later he couldn't remember a thing. Diamond. That day he was pretending to be a real person, someone quite rightly outraged by the scum littering up the garden that I so dutifully tend to. A disgrace! The Major of London will hear about this! I'm a friend of his, you know. The *Major* . . . And on and on it went. Then he gave me a tip on the donkeys, told me again about his friend Bailey, almost slipped over, and finally tried to take a piss in a bush before he wandered to the off-licence. *To* the off-licence. I shut the door for his return journey, safe in the knowledge that he probably wouldn't remember the previous ten minutes anyway.

There is an outside chance it could all be true. I mean, someone has to own all these hotels, don't they? And lots of people were or are fashion photographers. *Bailey* would definitely have needed a haircut at some stage of his life, and why couldn't that be courtesy of the be-scissored Alan Ashby? It stands to reason. There's no reason to not believe it. Don't all creatives from that generation descend into alcoholism and/or other vice ridden diseases? There's this lovely old Indian fellow from South Africa who hangs about Little Venice, who openly and modestly discusses his breakdowns. He owned a salon in the West End during the swinging sixties. There are photographs to prove it. And he cut Michael Caine's hair once, only the once, but that's one more time than Alan Ashby.

The thing about Alan Ashby is: Has he ever been a somebody? Did he lose it or did he never have it? Those are the questions. But alcohol confirms delusion, so I don't think he's ever been a somebody, not even close.

# 32

Do you know, I think I might kill myself. A mate of mine jumped in front of a train *and* hanged himself off a bridge. That was thorough. A bit messy though, isn't it? I don't think I'd like to leave anything behind to clear up. And that's the problem, the clearing up process afterwards. Some poor pleb scooping the bits up into a black bin bag. Maybe even someone like me . . . You may wonder why I'm thinking these things, why I'm suicidal. Well, the honest answer is that I don't know. I'm just tired. I didn't sleep very well last night; and even though I'm only a few days into my shift, it's ages before I can have a lie-in again. Not that I stay in bed anyway, I'm very much a getter upper.

No, I still think I might kill myself, because it's not the tiredness, it's more than that - it's circumstance. Mmm-hmm, I'm bored. I used to have something to do and now I don't do anything. I just do nothing. You see, there used to be a reason I was doing this. A reason why I could get up at 06:30 seven days a working week. A reason to empty bins and bury tramp shit. Now? Now I'm struggling to remember anything. Each day that goes by, every hour that passes; I'm shutting down, slowing down mentally. I can feel it crawling around my head, piercing my skull and pushing its way between the dying sections of my brain, settling right in the centre. It's not the tiredness. I'm not tired today, I'm wide awake, *wired* awake.

Okay, so I know I'm a bit oblique at times, but I CAN'T HELP IT! It's part of who I am, who I used to be. So okay, I suppose this is the time for a bit of disclosure, a bit of background. Yeah, I know, there's quite a lot to get through, isn't there? It's not just about all this stupid work stuff, the job, it's more about other stupid things like art, relationships, how, where, why, what . . . Hang on, some kids are racing their bikes around the garden, using the path as a track. Little fuckers are riding on the grass as well! SHIT KIDS! Hmm, wait a sec . . . wait . . . just . . . a second . . .

Oh, may God forgive me. Just killed a shit kid. And now I may have to jump in front of a bus to avoid being arrested. I charged outside, grabbed the lippy little fucker and, I'm not sure how, but I broke his fucking neck; like in the movies. SNAP! It doesn't make that noise. It's more of a crick really, a wet crick. His body went limp almost immediately, and as I looked up, the other shit kids screamed and pegged it back to their council flats on their bikes. So people really do scream when they see actual horror. I put his head in the bin and threw the body under a Mahonia. You may have guessed by now that I am joking. But you see, that's how I felt, just how and what I felt and wanted to do.

I'm tired today, so very tired. I didn't bother going out to ask, yeah, that's right, *to ask* the shit kids not to ride their bikes; it's not worth it. So I closed the hut and went and sat down in one of the other gardens. Not _____ Square, the other one. A nice quiet garden only occasionally occupied by one single homeless guy.

When I got there he had unravelled the hose pipe and was phantom watering the flower beds. Moses is cool. He always puts the hose back tidily.

'Hey, Moses.'

'Oh, alright, Jonathan. How are you? You know, I was reading the paper this morning and it's terrible, isn't it? The things people do. You know, back when I was living in Coventry, this is in the seventies, Jonathan. Back then there was a young man like you working in the same factory. You could always get a job in those days, you know, the cost of living was so much lower then. And there was this young man, I'll never forget, his name was Jim, and he was like you, very intelligent. I saw you the other morning coming in to work, and from the distance you looked just like him. From the back. He was slim too, and dark haired. Well, he disappeared one day. One day he was at work, the next . . . He didn't turn up, didn't turn up for a week. He'd died. Just dropped dead one day. Can you imagine, Jonathan? He was such a lovely lad. And even when I was drinking, and I did drink, I'm not going to lie, I was a terrible drinker, but even when I was drinking I thought of him quite often, and wondered what might have happened, not just how he died, no, that's morbid. No, more what might have happened if he hadn't died. You know, Jonathan, life's a funny thing, isn't it? Good people die young and yet people like that Conran and those others . . .'

'Do you want me to turn the water on?'

'I'm nearly finished, Jonathan, thanks.'

'Okay.' And I left him to it.

After about an hour of sitting on a bench and taking in the sun, I made my way back to the hut. The shit kids had gone. The only visible evidence of their visit was a few discarded crisp packets and crushed up cans of cheap pop. I put them in the bin, said hello to Conran, who was shit-faced, I mean *absolutely wankered*, and sat down in the mess room.

The thing about this job is there's always something, always someone, some tragedy to talk about. How about that for cheering you up. Moses always tells me about Jim. Every time I see him down at _____ Gardens. Whatever it is that Jim represents to Moses, it's so strong, so powerful, that he never tires of thinking about him.

Moses used to feed the pigeons. He'd stand on the corner by the pub opposite the Angus Steakhouse, his shopping trolley parked neatly by his side. And he'd feed the pigeons every day, a flock of them, and he'd be happy, chatting and sharing his bread with the filthy birds. One day I was watching this, and there was a big crowd of pigeons, loads, and I saw out the corner of my eye a van driving down the road. The van suddenly roared and accelerated straight through the pigeons, killing, flattening, destroying a large number of them. I looked at Moses. He was lost for a second, the whatever it was that had just happened not quite registering yet. People just walked past him as he stood there, holding the bread.

I didn't know what to say or do. These things sort of just happen, don't they?

# 33

You know, I'd never seen her before. Never. Ever. Seen her. Before. I've been here in this garden for three years now, and I'd never ever seen her before. Who? The prozzie of course, Santa Maria, that sweet little thing. And now it's like she's a daily visual treat, passing airily through my world. It's amazing isn't it, the not noticing people thing. She knew me though, oh yeah, she'd seen me about, of course. 'You've bin ere fuh years aven't ya?' she said.

Yeah, well, I work here . . .

Now I see her nearly every day, on the way to the Cabaret Project or her favourite corner, flouncing about. Yeah, flouncing. That's one confident prostitute. She told the plod she were the number one round here those two year ago. She were the top dog all right. Luckily, without the plod to facilitate communication, she can't stop to chat to me today because I'm hiding. I'm doing this because it turns out I've been flirting with a prostitute. Yeah, I know, what an oxymoron. It dawned on me the other day. What world do I live in that I end up flirting with a prostitute? How unnecessary is that? She told me that depending on how she felt she charges a hundred for an hour or sixty quid for half an hour. Now I worked this out. That's thirty quid for fifteen minutes, ten quid for five, and two pounds a minute. You don't have to buy her a drink and you don't have to warm her up - hey, you know what I'm saying . . . Even if you go over, that's a maximum of six quid.

Come on, we're not talking about *making love* . . .

That other day, you know the one, when it dawned on me I was flirting with a prostitute, well, Santa Maria came by the mess room and I'd made the mistake of leaving the door open.

She paused at the door. 'Oahh, lazy bones! Look at ya jus sitting there!'

'Hey, how you doing?'

'Ah've broken mah leg.'

And she had. She was on crutches. A fairy tale Princess, all dressed up with nowhere to go and no Prince to kiss.

'How'd you do that?'

'Ah got run over bah a big red bus!'

'How did you get run over by a bus?'

'Ah were runnin fuh a bus and ah got run over bah anotha wun that were right behind me. It right fuckin urt. Ah were like, on the street goin, "Ya bastud, ya bastud! Ya broke mah leg, ya bastud!" And then they got me an ambulance.'

'How's it affected business?'

'There ain't bin no business!'

'Surely someone would be interested in a *specialised* service?'

'Why? Does it turn you on? Are you gonna pay me?'

'I'm busy. I'm on duty.'

'You're gehh anyway . . .'

'Are you trying to trick me? I've been tricked before . . .'

She laughed. A real laugh. 'Anyway babe, ah've gotta love ya and leave ya. Got an appointment, aven't ah? At the Caravan Project. Ah'm bein' a good girl. They're gonna help me with mah claim fuh com-pen-sation.'

'How much could you get?'

'Two grand they reckon.'

'Two grand?'

'Yeah, gonna go on holiday. Gonna go to da CARIBBEAN. Do some whahndin and a grahndin . . . !' she *winded* and *a grinded.*

'Watch your leg.'

'Dunt urt so much now,' she lamented, sighing, 'Ah've never had mah legs shut fuh so long.'

'Good. Next time you come through here I expect to see you

doing cartwheels. All the way down the path and past the hut.'

'Ah can do more than cartwheel . . .'

'Yeah. I bet.'

'Seeya, darlin. Gotta go, seeya!'

'Take care. Be careful.'

You didn't believe me, did you. See! *Flirting*! With a prostitute! Oh I know she still pimped me for a trick, but did you see that, the attempt at the dare? I have actually been tricked before. Well, sort of, it's not much of a trick really, is it? The "You're gay anyway" line some girls use. *Oh you're so right, please straighten me out . . . I'm . . . begging you . . .* Yeah, that's what wearing New Wave style mascara and eyeliner does for you in your twenties; ahhhh, the smell on my fingers of that nostalgia.

I remember I was at a mate's birthday drinks last year, and this pretty older bird was eying me up (probably about five or six years older). She was petite and well groomed, and while being pretty on that night, when she was younger she would have been very, very pretty, bordering on beautiful. Oh, I could tell she wanted to speak to me, I could see it in her eye; but not of the tiger. Anyway, me being so approachable and the like, she edged closer and closer, sort of eventually standing next to me. As a friend and I chatted, I could tell she was earwigging, waiting for an opportunity to add something to the conversation. And, after a few casually accidental looks, I used the word "sorority" and in she jumped.

Do you know how older women chat up blokes? Expertly. That's how. No dares, no challenges, no attention seeking spikiness. Just the expertise of experience and confidence. It was a joy to behold. A verbal and body language masterclass. The timing of her tactility, the assertive eye contact . . . There's only one way to reward that sort of effort . . .

I know what you're thinking. Oh yes I do. You're thinking: Fuck the prostitute, this other shit, and the Rain Man! What about that Erica? Well, what about her? What's it got to do with you? Nothing. It's none of your business. What does it have to do with you?

Everything.

# 34

Shhh, shhh, Erica's just gone to the toilet. We're having a *meal*. I can't remember the last time I had a meal in an actual restaurant. I hope she's paying . . .

We were only meeting up for a quick drink. To have a chat, you know, just casual, nothing in it. So, earlier this afternoon, I caught up with Erica in a quaint Covent Garden pub for a glass or two of wine. Or three. Then we decided we were hungry, and so now we're having a meal somewhere in Soho.

Even if I tried, I would never be able to find this place again; I have absolutely no idea where it is. It's quite nice though, and busy too, with its soothing, clinical interior, all burnt orange and silver; the waiters and waitresses complementing their trend setting hair styles with a uniform probably designed by Stella McCartney or someone. Cool. I could get used to this, really I could . . .

Erica smiled as she sat down. 'You were saying?'

'About what?'

'About regurgitation. About how artists innovate then regurgitate. I sort of agree. But are you sure you're not mistaking regurgitation for thematic exploration? And anyway, if that is the case, then it doesn't just apply to artists. Writers, film-makers, they all do it too.'

I thought for a moment. 'What, like Tarantino?'

'Ah, but he's an accepted parodist.'

'Bergman explored. Tarkovsky explored. Tarantino has never innovated, he's always *renovated*.' I paused, sipping my wine. 'I think calling him a parodist is a bit cruel though.'

Erica tutted mischievously. 'You're right. If he's listening, I apologise. But I'm not sure *renovator* is any better.'

I shrugged and finished my drink.

Our waiter came to the table, and with a slight European twang, he said, 'I hope everything has been to your satisfaction. Another drink, sir? Your wife?'

'Someone else's wife. And I'm fine, thanks.'

The waiter, smiling, did a sharp bow, and then wandered off.

Erica kicked me from under the table. 'You're horrible.'

'You have met me before?'

'Shall we have a dessert?'

'Are you paying?'

She laughed. 'That's very modern of you.'

Looking at the menu, I said, 'How can I possibly choose just one?'

'Anything in particular take your fancy?'

'Cheesecake. And tarte au citron.'

As if accusing me, she said, 'You could still eat two cakes?'

'Yeah.'

'I hate you.'

'Why?'

'Eating as many cakes as you like. It's depressing.'

'If it makes you feel any better, I'll help you with yours.'

Rubbing her foot against my leg, she purred, '. . . You'd . . . eat my cake?'

My eyes watered as I restrained a giggle. 'Yes.'

Holding my teary eye for a very long time, Erica said softly, 'I didn't realise you were such a slag?'

'I'm not. I only finger on a first date.'

'That's not true.'

'That wasn't a date.'

'And this . . . ?'

'Erica . . .'

She wet her lips. 'Yes?'

'What's your favourite colour?'

93

'Crimson alizarin.'
'What's your favourite smell?'
'Freshly cut grass.'
'What side of the bed do you sleep on?'
She bit her cheek. 'You know what side.'
'Yeah. You're right. I do.'

# 35

Just found a handbag. Muggers and bag snatchers often come in the garden to divvy up, chucking anything they can't use in the shrubs. The more diligent of the breed of scavengers put the unwanted personal effects and belongings in the bins. Yeah, in the actual bins! I like that. That's tidy of them. Anyway, I've just found a handbag in the bushes. There's a purse and some letters, a Mabelline lipstick and a Rimmel mascara, a tampon, a packet of Wrigley, some receipts, a pen from one of those charity shop envelopes from Scope, and a bit of Blu Tack. I'm suspicious this bag was thrown away and not just stolen and dumped. It's because of the purse, the purse has money in it. Fourteen quid in change. There are a couple of bank cards too. Muggers or bag snatchers would have rifled through all this, the fourteen quid almost enough for a brown or a white. No, this handbag was thrown away by the owner, I can tell. How? Not a difficult question to answer. You see, I've read the letters.

In order to perhaps locate an address, or at least contact the owner, sometimes you have to check out the personal effects; you know, to find a number to call or something. If I just give it to the pigs I'll have to (a) talk to them, and (b) give them my name etc; and I don't want to do that. So instead, I read through the letters. They weren't posted, they were hand delivered to, let's call her Jane. They were hand delivered to My Beautiful Jane . . .

The first letter I read went like this:

My beautiful Jane,

As I lie here in hospital the doctors aren't talking to me that much. I'm scared. There not telling me anything and I am preparing for bad news. I know you didn't mean what you said. I think we both said things we didn't mean. The nurses have been very nice to me and B****a has visited me and will give you this letter. I hope you will read it. I don't want to upset you. I just want you to know that I understand.

Will write again soon,

love J.

The next read:

Dear Jane,

I'm sorry you don't want to visit me but like this in hospital might be difficult for both of us. I'm in a lot of pain and the doctors haven't told me anything yet. They talk about me but not to me. Which is a bit like you, ha ha. I didn't mean that, I'm just so sad here and in alot of pain. B****a told me you have been crying. Dont blame her for telling me. I am sad you are sad.

I miss you anyway.

love J.

The next had been crumpled up and then flattened out.

Dear Jane,

The doctors told me that I might lose my legs. I don't know what to do. I wish you would visit me but then I know thats imposible because of what you did. I had to tell them that someone hit my legs with a steel bar and they said that made sense of the damage. You smashed them up really well. The police have visited me but what could I tell them? I know you didn't mean it or those things you said. Sometimes you don't know what your doing and I'm not blaming you. I know its what you are like sometimes because of what I am like.

I'm sorry.

J.

Love hurts, apparently. Can you imagine? What the fuck was all that about? Talk about a guilt trip. There are two more letters, but they're unopened and I'm not keen to change that. Some things are private after all. Even I have boundaries, especially for personal horror. I fucking do.

It's annoying though, isn't it? I mean, what do I do now? Do I give the handbag to the pigs, or take a chance and drop it in at the hospital round the corner? Perhaps I could trace her through the bank cards? Considering the effort she's put in to avoiding the poor bastard, should I even bother trying to find her? How much *effort* should I put in? The most recent receipt is dated three months ago. It's from Waitrose. And that day she bought a mozzarella and cherry tomato sandwich, ready salted crisps, a bottle of whisky, and a bottle of Lucozade . . .

Those unopened letters . . . It feels really wrong, sitting here, holding them. I could . . . perhaps I should . . . No, I'm going to leave it for now. And anyway, I've just noticed it's nearly closing time. I'll save them for tomorrow if I'm bored.

# 36

Hours go down in two days. That means it's almost August, and that means garden closes at 21:00 on Thursday. I'm off for those days, Wednesday and Thursday, so I'll have the pleasure of trying to kick the tramps out early over the weekend; can't wait for that. Anyway, I opened those letters. It's not good. I'm not sharing. In fact, it was a Herzog moment. Like in his film about that bloke and the bears.

Those letters should never have been read, and I don't know how I'm ever going to forgive myself for it. But I have learned a lesson, it won't happen again, I promise. Some things are private, and personal horror and tragedy really is one of them.

Still, I wasn't quite sure what to do with the letters or the handbag. I sat quietly for a long time yesterday wondering whether or not to just throw them all in the black wheely bin. Or burn the letters so no one else can ever read them. Is it my responsibility? When Our Beautiful Jane threw the bag in the bushes, she must have known someone would find it, that perhaps they'd contact her and give her the bag back. Did she come back for it? To try and find the bag, realising the selfishness of her act, only to discover it had gone? She only needed to come to the hut and ask for it. Would you? Would she even remember what she did?

What she'd done.

The content of those two previously unopened letters, I'm not embarrassed to admit it, I cried. Well, not cried, obviously. More like welled up. The honesty, the . . . invasion I felt, my invasion. The callousness of my reaction, the grim hilarity of it all. What is that? What is it? Guilt? A realisation that I'm not human anymore, not a human being? Surrounded by monsters, have I become one as well?

This is all about community. Surround yourself with monsters and become a monster. Surround yourself with . . . With what? With who? Aren't we all monsters? I've tried, I really think I've tried hard to not get involved, to shield myself from the horrors; but I don't think it's worked. Not yesterday anyway. Yesterday was a bad day. Yesterday was the worst. Oh, it was the worst. God help me.

# 37

Ow. Erica just crawled over me to get out of bed, and in the process crushed my cock - which is quite sore enough as it is, actually. I know, I know, but . . . Yeah, you're right, there are no buts.

Erica texted me yesterday. Then she phoned. Then, probably out of some sort of guilt, I suggested that perhaps we leave it be, and she suggested that wasn't what she wanted. So I thought about it, for about fourteen seconds, and then decided to meet up with her. Not for any funny business, just out of some sort of formal courtesy. That then turned into some very *informal* courtesy . . . A courtesy call, you might say. Well, maybe not.

I know what you're thinking. And you're right, it is getting a bit serious. She's been on my mind quite a lot recently, and not always in a good way. Yeah, I'm having some doubts. So when she contacted me I was a bit reluctant, a bit . . . I'm not sure I want this, this *connection* to someone, to anyone at the moment. Not while I'm . . . it's not . . . I just don't know. Fuck it, I'm too tired to think about it now; and my cock hurts.

I like *Erica's flat*. Erica's flat. She shares with someone but I can't quite remember who it is . . . He's away or something. Anyway, it's weird here, because there's no discernible masculine or feminine feel to Erica's Primrose Hill flat. There are books everywhere, but apart from that, it's quite minimalist; except for the odd design classic. A charcoal and cream Florence Knoll sideboard in a sparse living room; the Eero Aarnio Bubble chair hanging in an open plan kitchen; and I'm particularly impressed with the modern day Venus de Milo I'm looking at right now . . .

Shhh, shhhh, Erica, dressed only in a tiny yellow t-shirt, has just sat down next to me on the bed, her hand stroking my thigh, brushing against my cock.

'What are you doing this weekend?'

'Why?' I said, stretching my arms.

'What do you mean why?'

'I'm working.'

She frowned. 'All weekend?'

'Yeah, it's my long . . . shift.'

'What about the weekend after?'

'Why?'

'Why are you always so difficult? Why do you always answer questions with a question?'

'Why do you ask so many questions?'

Erica went quiet, tapping her foot quickly against my leg. 'I want you to come to my studio.'

'And see your little work of art? I'm sorry to tell you this, but I can see it from here.'

'You're so horrible.'

'Yeah.'

She waited for a moment. 'What have you been doing?'

'What do you mean?'

'See? Question with a question! What *work* have you been doing?'

'Nothing.'

'Nothing?'

'Yeah.'

'Nothing at all?'

Grinning, I snorted, 'What's it got to do with you?'

'You're horrible.'

'Yeah, you've already said that.'

She shifted, crossing her legs and positioning herself so she could see me better. 'I remember seeing your work, I think it was about six years ago, in a group show off Brick Lane. Those pieces were really beautiful.'

'. . . Thanks. Which pieces?'

'A triptych. Really beautiful colours. Abstracts. Like gas or liquid.'

'Oh yeah, I remember those.'

'Where are they now?'

'Don't know.'

'How can you not know where your work is?'

'Lost them somewhere.'

'Don't you mean someone probably bought them?'

'Maybe.'

Pleased with herself for some reason, she said, 'You didn't know that, did you? That I knew your work.'

'You must be very, very old . . .'

'Fuck off.' Then, carefully, she took my hand in hers. 'Will you come to my studio?'

'Are you trying to trick me? I've been tricked before.' But, feeling like I should concede a bit, I said, 'Do I have to?'

'I want you to. I want you to see what I'm working on.'

'Don't you find that showing people your work before it's finished spoils it? I always thought it was like an invasion. There's a time and a place for sharing pieces. Like later, when you've moved on, exploring something new.'

She shook her head. 'Why don't you work anymore?'

Laughing, I said, 'I don't want to talk about it.'

'Okay.'

'Really. I don't want to talk about it.'

'I said okay.'

I ran my fingers along her thigh. 'I like your t-shirt.'

She smiled. 'What do you like about it?'

'It's like the best wrapping paper in the world.'

'You're so dirty.'

'Give us a kiss.'

'You give *me* a kiss. You owe me one.'

'Where do you want it?'

Straddling me, Erica pulled off her t-shirt. 'Anywhere you like . . .'

# 38

Undefeated City Of Westminster Parks alcoholic John "Wig Wham!" O'Reilly has just had a fight with a bush, and lost. In he came, throwing a right jab, then a left hook. An uppercut missed but he wasn't punished. The Mahonia bobbed and weaved in the wind, a vicious gust energising the branches! It lurched forward, catching John "Wig Wham!" O'Reilly with a stinging right hook. The champ staggered back. A kitten punch, he growled! A flurry of blows! A storm of pain! rained down on the challenger, each smarting less than the last. The champ swayed! The exertion clearly taking its toll. Tired arms, arms like lead with a head to match! The Mahonia sensed its chance, stealthily rooted to the spot, it dummied one way, veered the other, and with a ferocity only nature can control, the Mahonia slashed a left hook across the champ's face - A CUT! A CUT! Wig WHAM! O'Reilly threw a retaliatory combination so slow the impotency of that endeavour rocked the champ backwards then forwards! His legs had gone! A sucker punch drew him close, then the Mahonia whipped in a barrage of telling blows to the Wig WHAM's dilapidated rib cage! The champ's hanging on! He's grabbing on for dear life! Someone throw in the towel! GET HIM OUT OF THERE! SOMEONE! But no! Wig WHAM has one last trigger to pull - YES! YES! Old faithful! THE HAMMER! The Mahonia's too casual, too relaxed! For God's sake don't stick your chin out! The champ sees the gap, this is the chance he's been waiting for, the last chance he'll ever get! HE'S MISSED! HE'S MISSED! The Mahonia saw it all the way and landed a fist-ful of dynamite of its own, shocking the champ with sharp left and rights! His eyes are rolling, his knees are rolling, HIS HEAD IS ROLLING! HE'S GONE! The champ's slumped forward and the Mahonia's holding him up, a sporting gesture no less in this battle between these great wooden titans! But no! The Mahonia's dropped him to his knees with a nonchalant thrash across the brow! He's down! He's DOWN! He's never getting up from that! . . . Mahonia wins by a knock out.

I like John O'Reilly. He used to be a contender. He could have been a somebody, and instead he's a nobody. He's not even punch drunk. He's the only drunk I know who crawls out feet first, sort of digging his heels in to pull himself forward, huffing and growling with the effort. Every time I see him he's been fighting that fucking squirrel that gave one of my AFICAN brothers his purple haze.

How many beatings do you want to take? Well? Well? For a start, stop having fights with bushes and pavements, that would be my advice. When he's sober he's the nicest bloke, really he is. One fucking drink and the bell goes. The cliché is unavoidable. But it's all he deserves; the dozy fucker. He made some excuses to me once, saying that he'd been in a fight. And when I said, Yeah, I know, I pulled you out of the flower bed, he went quiet and smiled, But I got in a few gud shots furst, dint I, pal? Yeah, you only lost on points, I said. Then he shadow boxed at me before limping away, his crutches awkwardly dragging on the floor. I don't know how he broke his leg, but rumour had it that he crawled out of the park into the road and straight in front of a van, which then ran over his legs.

He's a whisky boxer. No 8.5% lager for the "Wig WHAAAAAM!" I call him that because he wears a wig. It's the best wig I've ever seen. And you should hear the other drunks, tramps, homeless and smackheads laugh when he gets going. That wig slipping further and further forward, or further and further back as he calls them out. Once, I saw him unbuckle his belt, shake it aggressively at everyone, carefully put it back on, then unbuckle it again, shake it

104

aggressively at everyone, carefully put it back on, then unbuckle . . . For hours. And they all just laughed at him. CONRAN, Skago-rexic Stuart, Ronald Polio, they all just pissed themselves; literally in some cases.

So who's he fighting? What's he fighting? *Whaddaya got?* There's someone in front of him when he does it, I know it, I can almost see him, the opponent. It's not Mr Whisky, I'm sure of that. No, not that demon. I'm sorry to say I think it's himself, or an alter ego, a mocking twin of evil; or of good. Apparently, he really was a competent fighter in his day. Well known on the circuit, well re-spected even. It's hard to picture after that demolition by the Ma-honia. One year, by one of the benches he'd been sitting on before getting filthily drunk and crawling out, I found a photograph. The familiar pose, the seventies sideburns; lightweight champion of the world. I gave him that picture the next time I saw him, and he looked at it like I had, not recognising who it was at first. Then he threw it in the bin.

# 39

Have you ever been disappointed? I mean *really* disappointed?
You talk to someone, or they're involved in a similar social or peer
group, and you think that the threshold for, well, for brilliance,
must be similar because it seems like you and that person are like-
minded? And they talk the talk, they walk your walk, and you hope,
you pray that maybe, perhaps, perhaps you have met an equal of
some sort. Ever had that? Ever had that happen? I'm not going to
lie to you, I have entertained this notion on a few occasions, and
the most recent of which *is* related to the deviously divine Erica
Monroe. And so, armed with this optimism, I finally agreed to visit
Erica at her studio. Yeah, I'm aware of how that might seem, but
she did ask so very nicely . . .

Anyway, it turns out her little work of art is a lot better than her
actual works of art. And the problem is that it's sort of affected
my, hmm, sort of affected my *interest*. I know, I know, who the
fuck am I, a professional bin-emptier and tramp-shit picker-upper,
to judge and be disappointed by an actual practising Fine Artist's
work? I don't know how to explain it, how to ignore the gut-drop-
ping, cock-shrinking horror of that realisation. It would have been
better to have never ever seen it. Never, ever, ever.

Thank God she's married and I can get out of all of this.

# 40

All right, I've been really busy today. Can't tell you what I've been doing. Okay, okay, I've been working. Yeah, hang on, I mean *working*. After visiting Erica at her studio, despite the shocking *disease* of it, I felt a slow burn, a gradual re-ignition. So today, on my Wednesday off, and after two very boring late turns at work, I've been busy.

I jumped out of bed. Oh, by the way, I sleep naked, have done ever since I was twelve years old. My dad had a shock one Sunday morning when, because no one else was up, he ripped my quilt off in that way parents do to get you out of bed, and flung it aside with the gruff immortal words: Come on, what are you doing? Can't rot in bed all day. Time to get . . . Okay. You're a young . . . *man* . . . now . . . And then he carefully put my quilt back and only ever *shouted*, "Time to get up" on a Sunday after that.

My mother continued to buy me pyjamas every year until I left home - which surprised me. I suppose some things are just between men, aren't they? It's a communication thing. Those pyjamas my mother dutifully laid out every Sunday night, unlike my sheets, were always clean for the next wash day. Strange that. Dirty teenage boy! Hey, some of it was nature! Come on . . .

Anyway, this morning I jumped out of bed, put the kettle on, dressed, made a mug of coffee, and ate an organic croissant. I live in a bedist. It's quite a good bedist. A large main room, and luckily, a separate kitchen. It's relatively inexpensive, well, on my wages it's just about affordable. I was charmed the day I found it. A typing error drew me to it immediately:

**W14, Large bedist, quiet house, nr tube, £\*\*\* pw.**

I just had to see it, because what the fuck is a bedist? Turns out the ad should also have said: 'No mod cons, no central heating, nothing.' Just a large 60's/70's style bedist in a derelict Victorian conversion with separate kitchen. The kitchen is actually bigger than some of the other bedists I've lived in; and to be honest, despite my public description of it as a rat-hole, it's actually pretty good; for someone like me.

The tall, polystyrene tiled ceilings, two huge sun-drenched in the afternoon windows, room for a double bed, three seater sofa, single armchair, double wardrobes, floor space - yeah, you're fucking jealous now, aren't you? In my kitchen, I have a 1950s dark green two seater sofa bed, a book cabinet, washing machine, plus all the required general utilities. See? Not that bad, not really a rat-hole at all. Well, okay, maybe a little bit . . .

After breakfast I felt restless. You see, because I was off at the weekend I decided to do something constructive with my time; and Erica's husband was up north on business or something. I wasn't really listening when she was telling me about it. Yeah, apparently he's a novelist or a film maker or whatever. Blah-blah-blah. Uh-huh, I wasn't really listening, me being too preoccupied with looking at the work.

Erica shares a studio with a fairly well celebrated member of Saatchi's New Painters; *her* work was interesting. Erica's . . . Well, her little work of art is the only jewel in her neatly groomed crown. It's not that it's terrible, it's just that it's mediocre; and you must remember my rule about mediocrity or brilliance.

Erica is a figurative painter. Her canvases are colourful, expressionistic works. She doesn't use a ground, preferring to work straight onto the white of the canvas. *She just paints*. She paints with freedom, but not with that much skill. Flaws in her technique are disguised by naive stylisation. So despite the brush marks being energetic, they serve only to camouflage her anatomical illiteracy.

Her use of colour is quite strong though; but generally . . . Mediocre.

Don't get me wrong, I've done my own time in mediocrity. But that moment of brilliance, when it came the first time, the touching of that Holy Grail - marvellous. You can't go back. There's no way. The kick you get. The sheer *knowingness* of that achievement; it's unsurpassable.

It's been a long time since those days and I'm living on reputation. You may have guessed this, I know, I talk big but can I walk big? That's the point. I can, or rather, I used to. That's why I walk into Private Views and studios and I'm treated like this is also what I do, because I'm a creative person, aren't I? Live it, breathe it. Have passion for my subject, for my work, for the whole fucking thing. Is that the truth? No. No, it isn't, because you see, I hate it. I hate it all because of the mediocre or brilliant thing. Now when I see people's work I just see the joins, the mistakes, the shitness of it. Oh yes, occasionally there's quality, a technical competence; and occasionally something, someone, stops me in my tracks and I FINALLY FIND SOMETHING INTERESTING; but really, most of the time . . .

Imagine knowing this. Imagine knowing this is true. How frustrating. But now, after an extended sabbatical, I'm far enough behind to start again; to begin the process, the journey to rediscover; to explore and chase brilliance again. I know this is it, the beginning of that horror, and it is a horror, because the last time I was evil. Hey, don't laugh, stop it, this isn't funny. I'm telling you something here. It's true. I was evil. I destroyed everything and everyone around me to do it. I have to be evil, it's my way, the only way I can achieve the necessary *quality*. Without it . . . mediocrity. And no one should settle for that.

Having cheered myself up with this realisation, I set about the first step to recovery. Is it recovery? I'm not sure, perhaps it's just regurgitation. Yeah, I'll have to watch out for that. I mustn't repeat, I mustn't repeat. It's important to avoid that trap, much too easy to fall into, and so many people do *exactly* that.

So, do you want to know what I did today?

I read.

Hey, I didn't say or promise it'd be exciting.

# 41

Morning.

I jumped out of bed, showered, put the kettle on, dressed, made a mug of coffee, and ate an organic croissant. Then I read for three hours. Then I opened one of my wardrobes, the one without clothes in. This one has stuff in it. Yeah yeah, it's a *wardrobe*. Well, the *stuff* in this wardrobe hasn't been in use for a long time.

Packed neatly away in boxes and double taped, these treasure chests contain my materials. Brushes, rollers, paints, jars of white spirit. Look at this one, look at the colour of the silt in the bottom; it's like gold. That's ancient white spirit, stained by the memory of activity. Five, six years it's been in that jar, undisturbed until today.

I taped the box back up, put it away, and closed the door to the wardrobe. Then I went to the shops, came back, and looked, gazed actually, at that wardrobe. Made a coffee. Ate a cake. Played some records. Had a sleep. Woke up and stared at the polystyrene tiled ceiling for about an hour. Watered my plants - can't remember the names, I just tend to call them baby or darling. Vacuumed. Did the washing up. Tidied a pile of newspapers and magazines; sat down.

Played some more records. Ate an apple. Then read through the articles I'd ripped out of the magazines I'd recycled. Stuck the telly on and watched Antonioni's *The Passenger* on DVD. Made dinner. Checked my emails. Ignored my phone; sat down.

And this is a good day, because that's quite close for me. I don't go through this ritual every week, you know. This is only because I've been inspired. But wait, something's wrong, I'm jumping the gun here; and that's why I put that box back and ignored all the others. I really need to start at the beginning, start from zero, start with exercise rather than statement; and there's only one way to do that, even though I'll have to wait until next Tuesday to do it.

I need to draw a naked lady.

## 42

Well, the weekend passed without incident. That's not quite true, there were lots of incidents, it being a really hot couple of days, and heat plus Special Brew plus mentals equals carnage. But I ignored it all, I stepped back, ran away even, because none of it mattered. The fighting, the defecating and vomiting. The fourteen drunks, shit-faced and laid out on the sunny part of the lawn like burning, stinking corpses by midday . . . That was a lifetime ago for me, because it's Tuesday, and later, I'm going to draw a naked lady. All I have to do is breeze through the day, keeping everything, everyone, at least at arm's length, and not getting involved.

There was a highlight of my weekend - Alan Ashby. Alan Ashby walked past me on Sunday as I was closing. He stopped, raised a finger and slurred, 'It's only. A joke.' Then, as he walked out the gate, I saw a piece of paper stuck on his back with something written in blue marker, which said:

I AM A FUCKER,
FUCK MY ASS!

I laughed. A delayed reaction of course, but I laughed as I locked the remaining three gates. Kept laughing as I walked home, and finally, let out a tired guffaw as I put my head down on my pillow. Not kick me. Not punch me. Not I am a drunk. I am a FUCKER, fuck my ASS!

It's only. A joke.

It was funny, because when I saw him stumble towards me, he had his jacket over his head, checking it. And I thought, What the fuck is he doing now? Come on, Ashby. I want to go home. And it all made perfect sense when he passed. He'd just left that note on his back, perhaps realising it was true, accepting it; I don't know.

*Someone* had stuck it on his back. Someone who knew him, someone he knew; and they had waited for him, wrote it out and put Selotape on it. And when they saw him, they stuck it on his back.

*And then he just left it there.*

Was he upset? Do alcoholics get upset? Alcoholics don't have friends, they just have people they drink with. Or not, in Alan Ashby's case. A definite home alone drinker. You know, in one of the seventeen hotels and three bed and breakfasts he owns. Were his feelings hurt? Did he think that maybe someone somewhere treats him like a human being, only to crush that delusion with a cruel, infantile joke? Once I'd stopped laughing, and it did take quite a long time, I felt sorry for him. For the first time in three years I actually felt sorry for him. The thing is, I usually ignore him as much as I can. Once, when the gardeners were in, he wandered over to us and interrupted our conversation to tell them:

'He hates me you know.'

'No I don't.'

'Yeah. He does. Why do you hate me?' He was laughing, joking about it.

'I don't know who you are.'

'See? See? He hates me!'

One of the gardeners, I don't know where he's from, smiled in an embarrassed eastern European way; and as Alan Ashby sank to his knees, throwing his arms out in mock despair, I blinked in disgust.

'He hates me! I don't know why! I don't know why I'm on my knees . . .'

'Listen,' I said. 'I know I'm the king of the jungle, but even the monkeys don't have to bow before me.'

The gardeners laughed (we have this king of the jungle/monkey gag), and when Alan Ashby struggled to his feet, not one of us helped him up. He God blessed us, and then went off on his way.

There, that's passed the time. It's nearly two. I'm going home.

## 43

Life Drawing starts at 19:00 and finishes around 21:30. It's held in a function room above a pub in Old Street. I like it here. This pub's still a bit dirty, a bit shabby, a bit rough. My sort of boozer. I haven't been in for a while, but Erica's been popping by recently, and she said the drawing was still on. She's not coming tonight though, I checked earlier. Her husband's back.

There's a chance I might bump into someone like Simon Tabernacle or Jocasta MacMillan or Sebastiane Flaw, but the drawing a naked lady part makes up for that threat. It's the sort of pub that, despite my previous commitment to disconnection, if I threw a putty rubber, I'd hit someone I knew, or know, or don't want to know.

I buy a pint of Guinness, and although it's been years, eight years, I recognise this dainty geezer standing next to me at the bar. We nod at each other, but we're much, much too cool to say hello. I remember he was on menswear at the RCA. Don't be impressed. My ex-wife went there, not me.

My *ex-wife?* Err, that sounds so weird. Am I old enough to have been married and divorced? Yes. Yes, I am. And I'm not sure why, but being, fuck, being *artists*, seems to make being married and divorced feel different; like it's not so two point four . . . Does that sound right? *Is* that right? Anyway, I have to go upstairs now. It's time to draw a naked lady . . .

114

Hmmm. Some things never change. I walk upstairs, and as I put my pint down, Lucy, a plain faced girl with a fantastic classic bob haircut who organises the session, hands me the clock and introduces me to the model. So I set the times, directed the poses and generally slip straight back into gear. My drawings aren't bad either, but sometimes it's the poses that makes the magic happen. This evening's model was a cheerful Australian girl with an athletic physique, capable of a variety of difficult poses. I like to demonstrate the sort of dynamic I want, and this leads me into direct mono et mono with the model. It's important for her to have someone to work with, to take the formality out of the situation. I'm good at that.

After the first few poses, I could sense that it had become quite a relaxed atmosphere in the class recently; but after I had strictly adhered to the times, and engaged only with the model, the mood changed from a dreamy lack of focus, to hardcore concentration. That's the sort of Life room I like. Don't get me wrong, I'm not a tutor, and it's an untutored class, people can do whatever they like; but once you set foot over that line and you have a model posing for you . . . You owe her your undivided attention; it's a power thing. And she must have that, because she is naked. The intimacy yet anonymity of that fact demands it.

Because I'm in charge, because I'm directing her, the model wants to please me; it's a power thing. And she did everything I asked her to do. We worked out the poses, discussed the options, and then I posed for some of them myself so she knew exactly what I wanted. I politely asked her if she was okay; if she wanted a drink; if she was warm enough. And then I laughed at how funny her toes looked poking out from under her crossed leg. Then I pulled an impossible pose, sort of balancing precariously; which she struggled to copy. And then I told her it was for forty five minutes . . .

Oh, how we laughed . . . all the way down to the bar and later back to her place. If only my everyday life was as civilised as this.

## 44

I was almost late for work this morning. Yeah, you know why. I managed to get in with just minutes to spare, and ran as best and as fast as I could around the other gardens to open them, so that we, as a company, didn't incur a fine. Four hundred pounds an unopened gate! If Mr I Come On Your Face Charlie Council came round at 08:01 and those gates weren't open . . . Yeah, trying to get in from so far away after such a late night was not a good idea. Fuck it. C'est la vie!

I'm tired. I am really tired. And it's a long day, 21:00 finish. It's going to be hot. And it's already busy, the garden being full of office girls; so I think I'll recuperate under the Indian Horse Chestnut, drink plenty of water, and think about my drawings.

Now I sort of remember why I stopped going Life Drawing: naked ladies and alcohol. I think the novelty blissed me out - and then look what happened! Not that it happens every time, I wouldn't want you to think that. But the whole hit of drawing again definitely blissed me out last night, and I can't wait to check my drawings later - but only after I've recovered a bit. Right now I can't even lift my arm to bring water to my filthy vagina stained lips. It's going to be a struggle today, I can feel it.

'How was life drawing?'

'Fantastic.'

'What was the model like?'

'She was sort of . . . athletic.'

'Was she any good?'

'Yeah, she was. Good poses.'

'Really. Good poses.'

'Yes, Erica. Really.'

'Did you stay for a drink afterwards?'

'Mmm-hmmn.'

'Yeah, sorry I couldn't make it. I was busy, what with . . . Anyway, Gina said she saw you.'

'Saw me what?'

'Nothing. Just said she saw you in the bar.'

'I didn't see her. Who is she? Doesn't she life model too? Have I met her?'

'Briefly.'

'Right. Briefly.'

'I have to go.'

'Okay.'

'. . . Bye.'

I hate phone calls. Considering the fact that telephones were specifically invented for communication, it strikes me as odd that in my world less seems to be said than more. I'm waiting. I'm sitting and waiting for the next call. And there will be one, because Erica won't leave it. The irony of all this. I know what she's getting at, of course I do; but this is what I was talking about, the commitment issue. I'm not ready for it, for an affair. Or more.

We've cooled a bit on the fucking part, and that's where it's been getting dangerous. We've been talking, not quite socialising, but you know, getting to know each other better. Much better. And I'm worried. So I suppose my clever id, superego or whatever, came up with a plot to sabotage for everyone's own good. Do I mean that? Yes. Yes, I think I do. It really should never have happened, to have reached this point, and that's my fault; because of my weakness for reconnection. Not with Erica, but with that world, a world outside of all of this.

For a time this was enough. I was satisfied, probably through novelty, with doing a pleb job every day, dealing with the different sort of problems it brought me. It seemed less involving, and that was my first mistake, because everything you do involves some form of commitment to the cause. After the breakdown of my relationship and subsequent divorce, the return to something simple was so enticing, such a relief, that I jumped out of bed every morning, leapt in fact, eager to mow a lawn or prune a bush or plant some Polyanthus. Not having to think worked well for a while. I accepted all the abuse, the condescension, the sheer ugly violence of the public and the tramps and the shit kids; I took it all. The anonymity I indulged in, the knowledge that I was hiding, or rather, camouflaged, was funny. I laughed at it all the time. When I found my rat-hole bedist, I laughed. When I closed the door to my empty studio for the last time, I cried with laughter. It was all so easy to do! I couldn't have escaped more obviously within plain sight if I'd tried! Oh, the thought of disappearance had occurred to me. Oh yes, the long walk, the falling off the edge of the world. I nearly did it too. Except that one night out with a mate, as he went to the toilet, I thought: This is it! I could walk out the pub and never ever return, just go, my name is Reginald Perrin, my name is Reginald Perrin . . . And the minute I envisaged that, the very fucking second, I knew I could never do it. So instead, I settled for semi-retirement, the shit job, the semi-shit take it or leave it life; watching those who *had* taken the long walk, *had* fallen off the edge of the world; vicariously living it through the filthy, the insane and the desperate. What is freedom? What is sanctuary? I had certainly learnt a lesson about escape . . .

My ex-wife, Christina, a Greek goddess of sorts, with strange, vacant blue eyes, was a printmaker. Mediocre or brilliant? Actually, just below halfway of mediocrity, sliding towards very mediocre. But ambitious, dear God, so determined, despite a lack of real ability. It's funny what hard work can achieve, isn't it? Turns out it achieves just about enough; which sounds a lot like mediocrity to me . . . Hang on, the phone's going.

My ringtone is some obscure Berlin brothel music I recorded via the telly from *Smiley's People*. Smiley, played by Sir Alec Guinness,

118

is surrounded by naked ladies in a strip joint called Der Blaue Diamant, waiting for someone to turn up. While he's patiently sitting there, in the centre of all the sex, the drinking, and some really terrible S&M routines, he orders a whisky, cleans his glasses, and looks thoroughly bored.

For me, *that* is brilliant. Because despite his temporary community, he is just, and only, focused on what is relevant to him.

. . . Aiyah bastard. I need to get a new phone, this one hurts my ear. Thing is, I'm not sure it was just the radiation giving me a headache. No, I think it was the noise, the sounds that were spilling, *seeping* out, penetrating my collapsing ear drum, forcing their way in to the centre of my skull, that hurt the most. It's like every word twisted another part of my brain the wrong way. By the end of that second conversation I was left bemused and, well, bored to be honest. Probably as a defence mechanism. I shan't impart the details of said conversation, but I will act it out a little.

Okay. The conversation ended like this:
Me, a pinched look of bewilderment.

A short text three hours later had this feeling to it:
Her, with wide and sad eyed melodramatic closure.

My reply text was like this:
Me, nodding in sterile compromise.

There. Stanislavski would be proud. How long this will last for, this agreement, remains to be seen. It's an agreement of disconnection. Our paths will no longer cross, our social circles will no longer overlap. Have a nice life. Okay, I will. You too. I will. Yeah, me too. Okay then. Okay.

I feel better about things now. Like a clarity has returned. Later, I'll be crying myself to sleep; but for now it's a tarte au citron and a mug of coffee to celebrate the inevitable. And it was inevitable, because where was it going, where could it go? Fall in love? Get married? Live happily ever after . . . ?

No. I'm not capable of that. Not yet.

119

# 45

I've been watering the flower beds. Not with water, with *tears* . . .
Not really, *come on*, you have met me before . . . Anyway, where are
all the young nuns? These two nuns just walked past the hut, one
about eight foot tall, the other, bent over, and three feet small -
both a century old. I see nuns in here quite often. At first I thought
I was hallucinating, like The Visions of Santa Maria or something.
What's that film called? Not *Black Narcissus*, that one about . . . was
it Lourdes or . . . ? Where the statue talks to the young girl . . . Is
that right? Or is it a vision, by a waterfall? Can't remember. Thursday night nearly time for closing blank brain syndrome. It's been a
long week, a trying couple of days, that's for sure.

I am hallucinating. It's the weariness starting to get a grip on
me just as the hours are coming down. I keep thinking I'm seeing
things moving in my periphery. Like a shrub was a rat. Or the sun
flashing on my arm was a little bird or something. I'll be okay after
a good night sleep. It always sorts itself out after a few days not
doing anything, and with only tomorrow to go until the weekend .
. . I have nothing planned. Not now anyway. I never do much after
a long week, there's no point, and Saturday is just a write off. The
brain, the ego, says yes, but 21:00 that night, I'm asleep on the sofa,
drooling all over my cushions.

*The Song of Bernadette.* That's it, *that's it.* I don't think she's a nun
actually. I think she's just a peasant.

# 46

Well, I just did some patrolling, and I found that as I walked the streets I was muttering, like this, under my breath: Prostitute. Smackhead. Bulimic. Closet homosexual. Wife beater. Kiddy fiddler. Pimp. Anorexic. Alcoholic. Prick tease - female. Prick tease - male. Caner. Boring muzo. Waitress. Attention seeker. Office worker. Bus driver. Hotel cleaner. Minge tease - male. Pea tease - female. Virgin. Can't help herself slut. Won't help himself slag. Rent boy. Project manager. Racist but pretends not to be - white. Racist but pretends not to be - black. Cock gobbler. Wannabe model. Wannabe actor. Wannabe but never gonna be pop star. Tourist. Sexually frustrated. Sexually liberal. Sad faced girl (don't worry, baby, I'll marry ya). Mummy's boy. Shit kid. Shit mum. Shit dad. Bad hair. Bad teeth. Terrible make up. Sportswear Neanderthal. Townie fuck. Foreign townie fucks. Euro trash. Americans. Tramp shit picker upper.

That'd be me, when I got back to the hut and looked in the mirror. But not just that, some of the above as well. I like to remind myself how important community is, and walking the streets really helps me to do that, with all the necessary spite and reflection I can muster.

I'm so fucking depressed I wish I was dead. Yeah, again.

## 47

It's a beautiful day. Would you look at that sky? I love Friday and Friday loves me. We love each other, and I am a very happy chappy right now. I don't know how, but I managed to have a really good sleep last night. I arrived at work quite early this morning, refreshed and energised, strangely raring to go. I sat under the Indian Horse Chestnut with a hop, skip and a jump in my heart, and finished work at 13:00. I'd just had enough of all the fun and the games, and told Graham that I was going. Any fucker comes round for me - bollocks to them. I'm off. I think Graham was slightly disappointed, mainly because this meant we didn't have our one hour chat about emptying bins and not burying tramp shit; or whatever else we usually talk about.

My mood was good. Sleep fixes gloom, clearly. I knew I was ready for bed last night because my whole body ached from the moment I walked through the door. I actually felt in pain, and I didn't even argue with myself as I hit the sack a minute later. Somehow I slept. My brain shut off, my mind slowed to an acceptable rate, and I closed my eyes, waking up only three minutes before my alarm. It was so unusual I thought I was dreaming. I couldn't remember waking up, like I do most work nights, at 01:11 and 03:56. Every night. Why those times? And every night? Oh, it's stress all right, I know that. But the accuracy of it all. 01:11 and 03:56; it's upsetting.

So last night I slept straight through, I'm sure of it. Perhaps it was because of the weekend, knowing I had those two days off to do nothing. Or do something, depending on how I feel. Perhaps I just needed to hide for a change, from myself and the recent events. Clever id, superego or whatever. King Kong. That's so fucking true.

# 48

Just found some slides. With nothing to do this weekend, I decided
to take a look at some boxes stored in my wardrobe. Yeah, *that*
wardrobe. And the very first box I opened had all these slides in it.
Slides of me, slides of my ex-wife, slides of us on holiday in Paim-
pont looking for Coetminias - oh, and slides from an exhibition . . .

Of my paintings.

I no longer have any of my old work. I either threw it all away,
left it behind in my studio, or just lost it. Something like that . . .
Anyway, out of a box of maybe fifty slides, this is all that remains.
Just three. Of three abstracts. They were based on this idea I had
about how the eye lets in light, about how it interprets colour. Two
of those pieces were like the effect of that exploration. But the
first piece, ah, the first piece . . .

It was a fairly small canvas, smaller than the other two, about
50 x 60 cm; just a test really. I certainly didn't expect it to work
first time. Initially, I used tertiary colours for the ground; wash
after wash, wiping off, wiping on. Finally satisfied, I limited my
palette, using tonally sedated reds and greens. I stuck to a basic
geometric composition, filling the space with semi-abstract shape
and form. The washes gave the piece a depth and a volume, but
those complementary colours, so, so dense; the eye, searching for
information; the pupil, a dilated chasm . . . BANG! Revelation. The

intensity of that moment in time. The sudden explosion of colour; from the void . . . to the vivid.

I tried it again. And then another one. Both times using different palettes. Oh, they were pretty, beautiful even, but they were the effect rather than the physical process; they were just wrong. They didn't work, not really.

These slides look so old, so dated now. Fuck, it's depressing. Look at Christina. She's almost happy in these slides. Idiot. Look at those shoes she's wearing. I loved those shoes, a pair of sap green platforms. We picked them up in Kensington Market before it was taken over by shitty European gothic chic. She looks pretty in this one. Her slim tanned face, long thin nose, and those acute angled but full lips, pouting at the camera. *And how curly is her hair?* Ha! I like her eyeliner in this one. She used to do it like that just for me, just because I liked it.

One day, about a year before we split up, we went life drawing. And afterwards, probably three months later, we were sitting at home, in our flat in Archway, and she stood up and disappeared for a minute. When she returned she had my sketch book with her. She sat down next to me and oh so carefully looked through my drawings. At various points I made comments like, "That's terrible," and "Line's not too bad on that one. The arm's okay . . ." You know, stuff like that. And, after the last drawing, she closed the pad, put her hand palm down on the cover, then hurled it across the room; the little pocketbook of doom slamming violently against the window pane; the BOOM from the impact shocking me.

I laughed.

*She* burst into tears.

When she stopped crying, which took quite a long time, and not exactly helped by me still laughing, Christina looked up at me with these tear swollen eyes.

'I hate you,' she said.

'Why?'

'Because my best drawings aren't even as good as your worst. And all you can do is say how awful and terrible your line is, and how . . .'

Then she started crying again. And I remember that as I held her, she sobbed into my shoulder, those relentless tears scarring my shirt; but not my heart. I wiped those tears from her cheek. Then I examined her closely, coldly, eventually searching her eyes, finding only a void. I knew in that moment, I knew, I realised, that I didn't love her anymore.

. . . I think I'll put this box away now.

## 49

Conran, one of my favourite drunks, has returned just in time for The First Day Of Alcoholic's Term. As we approach September, the beginning of most academic years, Conran is back; and how I've missed him. Conran has been in rehab. Oh yes he has! He's been in rehab. And for the three weeks before he went, he drank so much that, rather than rousing the beast, I left him, every single night, where he had dropped. The others all gave him a glorious send off, a fanfare of 8.5% vol proportions. And now, after just four days, *four whole days in rehab*, he's back.

'I thought you were in rehab,' I said, as he paused at my door.

'CONRAN WAS! CONRAN WAS IN FOOKIN REHAB, MAN!'

'How was it?'

'STUPID.'

I laughed. 'Why?'

'Oh, man,' he said, quietly. 'They made me draw a dog, man.'

'A dog?'

'Yeah, man. I can't draw. CONRAN CAN'T DRAW! But they said it dint matter. They said just draw a stick dog. So they gave me a black pen and said draw a dog.'

'And did you?'

'Yeah, man. And then they said, What is that dog saying to you? And I said, GO AND GET A DRINK!'

'No! Really? What happened then?'

'Then they said draw another dog, this time in red. So I draw this stick dog in red, with a red pen, right, and they say, What is *this* dog saying to you? And I said, GO AND GET A FOOKIN DRINK FOR CONRAN, MAN!'

Then he hee-hawed loudly, a phlegm filled throaty hee-haw that would choke and kill a real human being.

'What happened then?'

'NOTHING, MAN! NOTHING HAPPENED!'

'Didn't they ask you to draw another dog? Perhaps one in . . . green, say. You know, as a contrast to the black and the red dogs?'

'NAH, MAN! WHY?'

'It just seems to me that the black dog is your depression. Why you drink. And the red dog is your anger, or the urge to destroy through drink. And a green dog could have represented calm. A calm, *clean* Conran. A symbol of the future, to represent change. The reason you were in rehab in the first place. The part of you that wants to change.'

Conran laughed, 'YOU SHOULD BE A FOOKIN SOCIAL WORKER, MAN! YOU'RE BETTER THAN A SOCIAL WORKER! I'D LISTEN TO YOU, MAN!' But then he paused for a second and sort of wiped his eyes. 'I tried, man, but it was too difficult . . . They dint explain to Conran what it all means. Not like you, man. Not like you just did . . .'

I nodded. 'Because you were in rehab for a reason, weren't you? You wanted to be in rehab,' I shook my head, 'and you can't do this forever, can you?'

'It's been a long time for Conran, man.'

'I know. There's always next time, Conran. There's no rush.'

'TAKE IT EASY, MAN! I'VE JUST GOT TO GO OVER TO THE EDGWARE ROAD . . .'

And score. 'Yeah, okay.'

'LATERS, MAN!'

'Yeah, take it easy.'

Do you know, he was terrified of going into rehab. OH YES CONRAN WAS! Sorry, please forgive the panto. But he was absolutely shitting himself. All summer he's been going on about it, and then when it came up? Look what happened. I do wonder, probably unnecessarily, why any of them bother. The drunks, the social workers, the people who run the rehab centres. Why bother, why do they fucking bother at all. From what I've seen, none of the drunks really want to change anyway, not really. It's too much for Conran to face up to what makes him who he is. What he has become. I've heard his sob story: the abusive father, alcoholic mother, a disability discovered during his teens; anything you want to believe, you can blame.

He's scared. He's scared of life outside this garden. The streets are alive with threat for Conran, and the only way he can cope with it is to be shit-faced. Or engage in aggressive begging outside the Post Office, the Tube station, or anywhere else he hasn't been ASBO'd yet.

This is the second time he's cried in my company. The first time was in May - but not this year, when was it, last year? Possibly. *Whatever.* Anyway, I was planting the summer beds (Chrysanthemum Gold Plate and Cosmos Sonata), and Conran was supervising in that way his type do, you know, with a can of 8.5% in his hand and a crack wrap in his mouth.

'HOW DO YOU GET IT SO STRAIGHT, MAN? THESE LINES, MAN, DIAGONAL LINES, MAN?'

'I've got a good eye.'

'THEY'RE SO FOOKIN STRAIGHT, MAN! EXCEPT THAT ONE.'

'Where?'

'THAT ONE, MAN.'

'I'll twist it. The plant's not symmetrical. The leaves are bigger on one side, see?'

'STRAIGHT FOOKIN LINES, MAN.'

'You and your lines, Conran . . .'

He hee-hawed. 'CONRAN LOVES LINES, MAN.' And he put his so yellow they're brown fingers to his nose. 'WHOOOOSH! DID SIX LAST NIGHT, MAN.'

'Only six? You're slacking.'

'YOU'RE SLACKING, MAN. YOU SHOULD HAVE FINISHED THIS BY NOW!'

'Listen, why don't you stop fucking supervising and give me a hand? Come on, get your hands dirty. Feel your muscles working for the first time in years! The sheer physical honesty of that! COME ON, gimme a hand! Wipe away the sweat of hard work rather than cold turkey . . .'

Conran went quiet. 'I want to, man. But I can't, I can't do it.'

'Put that can down and chuck me those flowers.'

'I can't. I can't do it.'

'Don't you ever feel like doing a hard days work?' I corrected myself, 'Or at least a hard morning . . .'

'I can't. I've got a bad back,' he said, pulling his cap down, covering his eyes.

'Yeah yeah, me too,' I muttered, bent over, on my knees, continuing to plant.

Conran shifted from foot to foot, swallowing, then cleared his throat. 'Nah, man, I have. A disability. When I were a kid my back got fooked up. I had phy-si-cal therapy and everythin. The doctors . . .'

'Yeah, I'm gonna need some physio therapy after this. There, finished. What do you think?'

'STRAIGHT LINES, MAN! YOU NEED A DRINK, MAN. CELEBRATE!'

'It's a minor achievement really,' I sighed. 'I'm going to have a cup of tea instead.'

And I did, not wanting to hear the tragi-comedy of Conran's life again. The thing about drunks is, they're never bored by autobiography. It's just *so well* rehearsed after all those countless alcohol fuelled phantom conversations you see them having.

I see Granny Smells doing it all the time. She comes in, makes a roll-up, hangs it from her toothless mouth, then talks it all out with her imaginary friends. I've watched her, and it's the same every time. The same hand gestures, the acting out, the drama. When I walk past, or check the bin, she stops doing it. Then, as I walk off . . . The thing is, she doesn't say anything out loud, she *mimes* it. Yeah, she mimes the whole thing. I don't know who she's talking to - a daughter, a husband, her mother, her father; but it's definitely a row, an argument about something.

She's as old as time, and smells like she hasn't washed since the beginning of it - really, it's true. If I spot her early enough, I leap up and slam the door shut, just so the unmistakable stench of senile piss doesn't invade my space in the few seconds it takes for her to pass by. It's a different odour to Ronald Polio, his piss smell is mixed with shit and vomit.

# 50

Do you remember when I said that if I threw a putty rubber I'd probably hit someone I knew, or didn't want to know? Well, I've just been life drawing again. And don't worry, it was a geezer. I don't like drawing men. Not for anti-bumfuckbrowncocklove reasons. No, not that. It's just that unless the body shape is interesting, like sinewy or toned, or muscular like Michelanglo's *David*, then the general male physique is shapeless and pot bellied. Mediocre. And by now we all know about the mediocrity thing, don't we?

So, to be honest, I've ended up with a lot of drawings of his legs. I tried to get him to pull dynamic poses but . . . Good models make good drawings. Bad models . . . Boring drawings. Anyway, I endured it, legs and feet can be interesting too; but really, my heart wasn't in it. So I finished the session slightly early, which was to everyone's relief, and then could barely wait to have a drink, recent events needing sedation. I shook the hands of the geezers playing pool, gave the thumbs up to a kid from a design studio over the road, and finally attracted the attention of the sweet little bar girl with neat eyeliner and a choppy crop. Some of the others joined me at the bar - Lucy and Kat, Peter and Colin; and we casually discussed the session while having that long awaited beer.

The pub was busy, getting a bit rowdy, it being nearly ten o'clock. And even though I had work in the morning, I thought: Fuck it, a few beers won't hurt. If only I'd known! If only I'd walked out the door after one pint, said my jolly farewells, pausing only to wonder if the Beatrice Dalle look-alike Kat wanted to fuck me. If only I'd done these things and gone home, preferring to lament my disappointment with the model. Or think about Kat's provocative eye contact and body language; if only. Instead, I gulped down the first pint, then a second. By the third I needed a piss. So off I went, released the torrent, and then made my way back to the bar.

I didn't see him at first, I mean, he was right in front of me, but it was like my eyes were ignoring what was standing not a foot away. When they did accept, it was like a detonation. AN ENEMY! And I still could have escaped if Kat hadn't called me over at that precise moment, bringing me to his attention. As it was, it was like a slow realisation, a doom of sorts. Like in *The Duellists*, the film of a Joseph Conrad story about two soldiers who, over a long period of time, stubbornly persist with . . . Well, with *duels*. It was like that, the inevitability of it. The inevitability of coming face to face with my best ever enemy: Andrei.

We gave each other a steely glare. One of those looks that knows everything about each other. And then I laughed, just beating him to it. We suffer from Doppelgänger Syndrome. I've made that up (not the syndrome, that really exists), I mean our pretend suffering of it. But there's still a discomfort in recognising someone like yourself, and feeling the need to eradicate their existence, their memory. We're similar looking, with similar hair, similar clothes, similar-similar-similar. And that's horrible. It's like two sides of the same tarnished coin.

'Not stopping to chat?' Andrei said, his sharp features cutting the room in half.

'No,' I replied, airily.

'But we've so much to catch up on. How *are* you?' Andrei slid a look at his dull new media new middle class companion, and then, with the worst acting you've surely ever seen, asked me, *'Who are you?'*

'Marley's Ghost, of course. Come with me. Step outside.'

'Ha! Not again. Cost me five hundred quid getting my tooth fixed.'

'You can afford it.'

Andrei smirked. 'But could you? You see, that's the question. Can you afford it?'

Pinched slightly, I said, 'I'm sure I mentioned the last time I'm too pretty to fight.'

'Yes, I remember, that did upset you. The split lip.'

'Quid pro quo, Clarice. My lip, your fake tooth. You, yelping like a dog . . .'

Andrei smiled, and said in a low voice, 'I've missed you.'

'That's because I'm brilliant, and the mediocre like to hang around with the brilliant.'

Pausing to think first, Andrei said, 'I heard you were emptying bins and burying tramp shit. Simon didn't believe you, but I did. I like a man who fulfils his limitations.'

Now, this might have gone on for days, or years, or until the end of time, so it was good that Kat interrupted it by handing me a pint and leading me away.

'Who's that?' she asked, looking at my mouth, not my eyes.

Replying as nonchalantly as possible, I said, 'Well, I'm sure he'd like to think he's King Kong. But then, we all know what happened to King Kong, don't we?'

'Seemed a bit tense between you?'

'He's just an enemy.'

'Do you have a lot of enemies?'

I snorted. 'Funny you should say.'

As I finished that pint, I strained with every sinew in my body not to accidentally look over, feeling that gleaming fixed tooth grin on the back of my head. Yeah. So anyway, I finished that pint, and I did say my jolly farewells; and I did wonder if Kat wanted a fuck, but she's a bit young for me, even just for that.

And anyway, I'm pining . . .

You want to find out more about Andrei, I know, I can tell. And the way things are going I won't be able to avoid it. But I think I'll keep it a mystery, at least for now, just for a little while longer.

Hey, *come on*. You're on my side, and by now you know what I'm like . . .

# 51

My boss just came round to tell me that there's a private party in the garden tonight. Well, thanks for the late fucking notice! Yeah, he forgot to mention it to me. Forgot to mention it to my supervisor. Forgot all about it. Until *yesterday*, when he received the confirmation email from Mr I Come On Your Face Charlie Council. So this morning, because the gardeners were busy elsewhere, I have been super tidying up the garden, edging, blowing, and a mowing.

One of the neighbouring hotels has rented this little piece of paradise for a function. This means that we'll be closed to the public between the hours of 17:00 to 20:30. I don't mind to be honest, it's easier for me. They'll bring in a security firm to keep the riff-raff out while the business and hotel sluts and slags wander around, drinking fine wine, and counting the calories of the posh canapés from Marks and Spencer . . .

I love these events. There are others too, like last week's music festival, organised by some big faced cheeses from some local business initiative. See how we work hand in hand with our community? I was off for that - unfortunately. And one year, can't remember when, we had, like, these arts and crafts people in, trying to get mums and kids interested in a bit of summer holiday distraction. You know, making stuff out of twigs and leaves, painting pictures, being creative! I didn't have the heart, I don't have a heart, when it comes to these brutally inept Art Club hobbyists, bemoaning the lack of numbers for their boring stencilling. Or chucking silver and gold glitter everywhere. The fucking mess they made. Oh yeah, they promised to tidy up, but what they really should have done was to promise to tidy up badly; yeah, better to make a promise you can keep, than one you can't . . .

An added bonus of this private party in the park, is that despite a projected finish time of 20:00, with half an hour to clear up, I know it will finish at *my* projected finish time of 22:00. Mmm-hmm, bet any money. My boss has already promised to pay me if it runs over. So, I'll let you into a secret: if officially I'm supposed to work until 20:30, then 22:00 means a whole hour and a half of overtime. Overtime with no extra rate of pay - I'll get paid normal time; and so for losing 90 minutes of my life, on an already torturous shift, I'll get an extra, oh dear God, I don't think . . . I can't say it. I can't. It's not even a tenner . . .

I love my job.

Rumplestiltskin is in charge. The real Rumplestiltskin, that is, not me. Tiny and medieval looking, Rumplestiltskin is the manager or something of the hotel organising this bonanza. That's unfair, she just looks medieval; I'm horrid. I spotted her the other day, wearing a very nice child's size beige suit, looking around the garden, planning where to put the marquee. Yeah yeah, nothing's a surprise to me; king of the jungle, remember? The only thing I needed to know was when, and look at the notice I received. Ha, I'm laughing at the sincere apologies from my boss now, but you know, why should I ask if there's something going on, why should I have to? Anyway, apparently there's going to be a harpist playing later. That'll be nice for them. Let's hope it doesn't rain.

Sitting here, under the Indian Horse Chestnut, reading my book (*The Loser*, by Thomas Bernhard), I can see the security guys debating with the tramps and the homeless exactly why they can't come in. I spoke to the security about an hour ago. They wanted somewhere to put their stuff, you know, batons, sprays, riot gas etc. I'm joking. Sort of. If they could, they would. I know that the tramps arguing with them right now would get a right Ballarding if this was a work of fiction. They said as much. I mentioned the *issues* we have to deal with and, with all the clichés you'd think they'd avoid, the security guys revealed a Ballardian type psychopathy about it. They would really enjoy it, that social cleansing. They don't seem to realise that those scum are my friends, at least, closer to me than they are, with their crew cuts and Gulf War placebo bravado. If it ever came to that Ballardian violent exchange, I'd be on the drunks, the tramps and the smackheads' side . . .

The party is starting to pick up a bit. The marquee is at the far end of the west lawn, the good lawn. My hut is at the opposite end, and as long as they don't stroll too far down, I think I can sit here until it gets dark, hidden away. Without any of the general public or riff-raff in this cordoned off part of the garden, there's a calmness, almost a pleasure about being here. It's the same at closing time. Once the gates are closed and I'm walking back towards the hut, I don't know, there's this beauty about the place; and I can't help it, I always mutter under my breath: *If only it was always like this, just me and the trees.* The streetlights break through the darkness of the bushes and the shrubs, and the moon shines down as I look up at the indigo sky. That quiet is so welcome, sometimes I feel like staying and sitting on the lawn, a private paradise all to myself. At last, I'd sigh.

There are probably sixty to seventy people in this half of the garden, but it feels like someone has stuck a bubble over us. This is humanity, civility, the human race at play. It's still early. After a few bucks fizzes or a couple of Pimms o'clocks, there'll be a surge, an increase in volume that only the sober can detect. But still, it won't include overhearing how many of your brothers you killed in Somalia, or who owes what, or how you bullshit everyone that you fucked over the pigs and the undercover tit-heads. No, it won't be like that at all.

Bollocks. I can see the shit kids fucking about on the east lawn, hoofing a football into the trees. Little twat attention seekers. Not only that, but Rumplestiltskin seems to be looking in my direction. Delegation of responsibility, isn't it? Shall I? Shall I approach, aggravate and walk away? What would be the worst thing that could happen to me? Being stabbed or shot, laughed at or threatened by a twelve year old? Okay, I'll finish this page and wander up. Any second. Deep exhalation of intent. I love my job, I love my job. Please don't kill me.

. . . Okay, well, at least I'm laughing. I casually walked up past the security, sauntered past this little chap with a clip board, dodged a pretty young blonde waitress holding a tray of champagne, then approached the shit kids. When they saw me, they stopped hoofing the ball into the trees and took up a defensive formation. Two of them, the big kids, gave me a disinterested glance, while the three remaining little cherubs looked at their feet.

'All right lads. Hey, why you kicking the ball into the trees?'

Big Kid A said, 'For summink to do, innit.'

'Listen, if you want to play for England, you should practise controlling the football. Left foot, right foot. Heading.'

'We don't want to play for England, man.'

'Who do you want to play for?'

Big Kid A thought for what seemed like ten whole minutes. 'Don't know.'

I sighed quietly under my breath. 'Well, anyway, if you are going to play football in here, even though you know it's not allowed, try not to destroy the trees, okay?'

'What's this party, man?' Big Kid B asked.

'Local hotel.'

'Can we drink some of dat champagne, man?'

'Oh,' I joked, 'so *you're* the special guests of honour?' The big kids laughed, and the cherubs laughed too.

One of the cherubs, the smallest, said, 'You don't come and tell us not to play football in here anymore.'

'No.'

'Can we ride our bahhkes?' Big Kid A asked.

'I'd rather you didn't. At least not this evening. Listen, just try not to destroy anything, okay?'

Then, despite trying to engage me in further conversation, I left them there. What do I look like, their fucking dad? *No thank you.* I'm not sure I ever want kids. I mean, come on, if they were half as talented and half as good looking as me, then they would be twice as depressed. And if they were twice as talented and twice as good looking, then *I* would be twice as depressed - and I don't think I could live with that . . . Although, depending on the mother, I suppose it *could* be all right . . Anyway, I walked past the pretty waitress, smiled, and being slightly distracted by her, didn't notice the chap with the clip board step in front of me.

'I'm sorry, sir,' he said, hiding a slight eastern European accent. 'This is a private party. I'm afraid this part of the garden is closed to the public.'

'Is it? Right, okay. Well, perhaps I'm on the guest list?'

'Certainly, sir. What is your name?'

'I'll spell it for you, okay? Ready?'

'Yes.'

'Right. First name: Eye. Double yew. Oh. Arr. Kay. Then surname: Aitch. Eee. Arr. Eee. There, am I on the list? Under Aitch?'

He scanned down his list. 'I don't seem to . . .'

The pretty waitress interrupted. 'This gentleman works here, idiot.'

He blushed. 'Oh, I'm sorry. Of course. So sorry! Please, go through.'

'Cheers, mate,' I said, winking at the girl, who was still shaking her head.

And so that's why I'm laughing. Fancy me being mistaken for an ordinary member of the public! Is it true? Do I look like I don't work here, don't belong? That kid has done me a favour! I suddenly feel so much better about myself; and what a rare feeling that is! Time for some dinner, then read the rest of *The Loser*. I think I'll have the time to finish it tonight, I can already sense it.

Listen to that. The harpist is playing. Despite the shrill giggling, hearty laughing, and the increased drunken volume, the music is dancing between the bodies, bouncing off the trees; those sharp notes cutting through all the hubbub on their way to my ears. It's weird, sort of like that party scene in *Rollerball* where they shoot the trees. A strange mixture of sophistication and baseness. The juxtaposition of abstract beauty and violent, destructive beasts. There's something apt about it, well, I probably mean ironic, that I'm reading *The Loser* as she plays. I won't explain why, I'm just going to keep listening to her. If I close my eyes . . . For a moment in time my world has changed, an ecstasy, a freedom; like when Andy plays a record for the prison in *The Shawshank Redemption*. I'm almost in tears, probably tears of self pity. Why does it take something random and abstract and beautiful to pull feelings of despair out of a box that you think is always locked away?

I'm tired and it's getting late, nearly 23:09. Oh, they're apologising. Yeah, they're sorry mate, won't be long now. I can't blame them. It's so peaceful here when it's late, having it all to yourself. The night air cloaking the violence and poverty that's slumped or staggering about in the streets right outside those gates. That energy isn't muted, it's *placated*, and we all appreciate that. It's why I can't, despite my own fatigue, get annoyed or be put out by the time they're taking to leave. This is a moment to savour, a rare opportunity to share that calm. It's good to be nice sometimes.

## 52

My boss paid me three hours of overtime. WHOOOO-HOOOOOO! That's nearly, wait, that's not even twenty quid! He wasn't happy about it, I can tell you, but I made sure I texted him as I locked the last gate to confirm my eventual departure, just so there's no argument. But to be honest, by the time I got home it was time to get up, or so it felt. Three hours of recovery lost; but look at what I had instead. I'm so calm this morning. Everything around me is insignificant compared to last night. Eventually I strolled out and sat watching the harpist as she played. The rhythm isn't unlike making brush marks on a canvas. You don't have to be frenzied to emote, the energy can be redirected from that into something that is still dynamic; it doesn't *have* to drain you so much. There was a moment, from out of her solipsism, that the harpist suddenly looked straight at me. Just for a second. But it was a connection I completely gave myself to. I think I fell in love for that second. And when she finished, before Rumplestiltskin and the others rained their applause over her, she gave me a coy, sad glance. And, almost matching that sadness, I stood up and walked silently back to my mess room.

Come on, why spoil it . . . ?

# 53

Shhh, shhh, quiet, don't make a sound, quiet like a mouse in a mouse trap; or silent like a ninja. I'm in the pub with some friends. Shhh, shhh, I know, but it's time for you to meet them. For ease we'll call Jonathan, Jonathan, and Jonathan, Jonathan - but she's a bird. Only joking. I'm in the boozer with Nick and Jane, and their friends Paul and Mette. Me? What about me? Well, you know how it is, I haven't brought a wife or girlfriend; you haven't forgotten have you, that I'm pining? Yeah, I think I remember mentioning that. It's always the way, isn't it? You contrive a separation built on disconnection and reconnection, and then the stubborn fucker matches your own    obstinacy and . . . Ah, well, anyway, you're not missing anything. This lot are discussing career opportunities in the big, bad world of new media and the like. As this is of no interest to me whatsoever, I'm just sitting quietly, sipping a pint of Guinness.

I saw a picture of a monkey once, about ten years ago, of a chimpanzee actually. All his fur had fallen out and he looked like he'd been sculpted out of stone. The definition of that physique - unbelievable. No gym time could ever match the perfection, the majesty of that proportion. Fabulous. Wait a second, it's my round. Three Guinnesses, one lager and a glass of wine for Mette.

Mette and I don't get on. It's not said openly, but I know it's true. I saw her roll her eyes once when I complimented her dress. *The*

142

*dress was lovely.* The first time I met Mette, she and I had a disagreement about a character in a book, and she's never forgiven me for it. Paul, drunkenly, excitably, spoke over her during our conversation; and after scolding *him*, she seems to have since redirected blame on to me. That was about three years ago. I don't mind. I'm easy in these situations. It's pretty rare that we're sitting at the same table actually. Usually Nick and Jane keep their universes separate. Today is either a test or a mistake.

So I'm being deliberately quiet, just to see what people talk about if I don't get involved. That's how it works, isn't it? Conversation. Subjects are discussed, and depending on who you're with depends on how expansive it all gets. Opinions are often regurgitated or confirmed, and usually there isn't any real opposition to those opinions. That's what being friends is all about. Often there's a hierarchy. One member of the group indirectly chairs the passive chatter, all the while cementing their position at the top of the discourse food chain.

Anyway, back to that bald chimpanzee. I think it was at Cotswold Zoo or something. He looked amazing, sitting there, all metrosexually smooth-chested! Oops, just sniggered and halted Mette's rhythm. Shhh, shhh, I am listening, really I am. Anyway, it was only temporary, the chimpanzee's baldness. Stress related, apparently. At least, that's what the zoo speculated.

There is another hairless chimpanzee, a female called Cinder, in America somewhere. But she's permanent. A full-time smooth operator.

## 54

I've been thinking about that harpist. What was she so unhappy about? What was her problem? If you're capable of making something so beautiful, so transcendent, then why the sad eyes? Poor old Sad Eyes. Melancholic or what? There was something lonely about her performance, wasn't there? Remember, I noted her solipsism, didn't I? Fucking hell, now I feel like I should have said something . . . Like what though? Let's see, hang on a minute . . . I know! I do know the answer to that! Ha! Maybe something like: *I understand. It's okay. I understand how you feel, really I do. But you see, and here's the thing, listen: I've given up! Really I have! No melancholy for me! Oh no!*

I love delayed decoding! She knows all about the brilliant and mediocre thing. She breathes it every time she sits at that harp. Just how close can you get! Beautiful. What a moment to cherish; and let me tell you, it wasn't love I felt in that second, but understanding. The party goers could appreciate the brilliance, but probably not the sadness. And love? HAH! Does love match brilliance or mediocrity? Oh, that has made me laugh. I am really laughing. Because usually it starts with one, and ends in the other.

# 55

Time moves so slowly, doesn't it? Like that Borges story about the guy who can see his hand ageing second by second. I'm not exaggerating, there's something chronic about the way that I just don't seem to be able to make time pass quickly enough; or without noticing. How do other people do that? It's not that I'm not busy, it's more that I'm aware, aware of time. I don't know, I can't work it out. It's been barely three weeks since disconnection, and while that's not *that* long, it really feels like it to me. No amount of deflection can help. The life drawing, work, a Private View tomorrow . . . An enemy crossing my path.

Enemies. How many enemies do you have? I'm not talking about your mum and dad, or your best friend. I mean *actual* enemies. The word "enemy" is so fantastic, it's like a bomb. I went to a Private View last year with a friend and some other people I didn't know. Halfway there I asked if any enemies were going and my friend said yes. My face dropped, pantomime disgust, and the others, a couple of girls, looked shocked and asked, all seriously, "Why do you have enemies?" I remember I laughed and said something like, "Look at me." And for a second, I think they became enemies too.

So, okay, let's finally discuss an enemy. I'd already met Andrei at a few parties, a couple of Private Views, and knew that it was best to avoid him really. On one occasion though, a party, I couldn't help it, it was too hard to resist. And so I listened in to Andrei's conversation, you know, just to see.

There he was, sitting talking to these two shit-faced teenage pop tarts. And despite the fact that there was no way they could possibly have known who the artists were he was going on about, it wasn't stopping him from super-indulgently amusing himself.

Anyway, eventually I interrupted. 'You fucking name dropper, Andrei.'

'How dare you!' he grinned. 'Knowing things is good, isn't it, girls? Girls?'

I cocked my head. 'Whatever. Personally, I prefer artists I don't know. Artists I have never heard of or *even seen* their work. They're my favourites. How many just want to get their faces on the next new Matthew Collings show like This is Modern Art? No, wait, *This* is Modern Art. It'll be said like that, won't it? *This* is Modern Art.'

'I had lunch with Collings the other day.'

'No you didn't.'

'No, I didn't.'

Andrei laughed. And then, ignoring the pop tarts, he smirked to himself, pointing to an empty Giorgio Cattelan bookcase.

'Where are all the books?'

'What books?'

'Very good. Empty bookcase - what a statement. What minimalism.'

'Hardly. Nick and Jane have just moved in, you pretentious fucker.'

'I could take that literally and you'd be upsetting some very unpretentious girls.'

'That can't be true if they've slept with you.'

'Nice comeback. You should write a book.'

'So should you next time.'

Andrei laughed, waving someone over. 'Erica? Come here, sweetheart. Have you two met? Come on, doll. Don't be shy.'

I watched Erica give Andrei a big smile, followed by a private flutter that made me feel like I shouldn't have seen it. Or wish I hadn't seen it. Then she turned and smiled at me. That was some performance, I thought, admiring her eyeliner.

'Hello,' she said softly. 'Didn't I see you at a screening a couple of months ago?'

'Doubt it. Sorry, didn't quite catch your name?'

'Erica.'

'Jonathan? That's a . . . lovely name . . . Jonathan . . .'

She laughed. 'Thanks. Do you tend to know a lot of Jonathans?'

'He's a novelist too,' Andrei interrupted, pulling Erica to him.

'Really? Never would have guessed.'

Andrei continued to spill words from his filthy mouth hole, but, as I pretended to listen, I caught Erica linger with a look that was despite, or perhaps because Andrei was holding her close.

'Who's your publisher?' he asked.

'I'm still writing the synopsis.'

'Still writing the . . . that's funny. Really. I'll put you in touch with my agent. Let me read your *unpublished* novel and I'll pass it on.'

'Andrei, you're so selfless. I don't know how I ever believed everything everyone always said about you.'

'Stick a gold star on my chest.'

'What, in the hole where your heart should be?'

'I'm all heart. That's just a pocket where I keep loose change.'

Erica sighed, shrugging Andrei off. 'You two should just get your cocks out.'

'That's a bit obvious, Erica, for you,' Andrei said, innocence personified.

'If you were being just a little less obvious, I wouldn't have had to say it,' she said, walking away.

'What do you mean? What do you think she . . . ?'

'You're on your own, Andrei,' I said. And with that, I walked off too.

Later, after a few more drinks, I caught up with Erica outside the bathroom. She was dressed in a beige knitted playsuit and long leather boots.

'I'm so sorry, I can't remember your name?'

'Erica.'

'Tony? That's a . . . lovely name . . . Tony . . .'

Erica breathed out. 'You're horrible.'

'We barely know each other and you've already worked out I'm horrible? How typical.'

'Is it?'

'One of my friends says I'm a sociopath, but I think he means sociable, because once he told me he'd seen my nemesis, and I said which one, and he said he didn't know, so I said what did he look like, and he said like you, and I said you mean *doppelgänger*.'

'I see. Nicely delivered. Is that from your novel? Andrei has that tendency too.'

'Tendency to what?'

'Use lines from his work. Testing it out. I think you know what I mean.'

'Yeah, I probably do.'

Erica leaned back against the wall, red wine in hand. 'So, come on then, what's this novel of yours about? Interest me.'

'Well, thematically, it's about misplaced creativity. Narratively, it's a fairly orthodox Joseph Campbellian hero's journey.'

Erica snorted. 'You fucking writers.' Then she laughed, slightly more than she meant to.

I watched as she composed herself, felt a jump in my gut, waited, then said, 'So, come on then. What is it exactly you see in Andrei?'

'I don't know,' Erica replied, sadly.

'Dump him. Go out with me. I'm better.'

Erica tutted, but briefly held my eye before looking down at her glass.

'Honestly. He can only actually be richer or have a bigger cock. That's it.'

'Jesus . . .'

'What?'

'Do you think I can't tell what you're like? All the looks you've been giving me. The signals. And then the jousting with . . .'

'I think you'll find we've been swapping the signals.'

'Yes, you're right.' She sighed, biting her lip. 'I must be drunk. I'm confused. I . . . It's complicated . . .'

'Look, I just believe in genetic attraction. Two people either like each other or they don't. Sometimes you just have to go with DNA.'

'You're so funny,' she said quietly. 'Do you think I could ever take anything you say seriously?'

'Do I look like I'm joking? This is my serious face.'

Erica shook her head. 'No. I think that's your poker face. And I think I'm going to fold . . . That's right, isn't it? Fold?'

She giggled to herself, paused to think for a moment, then placed a hand on my arm, lingered with that look again, and pulled me into the bathroom.

Now you see, at that time I didn't know Erica and Andrei were married. I can't remember if she was wearing a ring; and to be fair I wasn't exactly checking. Hmmm, yeah. Thing is, I *had* recognised her from that screening she mentioned (well, why wouldn't I?), and we'd exchanged enough glances, you know, in that way; and I don't know, it was wrong but . . .

When I said I didn't know who her husband was, well, I lied. I just didn't want to talk about it. Do you want me to apologise? I could but I wouldn't mean it. I'm not that nice. And yes! Do you think I've forgotten? Remember, I said I used to have something to do, way back when we first met, I used to have something to do. I've misled you, I know, and it's horrid of me, but let me explain.

I gave up *art* to write a novel. The novel was too ambitious, too . . . too everything. Maybe it's just rubbish. So now, having abandoned all hope of being published, I'm settling either for emptying bins and burying tramp shit for a living, or coming out of retirement and attempting to jump back on the pain train to Artsville.

And, oh yes, *Andrei* is a published novelist. Some pop culture based cult fiction bullshit which I'm not jealous about, oh no. And he also works in film or television or something. I don't really care. Fucking all-rounder. We had a fight once, arguing about the pursuit of truth . . . Have a guess at how drunk we must have been for that.

Truth is, it was at that Private View that I found out they were married. I think I just about hid my shock, I'm not sure. But then I'm lucky that my reputation and sense of humour go before me. So when I laughed as Erica introduced Andrei as her husband, I managed to cover it by spluttering, *Why?* They laughed, I laughed, everyone laughed; and still Erica threw me a private look. Of course, I avoided her after that, but *of course* our paths continued to cross. Then, well, you know the rest of the story.

So, there you go. That didn't take long did it? Not such a slow bleed this time. I don't know why. Perhaps I just needed to get it off my chest, that burden of selective confession. We're so confessional now these days, aren't we? It's funny to think that I've kept some secrets from you. Indirectly, directly, delayed decoding . . . All these traits I indulge in. The anecdotal bombardment; a narrative, *my narrative*.

And there's more. Like the reason Erica has been unfaithful. And why I've colluded with her. And how that last telephone conversation really went. I know, I know, my narrative pokes its deceitful head out again. Selective confession wins! It really is the best! I love it and it loves me, and that's a very good job, because no one else seems to.

Come on, cry with me . . .

# 56

Was I drunk or just tired? Yeah, you may have guessed that I'm regretting letting some truths slip. It doesn't come easy to me. But you know what? I was *tired*, and there's no hiding from tiredness. Drunkenness - yes. I've never believed in the claim that you tell the truth when you're drunk. God knows I've been at my most fraudulent on those numerous occasions. But then, I live a lie every day, every waking and sleeping moment. You don't trust me now, do you? I've spoilt our bond, haven't I? Come on, you must have known it would end like this. I mean, look, it's so close to the winter shift now and I'm about to go into hibernation, that it's probably a good thing for us to have a break.

Mmm-hmm, not long now. Come the middle of October the shift changes, and I'll be left here all on my lonesome with just the billions of leaves to keep me company. Day after day of bagging the leaves from my fourteen towers of green armour - Ha! Green no longer. Red, yellow and brown. That slow descent from the top of the tree to the ground; a journey that only the leaf can fear. And I'll be waiting for it, for all of them. The billions of leaves that I'll blow into piles to bag up. Sticking them out the front for the recycling trucks to collect. Hoping in vain that my efforts will at least result in some composting for a greater good. My boss reckons that the leaves just get chucked down the dump in Battersea with all the rest of the rubbish. It saddened me the day he said that. Like discovering there's no Father Christmas. Or that *Picnic at Hanging Rock* is a work of fiction. Or there are no fairies at the end of . . . Wait, that one's true isn't it? Although, the Irish Fairy has gone to Belarus for a month to visit some young kid and his family; like on a quid pro quo, an exchange of some sort. I dread to think what he'll actually want to exchange . . .

Yep, it all goes into hibernation for the winter. No fairies, no tramps, no smackheads. They all fuck off back to wherever it is they come from. Why? Because it's *cold* during the winter. Yeah, tell me about it. Without all my favourite fiends, it's just going to be me and the trees for five months. Seven days on, three days off, seven days on, four days off. Closing times come down by half an hour every fortnight until the end of British Summer Time. Then from November it's a glorious 16:30 finish! Yay! Look at all the free time I'll have in the evenings! All that extra time to freeze my bollocks off in my rat hole bedist because I can't afford to put my heater on . . . Yay! Bring on the winter pain! I'm nearly ready, after one last necessary disclosure. Come on, do this last duty for me. Listen to this final story of a lying man. You will? Oh, thank goodness for that. Look, I'm not promising anything, and it might not be worth it, but . . .

Two days ago I met Nick in a pub in Brick Lane for a sharp half (I never drink halves, so it was a pint . . .) before moving on to a Private View. Nick is a photographer. I don't ask him what sort of photographer, or what he's doing, because we don't really have time to talk about banal everyday activities. Ah, the power of conversation! Once you stop talking about your job or your problems, I find that you end up talking about ideas and thoughts, art or history or time or . . . Who would want to talk about what's right under your skin, like a poisonous inflammation? Or perhaps seeping out, like some sort of tedious sweat? Why not delve deeper, or at the very least do your best to *avoid* that banality? Anyway, we chatted briefly about the fear of dying from a verruca in the fourteenth century, then made our way to the Private View.

We walked in, grabbed some free beers, and then strolled around the trendily derelict gallery. A group show of Painters, Photographers and, I'm laughing as I say this, *Illustrators*. It was a small space and thankfully dominated by the Painters. I mean, I say thankfully, but really even that was only the smallest mercy. Not that the work was terrible, it was just that it wasn't brilliant. And so, surrounded by a peerage of mediocrity, I nailed a couple more beers while chatting merrily to some unfamiliar faces that seemed to recognise me. As we exchanged dismissive views on the work, I felt my guts plummet as my radar flickered into life.

In a room full of women, all of a certain type, all belonging to the same scene, in a room like that, the briefest visual contact, the barest glimpse, turned my heart and my cock inside out.

Erica walked past with that face, you know, the tight face, the one that says I always walk past people I'm not ignoring like this. I scanned the immediate area for Andrei; I didn't see him, so I closed my eyes and tried to locate his presence with the power of my mind - but still couldn't. The truth is, I closed my eyes in trauma. My DNA was jumping. It's true. And the horror of that realisation devastated me.

Love. Starts with brilliance and ends in mediocrity, doesn't it? I knew I'd lost. And my clever id, superego or whatever, then forced me to return to the Private View, where I was met by Nick's knowing and accusing visage.

'What is it?' he asked, suspicious.

'Nothing. This work's terrible.' I pointed to an illustration of a bunch of nuns as tents.

'That's not it,' he snapped. And as Nick looked around, piecing together the evidence, I could see in my periphery that Erica appeared to be facing in my direction. 'Is it Erica? Don't . . . You *haven't . . .*'

'What's it got to do with you?'

'Oh, that's fucking perfect.'

'Calm down. All I said was what has it got to do with you. Last I checked, that's not exactly an admission of guilt.'

'No,' he squinted. 'I recognise that look. I can't believe it.'

'Listen to me. Erica? Come on, she's not even my type.'

'Yeah, I know.' But he said it like he didn't believe me, like, *Oh yeah, as if . . .*

I shook my head. 'I can't believe we're even having this conversation.' Then, may God forgive me, I sighed, 'She's *married* for goodness sake.'

'Yeah, you're right. How stupid of me.' But again, Nick's tone didn't match his words.

'All right, Sherlock. Is there something you're not telling me?'

Nick huffed. 'Like what?'

Some plebs I used to know from the Royal College interrupted us, which was really irritating because I prefer to get things sorted out straight away (especially after Nick's tone of voice) . . . And because of that, it became increasingly difficult to concentrate on the cheery conversation I was having with those plebs. When I say plebs, I mean two of the painters showing at the Private View. Am I horrible? I don't feel horrible. Anyway, being asked my opinion is a dangerous request, because who *really* wants to hear the truth? NO ONE. So instead, I complemented the girls on their beautiful sixties style dresses - and do you know what? *What paintings?* Dresses trump art, clearly.

I tried to get away. I needed to get away and find out what Nick knew, but Janai and Carla wouldn't let me. Every time I almost had a window for escape, one of their friends would come over and I'd be introduced and . . . This happens to me quite regularly. I join civilisation and guess what happens? Civilisation likes me. It's true, I swear. Civilisation likes me, likes my company, likes my ways. I spend so much time with the mentals and the degenerates, that I forget that I'm part of the real world too. I wouldn't say I'm everyone's favourite person, but I have my moments, like just then, surrounded, quite frankly, by four decidedly pretty young ladies.

But the air was thick with discontent. Why is it that when you're being ignored you feel even more self-aware? And even more than that, aware of the slightest movements, like an acceleration of your senses. It's periphery. The power of periphery. I mean, Erica wasn't hiding or anything. She didn't leave when she saw me, and she didn't avoid me completely either. In fact, she practically stood right next to me on more than one occasion. And that peripheral tension radiating from her...I had two choices. Ignore her, or say hello, acting all chummy, like a long lost *friend* or something; still perpetrating the complicity of our previous deceptions. So I decided to ignore her. What else was I supposed to do? We'd disconnected. We had an agreement. Our paths would no longer cross. And if they did . . .

'Hey, how are you? Haven't seen you for ages.'

'Fine,' Erica said, not looking at me.

'Do you know Carla and Janai? And these two? Sorry, I've forgotten your names, Jonathan and Tony, isn't it?' The girls laughed. Erica didn't. She just gave me a really hurt look.

Recovering, she replied quietly, pointing. 'I know Olly. His are the photographs.'

'Yeah, they're okay. How's your work going?'

'How's *your* work going?'

'Hey, I think you'll find I asked first.'

Carla interrupted, 'We're going to the pub after. See you there?'

'Catch you later,' I said, winking, knowing full well that the peripheral tension had evolved; and Janai, Carla, and Jonathan and Tony, knew it as well.

We were quiet for a minute, me and Erica, sort of just standing really. Two people who had shared so much, swapped so many words and smiles and the body to body warmth, now stood next to each other as Siberian strangers. That's how it felt. Without that magic ingredient, whatever it was, we now really knew we were disconnected. Only one thing could or would change it. But to do it, to show that *affection* . . . We'd be exposed, and she didn't want that - that's what she said. I don't know if she was calling my bluff, if it had been a test, but I don't like tests. Never have.

I've let everything go. Anything that ever meant something to me. When it wanted to go, I let it. Erica. My ex-wife. Other girlfriends. Art. The minute they wanted . . . It's not commitment, it's something else. The minute they wanted . . . To me it seemed like confirmation. How much confirmation do you want? Or *need*? I'm a simple man, really I am. There's no need for trauma or drama, don't ask that of me. My actions should be enough. Perhaps I seem noncommittal, casual, relaxed or safe in the knowledge. Maybe that made Erica feel like I was joking, like it meant nothing. When she told me she loved me, I didn't laugh, I told her I loved her too. But

155

she gave me a look like she didn't believe me; I've got an unbelievable face, haven't I? Come on, bear with me, be on my side, even if I've just given a precise example of what might be a big part of the problem.

The fact is, she'd already made her mind up about me. She'd decided that first time what I was like. And me being a chameleonic sort of chap, I just slid neatly into the role. I wasn't the way out, I was the way *back*. It wasn't confirmation from me she was looking for. It was confirmation that Andrei was really what she wanted. You know, what with me being a professional bin emptier and tramp shit picker upper. Oh yes, we'd had that conversation. I'm thirty four remember, and a pleb; the most talented pleb I know, but still a pleb. Yes, that's right. I was a way back, a reconnection to the life that Andrei provided full security for.

'I have to go,' she said, eventually. Although in real time it was probably only a few seconds after the girls had evacuated.

I nodded. 'Okay.'

See what I mean? *Just let her go.*

Nick had been occupying himself during all this by actually looking at the work. I know! It's funny what we do in the face of delayed confrontation; the deflection we put ourselves through. As the Private View started to thin out and people made their way to the nearest pub, I caught up with Nick, who, to be fair, was still loyally waiting for me outside.

'Where'd you disappear to?' I asked.

Nick shook his head and said slowly, 'You're a disgrace.'

'I know.'

'What pub we going to?'

'It's up to you,' I said. 'Where's good?'

'I dunno really. All the pubs round here are full of Time Out readers these days.'

I laughed. 'Pub plus beer plus friend equals why does it always have to be this difficult? Carla and Janai are in The Old Blue Peg. Let's go there.'

After some rather irritating but fairly typical indecision, we shrugged and went to a different pub. I found it difficult to ask Nick about Erica. Firstly, they're sort of friends, and secondly, Nick admires Andrei. Not on a bumfuckbrowncocklove level, but in an even weirder way, like, because he's talented! *What?* I've never admired anyone because they're talented! Why would I? . . . Not a peer anyway.

Three pints later and Nick was starting to get agitated, sort of impatient and pensive. It felt like we were deliberately avoiding the subject (I know I was) in that way, you know, the way that says I can't wait to talk about it.

'So . . .' I muttered, barely concealing a smile.

'Mmm-hmmmmm.'

I took a deep breath, smiled at the bar girl, and swilled the last of my pint around the bottom of the glass. 'Another pint?'

'I shouldn't really.'

'It's my round.'

'Go on then.'

I ordered two pints. 'Who's your favourite Sherlock Holmes? Rathbone or Brett?'

'Brett.'

'Good choice.'

'I know where you're going with this.'

'What do you mean?'

'Yeah yeah, you called me Sherlock earlier. I know what you're like. I'm sure you think it's really funny or something.'

'What's really funny?'

Nick sighed. 'Look, it's not my place to judge, but I just don't know what it is you think you've achieved by doing . . .'

'Doing what?'

'I knew something was going on. It's always the same when you're up to something. You're always so . . . Like that selective confession concept you kept pedalling a while ago.'

'. . . !'

'Don't pretend. Just don't even bother.' He stopped for a second, rethinking his next line. 'I can't believe you sometimes.'

'Is it because I have an unbelievable face?'

'You're a disgrace.'

'I know.'

'But *do* you?'

'I'm the king of the jungle. I know everything.'

'Really. And do you know Erica's pregnant?'

I looked at Nick. A fraction, and I mean a fraction of a second later, I shrugged. 'So?'

'So, if you and . . .' Nick looked over both his shoulders, then whispered, 'If you and Erica have been having an affair and now she's up the duff . . .'

'. . . Not mine.'

'How do you know?'

'How do I know . . . How do you think I know?'

'Andrei's over the moon.'

'Good. Nothing to do with me. My conscience is clear . . . Clear-ish, obviously.'

'I shouldn't have told you. This was a mistake. You got me drunk and now I've told you and it's not really my fault. Even if I put two and two together, you could still tell me you haven't been fucking her and then it's all just drunk talk. Tell me the truth. You have to tell me the truth.'

'My conscience is clear . . . Clear-ish, obviously.'

'That's not . . . That's not an answer . . .'

'It is.'

'No, what you should have said is: I've done nothing wrong. Or: That's not true. Then even if it's a lie, I can accept it. Then *my* conscience is clear.'

'Ha! Clear-ish!'

'Obviously.'

'Look, I can't be bothered to go into it, and there's nothing left to say really. When something's over it's over. And Erica and Andrei are having a baby. That's it.'

'And you're sure you're not the . . .'

'Yes. I'm a cunt, not an idiot.'

That seemed to placate Nick. People can do bad things. People can be evil and fuck things up, be fucked up. But in the end, as long as no one else has been hurt, as long as it's over and we accept that, then we can be forgiven. We can, can't we?

I filled Nick in with some of the details - selective confession wins! There was no need to tell him the whole truth. He didn't want to hear it. He wouldn't feel bad about it if he didn't know just how intense it had been. See? Just make it seem casual, a moment in time, genetic attraction. Just something adults do sometimes and then it's over. Job done. If we talk about our problems, our pain, then it seems really terrible, really bad. There's just no need to confirm the trauma, massaging it into a little monster that never shuts up. And that's editing. This is all about editing. Those few minutes of edited highlights put Nick's mind at rest. It didn't seem that bad. It seemed sort of okay with every word that fell from my filthy mouth hole. If you tell it as a story you can believe, you'll believe it.

*Believe me.*

Unfortunately, even though I had a conscious desire to practise what I preach, I didn't believe it. Couldn't believe it. And as Nick changed the subject, I found that despite looking like I was listening, my mind was elsewhere. Erica was pregnant? How? I mean, I know how, a mummy monkey loves a daddy monkey . . . But with Andrei? She told me they weren't sleeping together, hadn't for ages. He made excuses. She made excuses. They were barely in the same room never mind the same bed over the last six months. I know what it sounds like, and I know I'm hardly the most honest person, but I took what she said at face value - *I believed her.* Even though barely doesn't mean never.

So that leaves what exactly? I think it turns out I'm both a cunt *and* an idiot. The first few times we fucked I used a condom. But later, during the most intense period of activity, she told me she was on the pill, oh God, my guts just jumped, and that she wanted that . . . that . . . *intimacy.* Of course at first I was reluctant. It seemed so fucking obvious, didn't it? So how did I agree, how did I . . . I wanted it. I wanted her, that's why. It was easy really. Because of the genetic attraction thing. And then I sabotaged it.

Perhaps I was testing her.

So there we are. My last story before the winter shift and the hibernation that comes with it. I pretty much fall off the radar for those five months, what with the bread-line pay and the way the shift fucks me about. Nothing to do but wait for the summer shift to start. It's boring all right. The day after day after day after day of bagging up the leaves. Or praying for the rain to start a pouring down so I can sit and read or listen to the radio all day. It's much too cold for all my favourite circle of fiends to come a visiting. But then, they know I'll still be here when the spring comes. I'm nothing if not consistent, at least in that.

I like the winter shift. I don't have to share with Graham       directly. He'll work my days off, splitting his own shift between here and _____ Street Gardens. He won't like it there. Too many people, even in the winter. And there's a playground and loads of residents that can't keep their noses out. And Mr Fuck You I Come On Your Face Charlie Council visits it all the time. No, he'll find that my filthy kingdom really is the best. A paradise to escape to. A haven for all of us mediocre.

There's nothing wrong with that. Sometimes I think there are too many people wanting to be brilliant, even if they're not. Leave them to it I say. I'm tired of all this. My brain just needs to shut down for a while.

And anyway, it'll all still be here when I wake up.

# Part Three

# 57

Graham's dead. Yes he is. He died three years ago. You know when. Yeah, you do. During the winter shift. Turns out he went to bed one night and never woke up. That's the ultimate in hibernation! Some people just can't hack the winter shift. Me? Guess where I am? Uh-huh, that's right.

I know what you're thinking. Oh yes I do. You're thinking I'm drunk or something and that it was a slip of the tongue? Well, my tongue has done its fair share of slipping over the past three years, I can definitely confirm that, but no, no slip of the tongue this time. This time, as I sit here under the Indian Horse Chestnut, I mean exactly what I said. *Three years ago.* Shhh, shhh, calm down, it's okay, I'll explain it all in good time. Don't I always? Good point, I don't. And yeah, three years *is* a lot of explaining to do.

Yes, so Graham died three winters ago. It's the summer shift now. It's July actually. So really he's been dead for just over three years. And I know I've been off the radar, and you have every right to be irritated, but it's better to be late than never, because Graham's not going to be telling us any more stories. No, no more Hyde Park anecdotes. None. Not ever, ever again.

Like that one about being given flasks of tea so they wouldn't have to walk all the way back to mess room for their break, only to then have to walk all the way back to where they'd been working;

thus taking said break for about an hour, and thereby costing their company at least twenty pence in wasted labour! How I laughed the first time! Flasks of tea! Imagine that! Oh, how I miss my best ever little helper . . .

We're not patrolling anymore, oh no. After my boss had phoned to tell me Graham had fatally hibernated, he then gave me the best news ever: I was to be a gardener again! Officially! All my dreams came true! Blisters, sweat, injuries, scratches from the bushes, choking on the dust and the blossom from the filthy London Plane; all these charming pros outweighing the horrific cons. I was even given a new and fabulous indigo blue polo shirt to do all this work in. How lucky can you get? Not that lucky judging by the plebs my boss sent me over the last two summers. One was a gypsy. No really, an actual gypsy, who spent the whole summer crying about his twenty children and begging me for money; all this despite living in a six bedroom council house for free. The other was a dim kid, who only ate Mars bars and drank Coca Cola, who smelt stale, and looked a bit like the rat people from Tod Browning's *Freaks*. I had the best time ever, really I did. They were just SO MUCH FUN.

My new monkey is a very pleasant fellow. A middle class, blond crew cut, bandana wearing ex-mental and smackhead. Hell, yeah! But it's okay, he's not like that anymore. His mother might be a little bit too close for comfort, and he doesn't like people staring at him, but he doesn't bottle complete strangers in the street anymore or batter cunts who are looking at him in a funny way. Hmmm, a funny way or staring - which is it? How does one tell? Come on, Bandana, explain it to me. It's an *instinct*? Okaaaaaaaaaay.

I don't know his real name. I'm not that interested. When he turned up on his first day we both went, All right, man. So now I just refer to him as man or pal or Bandana. This seems to sedate him, allowing us to cement our working relationship as bestest, bestest buddies. We like similar music and reading similar books. And we both enjoy talking about the pleasure and pain of female company. Bandana knows a lot of slags, actually. Real slags. King Kong show ponies of the breed. He swears blind they're not crack honeys or crystal meth babes, but when they come round here asking for him, that hollow, rotten faced confession says it all . . .

I've grown a beard. Fourteen months and counting. It itches sometimes, but that might just be the wildlife. Do you know why some men shave every day the older they get? I worked it out. Grey bristles. Grey bristles make you shave every single day. After years of doing this, I have to say that I had a change of heart and image, gave up the daily trial and gave in to nature. So I grew a beard. A thick mixed badger bush on my face. A dense forest disguise; and I know what you're thinking, you're thinking: Why the disguise? Ah, well, I sta . . . Sorry? That's *not what you're thinking*? Tough luck. It's what I'm going to talk about.

So, where was I? Oh yes . . . I stared at the mirror and was devastated by what I saw. Not age catching up with me, oh no, it wasn't quite as simple as that. I looked in the mirror and . . . Hold on a minute, someone's asking me where the Tube station is.

'Excuse me. Could you direct me to the nearest Tube station please?'

'Wenl, iffe yu goh dummm theern, tum righhh, themmm itfz rih inm frommft offf yu. Okahhy?'

'Sorry? I didn't quite catch . . .'

'Wenl, iffe yu goh dummm theern, tum righhh, themmm itfz rih inm frommft offf yu. Okahhy?'

'Umm. Okay. Thanks for your help.'

My pleasure. Right, so where was I? That's right, staring at my face in the mirror. You see, I've grown a beard to cover up my deformity. Hmm? My deformity. From my operation. Basically, I had an operation to remove a difficult wisdom tooth. Yep, that's right. I went to hospital and they rather magically fucked it up and managed to sever a nerve in my face. Insubstantial compensation apart, I wouldn't have minded, but it was my best side, the left side. So my best side is now my worst side and my worst side is now my best side. Oh, the irony. I don't speak quite as badly as I demonstrated to that polite young Australian tourist, but it is fair to say that I have to concentrate very hard indeed to coherently form my words. It's been quite an education, I don't mind telling you.

I went through all the predictable reactions. The killing myself, the running away, joining a monastery . . . Then there was the depression, the self-pity, the self-loathing and self-destruction; the crying myself to sleep at night. Every night. Tell me, what else was I supposed to do? Two of my three best virtues had been my arrogance and my vanity. I'm saying that with a fairly straight face, severed nerve excluded of course.

So, what else could I do? . . . Nothing. After an all too brief I'VE GONE FUCKING MENTAL sabbatical, I decided to come back to work, to this job. I could have gone somewhere else, to a different garden with people who didn't know or recognise me, but I felt I had to face up to my fears. In the end there really was no point in hiding. And by the time I'd hit rock bottom and crawled back up, it didn't seem that bad by comparison. It was a perfect fit. So I stopped shaving, put up with the stale, caffeine enriched Ratboy monkey of last year, then fucking got on with it.

And anyway . . . Beards are in, apparently . . .

## 58

One of the Mohameds just came by. Most of them are dead now. Or deported. This poor fuck (at least he's wearing a cycling helmet today) has just wished me good health as he passed by. I hadn't seen him for a while, and to be honest, I must say I hadn't particularly missed him. Anyway, a couple of months ago he walks by the mess room, and I could just tell, I could almost have written it down and sealed it in an envelope, that he would pop his head in. Now, this is a pun. Because Mohamed was in a coma for six months. That's what his AFICAN brothers said. He was in a coma because he was drunk and spannered on crack when he collapsed, dead weight, in the street. Okay, you may think that's not too bad, a scuff here, a scratch there, nothing serious. You might think that but you would be wrong. Mohamed fell crossing the road. Specifically, almost having actually crossed the road. As he fell, because of his wankered condition, he neglected to put his hands out to save himself, and used his head to cushion the dead weight impact instead. Specifically the impact on the curb. And now his head has a curb shaped dent in it. That's right. A curb shaped dent. He broke his own head.

So now, whenever he comes by, he takes off his hat or his helmet, and shows me his head. Every time. He hasn't noticed my own disfigurement, he's too busy slurring himself. I suppose that in relation to his deformity, my own is negligible; but I'm sort of hurt, he shows off his curb shaped dent like it's better or something. I know, I know, I've grown a beard, my dense forest disguise, but still . . .

Another thing is, his right eye bulges out on that side. So there's more eyeball to see, and that's where the added horror lies. It's not just the curb shaped dent but the reshaped eye socket that has altered poor old Mohamed's image. He is in a sorry old state. That first time he showed me his head . . . You've guessed it - I felt stupid. My deformity, my problems, *were* negligible in relation to his.

I am still his brother, apparently. Before, I was like a spiritual brother. Someone who understood that we are all brothers in this world; that we all share the same space and God's own air. I didn't drink White Ace or shoot up or live on the streets, or fuck that old slag Elizabeth, but... but now? Now I'm not so keen to be his brother. Why would I?

Bandana fucking freaked when he saw Mohamed. Went absolutely fucking mental. He couldn't handle that reminder of physical fragility. I think he wears that bandana to hold all his thoughts in his head or something. Hmmm. Anyway, I know what freaked him out really. Where, oh where, is Mohamed's brain? The curb shaped dent seems to be deeper than you feel the size of the brain would be visible by. How big is his brain? If the dent takes up a third of his head, then why can't we see the brain? Or at least a visible bump in the flattened part of the scalp or something? It *is* weird. He can probably touch his own brain through only a few thin layers of skin. How about that! It would be like holding your heart or something. Feeling it throb. *Beating in time.* That proximity to your own mortality. Wow.

Mohamed's lucky really. I think it's actually a gift, even if it's one he doesn't yet realise or appreciate. Sadly, and (mis)guidedly due to the medicine called White Ace, he probably never will . . .

## 59

Okay, so I'm sitting under the Indian Horse Chestnut waiting for Bandana to come in. It's Friday, and all the jobs are done. The edging, the blowing, and the mowing. But what's going on with the weather? Hot one day, cold the next; is that what they call Global Warming? Where's the sun? I need sunshine if all my Esmeraldas are gonna come by, walking that way in and, oh, walking that way back out. Yeah, not so many of the pretty pretty walk this way anymore. I don't think it's horror. I think it's pity. The once great lion of the jungle, shorn of his metaphorical mane. Wait, a lion shorn of his mane would look like a lady lion, a lioness, so really that analogy doesn't work . . . Plus, the beard suggests I've *grown* a mane rather than . . . than . . . so . . .

I've become accustomed to my new status, actually. Yeah, it's taken a long time, but I'm resigned now; there's no point thinking about it all the time. Well, I'm trying not to, honestly I am. Frenchie doesn't come in anymore. No, I think she's left her job, whatever it was. She was my favourite. So slim and tiny. I would liked to have drawn her if I still . . . A bin needs emptying, it's overflowing, but I think I'll wait and see if Bandana will do it when he crawls in. How long can I leave it? How long will my conscience allow me to sit here? What if a boss came round and saw . . . Wait, an office worker is pushing the litter down with her own rubbish; bless you! Thank you, God! Thank you for sending me an angel!

Talking of angels, look at these hollow faced fucks. Oh Bandana, would you like a paracetamol? No? Does the dead eyed rotting excuse for a carcass next to you want one? Nah, it won't help. Do you know, I remember as a boy watching an old black and white film on a Saturday afternoon. One half of a BBC2 double bill. And this rabid dog staggered down the middle of some American dream of a town high street or something. Snarling and shaking in equal measure, it dragged its skanky remains onward and onward, oblivious to the fear it was spreading to all the little American children, their eyes covered by a teacher or librarian or something. Gregory Peck shot it. Where's Gregory Peck when you need him?

'I am fucked,' Bandana cackled, throwing his bag in the mess room with more force than was necessary.

'Who'sx thisx?'

'Who? Her? I don't know,' Bandana sniffed, sort of snorting afterwards. 'She followed me here actually.'

'Babe,' it said, feigning injury.

'What'sx your naymn, darnn?' I asked, as best as I could.

She pulled close to Bandana. 'Babe, what's wrong with this dude? Is he drunk or something?'

Bandana blinked very very quickly. 'Fuh - king bitch. BITCH!' he shouted. 'Do you know who this is! This is my FRIEND! Who the fuck are you! Who the fuck are you! FUCK OFF, PUSSY HOLE! FUCK OFF!'

'But babe . . .' she bleated, shocked.

Then Bandana violently pushed her off him as she made tentative calming gestures. Pushed her off and prodded her, forcing her back and out towards the gates; all the while cursing at her, asking her time and time again who she was. Then, as she fell over and struggled to get to her feet, he aimed a pantomime kick at her, but actually caught her in the face. She got up, and seeming not to notice the blood dripping from her nose, wandered off into the heart of darkness. Bandana had already come back over by the time she'd stood up after that accidental boot in her pretty pretty. He was phoning the supervisor. Oh, he'd arrived all right. He was definitely in.

170

'What you doing this weekend, man?' Bandana sniffed, sort of snorting afterwards.

'Nothingg. What you doingg?'

'Chilling the fuck out! That bitch. I fucked her sister last night. And then I fucked her. It was bad, a bad situation. I like her sister. I could marry her, I really could. You've been married. What was it like? No, don't tell me, I don't want to know, it's irrelevant. Can I read your book? I haven't brought one with me. Can I read it? I promise I won't crease the pages or leave sweat marks on the pages where I've held it. I know you don't like that. I'll be careful, I promise. God, I've had a bad week. It's not good. I'm fucked, totally fucked today. Thank fuck I'm at work, get some time to myself, yeah? Is it okay for me to borrow your book? I'll finish it by Monday. That's okay, isn't it? I have to confess, I stole a look through it last shift. It's fantastic, that whole pianist genius thing. I can't wait to read it. Why's it called *The Loser*? No, don't tell me, I'll read it. I can't wait. I'm going to the shops. Do you need anything?'

'No.'

'Cool, man. See you in an hour. I'll be back before you need to leave. I swear. I swear on my mother's life . . . the fucking bitch. I'll swear on something else . . . Wait, I'll think of something. Wait, yeah, that's it. I swear on *The Loser*, on your book, that I'll be back before you need to leave. There. Now you know how importantly I'm taking this pledge.'

'Yep.'

'I'm sorry about that rude bitch, man. What she said.'

'No problemn.'

'We're cool?' Bandana sniffed, sort of snorting afterwards.

'For fuckingg everr, man.'

'A1! See you in an hour. I just have to find her. Get a blow job or something. Where's my fucking phone? Where's her . . . There's her number . . . Jess? Jess, babe. I'm sorry. You know I love you, you know no one will ever love you like I . . .'

I'd forgotten about *The Loser*. It's right here on the table along with a couple of other books, Zola's *The Masterpiece* and Auster's *The Music of Chance*. Do you know what they all have in common? No no, listen, it's nothing clever, don't be so pretentious. Do you know what it is? *I haven't finished any of them.* Nope, not one. Nearly, oh yes, nearly read them. But to be honest I'd forgotten they even existed. They've sat here all this time, untouched and unloved.

Bandana is more than welcome to read them. I'm glad he's excited about it. It may take his mind off some of his little eccentricities. Bandana sniffs and snorts all the time. I recognised this melodic, rhythmic signature of an obsessive compulsive disorder, the very first minute we met. It's all right, it's only out of habit. I don't think that he's regulating his breathing. I think it's the activity, the love of doing it; feeling the back of his throat spasm with each flex. I tried it myself - it's a bit boring really. So then I tried a swallowing version, and found that equally dull. Some people are made for OCD and some people aren't. I came in to work once and found a fork balanced perfectly on top of the cold and the hot water taps. I left it there. Why should I move it? When Bandana came in from weeding or something, he said good day to me but looked first and foremost at the fork, checking it. He breathed out, sniffed, snorted, sort of coughed sharply, then moved the fork slightly. Then he put it back.

Because I'd left it where it was, and hadn't asked any questions, Bandana decided to confide in me, telling me everything, his entire life story. This was the second day! First day, of course we're all normal. Second day . . . disclosure exposure extreme! If only everyone else believed in selective confession. How my life could have been different.

It's nearly three o'clock. Gone are the days when I'd leave an hour or so early on a Friday. I think it's because I've gained a sense of responsibility over the last few years. Also, and most obviously, Bandana is still missing in action. I can leave safely at three, my conscience clear, or clear enough, that I've given him the longest time possible to return. It's his time from then on, bless his protective socks. His risk.

172

# 60

What a quiet weekend it's been. They all are these days. Back to work tomorrow, and I can't wait. The weekends off just get in the way, it's like a blank entry in my calendar every fortnight. Really, there's nothing to tell you even if I wanted to. I didn't do anything at all. I stayed in both days. I still live in my derelict bedist, and last year the ceiling started to leak when it rained. Oh, how my landlord cries tears of pain when I remind him about it; so I've stopped mentioning it, I just put up with it. He's very old and very sweet, but very reluctant to spend proper money to get it fixed. Never mind, it's not worth worrying myself about. Although, having said that, I do tend to wait for the leaks to start. Yes, when the rain outside wakes me up during the night, I lie there, waiting for it.

First the ceiling clicks, or taps, gradually increasing in rhythm. Tap-tap-tap. Then I throw an arm up and feel the wall above my head. If it's wet, then the corner has soaked through and stripes of discoloured liquid streak my wall. Enjoying this added special water feature, I wait for the drips to begin. As the taps and the clicks quicken, there's a moment when I hope it won't happen, hope that for some reason it's fixed itself and there'll only be my streaky wall to contend with. Alas, I'm always disappointed. Because about a foot in from the corner above my bed, the taps finally build to a point of no return, and a steady, consistent ejaculation of rain water drops right on my face. Even when the rain has stopped, this dismal torture continues until the final dregs have been drained from wherever it is they come from.

I've been up on the roof, you know. Oh yes, I've checked it out. I like the view from there. Don't worry, it's a flat, gravel style roof; there's not much chance of me falling off . . . It's pretty high though, I mean, my building is three stories! In the event of a fire I'm supposed run up the stairs, shimmy up an emergency ladder, leap through a sky light, then slide down the converted roof and on to the adjacent neighbours side. From there it's anyone's guess what to do next - apart from stand and watch the flames tear at and devour this wretched derelict . . .

Yeah, I've been up on that roof quite often over the last year or so. I've stood, bewildered and pinched at the lack of any discernible exterior evidence of deterioration. It's a definite mystery. Yep, uh-huh, a mystery all right.

. . . It rained over the weekend.

# 61

It's Monday afternoon, it's 12:38, and I'm already sitting under the Indian Horse Chestnut. Bandana doesn't mind me being early. He likes it. He thinks it's really cool, really great, and that we can have, get this, *even more* of a chat and a laugh; you know, what with us being bestest, bestest buddies and everything. Bandana seems on good form actually, mainly because he's currently all loved up with everyone's favourite fetid fiend. Apparently, when he caught up with her, she was crying her best heart out down an alleyway. And let me tell you, he didn't hang around in confessing that he was weeping sticky tears of his own not long after . . .

Bandana has rearranged all the mugs. It's an invasion I'm not that fussed about. I've long since given up any sense of territory I used to have. It's not important to me anymore, not in the slightest. I have to say that my general demeanour is that of a tired, old lion. One that just wants to sleep while the world spins wildly around him. And I am tired.

Bandana sort of looks after me. Did you notice that? He does. He sees me as an elder statesman or something. No threat to his self-obsessed generation, but someone to still have some basic respect for. I think it's to do with my problem. He has his issues. I have mine. And we've bonded through trauma, conflict and friction.

He's unstable. No, really, I mean it, I haven't lost all my senses. I think we get on so well because I bring consistency to his world. I'm always here, always ready with the right words (if I can pronounce them properly), and most importantly, I'm always on his side. Yes, my greatest achievement is to provide unconditional support to my favourite ever monkey. It doesn't matter if he kicks some skanky, rat haired crack whore slut in the face. Or tear-jerkingly confesses to accidentally creasing the cover of one of my books, despite promising not to (*The Loser*, the bastard) . . . No, we're in this together. A team, a duo; a novelty freak show. Paths crossing every day because it's what we deserve.

I'm looking at him right now, sitting in the mess room snorting and sniffing, coughing sharply. Do you know, he has a new trick, brand new today. He's making his eyes bulge. He's been blinking then bulging his eyes, snorting and sniffing, then coughing sharply. I'd ask him how he is, if he's all right and that, but the effort it would take for me to formulate the words . . . I can't be bothered. Suddenly, and this is quite rare, suddenly I'm quite relaxed sitting here under the Indian Horse Chestnut. An inner peace has arrived. My god, I've just . . . I've just had a moment of nostalgic reconnection! A recognition of something. Contrast. I've just recognised contrast! What a weird feeling. It's been ages since I've . . .

Looking right now at Bandana, I suddenly see him for what he is; and despite my own issues, I'm not like *him*. Not like *that*, am I? What is happening to me? What *has* happened to me? What am I doing here? Oh God, I think I might cry . . . Wait, it's okay, it's all going to be fine, he's going. It's 14:00. Time for him to go. Thank God, thank God. Everything will be all right in a minute. The very minute he's gone, I'll forget this feeling; the very minute . . .

# 62

Yesterday was weird; that's tiredness and old age for you. Thankfully it's passed, normal service has resumed. Even better than that, I've some great news: Ronald Polio is back! Le Retour de Ronald Polio! He looked very smart in his white chinos and blue hoodie. Well, when I say white chinos . . . White and brown, obviously. You know, I'm surprised he's still alive. How many years do you reckon they can live for, the alcoholically afflicted? Years and fucking years it turns out. Little fucking spazzer fell over and slept where he hit - the cunt. Yeah, I'm slightly hateful towards him to be honest. He's a reminder of the olden days, of happier times. Perhaps I should kill him.

Hey, *of course I'm only joking* . . .

Look at him. I remember once, a few years ago, he was asleep just like that, snoring and drooling on the grass. Some drunks, CONRAN and another, a dark haired Irish kid who always denied he was a crack head, waited for Ronald to collapse and engage in that 8.5% slumber; a shit stained sleeping beauty. As he slept, they surrounded him, chatting in low voices, as if respecting his moment of rest. Slowly, so slowly, they manoeuvred around him, still chatting, like this is what they always did, you know, looking out for a fallen angel. I watched from the mess room window as the Irish Kid carefully slid his fingers into Ronald's trouser pocket, all the while chatting quietly. With a nimbleness you'd actually expect, the Irish Kid pulled a fiver from Ronald's pocket. Then a tenner. Some change fell noisily on to the grass, and the cheeky, thieving scavengers giggled, nodding, a signal to say, We'll leave that. He'll think he's been lucky to have such good friends. Two good friends who haven't stolen the last few pence from his pocket.

Yeah, they laughed and Ronald stirred. He sat up, and they pointed to the change, then asked him if he wanted a beer. They'd get it, no problem, yeah? Of course, he said yes. And when they'd walked off, Ronald picked the change up and put it back in his pocket. Then he felt his pocket. Then he felt it again. Then he stood up (eventually) and emptied his pocket, checking for the money. He stared at his hand, his good hand, then fell backwards, limbs flailing in the air. It was quite a thud, I can confirm that.

CONRAN and the Irish Kid didn't come back, they had fucking pegged it. Law of the jungle. Ronald didn't think he'd been robbed, he just thought he'd spent the money on beer! And couldn't remember! He actually just assumed he'd drunk it all away!

I rescued him once. I watched him fall over three times before, on the fourth, I grabbed him, one handed by the shoulder and leant him up against a bin. He looked at me and told me, 'Ah've git a flat in Victoria! Can yu spare sum change, pliz?' Now, do bear in mind that the second time he fell over he was in the middle of having a piss. As he was pissing in the bushes, he lost his balance and crashed through the shrubs by the Indian Horse Chestnut. Did this stop him from pissing? No. No, it didn't. By the fourth time I'd seen enough. I couldn't let him fall over again, I just couldn't. Three times, yes. But not a fourth. Shit and piss soaked, he stumbled out, smiling at me, thanking me. I watched as he crossed the road and swayed uncertainly outside the kebab shop, begging for money or fags. Then I locked the gate.

And here he still is! Years later. Still flapping that paw, still . . . here. My best ever hero; a barely living god. He comes in rarely nowadays though. There's no one here to drink with anymore; it's mostly families and tourists. CONRAN died. Skagorexic Stuart died. The Irish Kid got into a load of drug trouble and now begs outside the Tube station in a wheelchair. My AFICAN brothers were either deported, or died. Last, but not least, my favourite mad old slag Elizabeth was sectioned, never to be seen again. Yep, Ronald Polio has outlived and outlasted them all. Bless the limping fool.

# 63

I am so glad the weekend is over and I'm into the easy part of my shift. Today and tomorrow is a three o'clock finish. Then *still* nine thirty Wednesday and Thursday. And finally, a three o'clock finish Friday. I've really grown to like the long shift, that intensity of so many hours over so many days. It's such a relief to have something to do, somewhere to be; and it's safe here in my private little paradise. The locals that still survive really make my day when they pop by, mostly in the mornings, just to say hello. I'm at my best first thing. I'm afraid my slurring gets worse the more tired I get. It's because I get lazy. It's very difficult to concentrate on forming my words so they sound okay as the day drifts towards closing.

I've done all my jobs for a Monday. Edged, blowed and mowed all three gardens, all before lunchtime. You'd be surprised how many leaves fall from the London Plane this time of year. And it's not even August yet! Oh, that has made me laugh. *Leaves.* I love leaves. Especially as we've been given a new blower. This new blower is louder than the old one but less powerful. It also runs out of two stroke faster. It's a real pain when you're all the way down the other gardens, and it splutters to a stop just seconds from finishing blowing the last of the leaves into piles. Once, I swung the blower around my head in frustration, like Leather Face at the end of *Texas Chain Saw Massacre*. Oh I was upset! So close to finishing, and I had to traipse all the way back to the hut and refill. Yeah, I was very upset actually.

Anyway, I upset myself today. For the first time in ages I upset myself. I was blowing the paths down _____ Square, and at first I didn't notice this bloke standing by some bushes. He'd been trying to get my attention, and then when I did notice him, I decided to ignore him anyway. I *was* working after all. So as I finished up and switched the blower off, I noticed that he was still talking at me. I took my ear protectors off, and, sort of dazed and confused, blinked as I tried to understand what he was saying.

'It's so nice to come to such a quiet garden,' he said to me again.

'Iss it?' I replied, as best as I could.

'Yes. So nice to come into such a quiet garden, and be able to think and indulge in the beauty of private, quiet thought.'

I looked at this grey, shabby haired bloke. With a black satchel containing binders thrown over one shoulder, he was wearing an ill fitting stripy red and cream t-shirt, garnished with baggy straight leg jeans, and sandals with grey socks. He must have been about my father's age, in his fifties, and spoke with an accent, almost a drawl, but not American. I then recognised the drawl as sarcasm . . .

'Well, you'll have plenty of time to think now,' I said, through gritted teeth. Like a ventriloquist, I suppose. It's easier to sound more coherent that way.

'Sorry?'

'Now I've finished. You'll have all the time in the world to do your thinking.'

'It was a joke.'

'Whatt?'

'A joke,' he repeated.

'Oh, wass it? It wass very funny. That joke. Usually jokes have a punchline or something. So you know when to laugh. If it's worth getting, that is.'

'Oh, I think it's more likely to be about numbers, as to whether you get it or not.'

'Really? What numbers? How do you assign value and meaning to these numbers?'

'It was just a joke.'

'A joke? Yess, you've said. Well, I work here, and that's not a joke. And I'm here for fourteen hours a day, whereas you're probably only going to sit here thinking for twenty minutes or so. A third of an hour. Twenty out of sixty. How are those numbers for you?'

'Well, I'd say you probably need to have to use numbers of over a hundred to understand a joke.'

'That's very scientific. Are you a scientist?'

'Well, I'm sort of a physicist, actually.'

'Hmm, that's interesting. Is it over a hundred because a hundred is three digits and three is a magic number? Like the Father, the Son and the Holy Ghost? Or like an approximate golden section in art? A third and two thirds?'

'No,' he said casually, 'just over a hundred would do.'

'Oh, I see. I'm talking about designating value or meaning to actual numbers, as symbols or signs, and you're simply talking about IQ. How original.'

Then Mister Physicist smiled awkwardly, walked over to my best ever bench, sat down, and pulled one of his binders out of his bag.

I cocked my head. 'Is that it? Seems to me like this conversation's gone a bit binary. On. Off. Looks like those are the only numbers we need, aren't they? Zero and one, hey, Mister Physicist?'

He didn't reply, which made me laugh. He put on a pair of glasses and started to read through his bits of paper and the like. Me? I stopped gritting my teeth and strolled as casually as I could out of _____ Square and back to the mess room.

I told Bandana about it when he came in. He wasn't happy. In fact, he was very *un*happy about it. But somehow, I managed to calm him down after he threatened to go and find Mister Physicist and do some number crunching of his own.

Find. Destroy. On. Off. It's all the same really.

## 64

I just spent the best ever thirty seven minutes with Alan Ashby. It's a long, long Thursday. And rather unusually in these days of Global Warming, it's hot. The garden was full at lunchtime. No Frenchie these days, but Poodle was in. And Friday Night Boy too.

I decided that after sweating my bollocks off mowing the grass and pruning some bushes, that I deserved a rest. So I grabbed a bottle and sat under the Indian Horse Chestnut. I was really dehydrated, so, so thirsty; and sweaty, so, so sweaty. My hair was wet. My beard itched like a fucker, and my underwear was sticking. But as I sat, hydrating myself as much as possible, I felt good, like I'd exerted for the first time in ages.

I was daydreaming to be honest, I won't tell you what about, I'm still not that confessional. Ha! Anyway, I was daydreaming when a flash of white and blue took my eye, and I looked over at that white and blue flash. It was Alan Ashby saying hello. Shocked and surprised, I said hello back. He seemed equally surprised by this and stopped dead in his tracks.

'Good day to you,' he slurred, wearing a shapeless white t-shirt, his eyes rolling slightly behind his sun reactors; the blue bag clanking.

'Yeah.'

'Would you like a drink, young man?'

'No.' My simple replies were designed to disguise my impediment. 'Wait here. I'll be back.'

And off he went. And I thought no more of it, because the likelihood was that he wouldn't remember he'd promised to come back anyway. About a minute later, he stumbled up to me and handed me a can of lager, a cheap one, but a can of lager nonetheless.

'Do you mind if I sit down?' he asked, as he sat down next to me, crushing a little bush.

'Yes.'

'I like you,' he slurred happily. 'I don't know why but I do. You're surly but a good chap, do you know that? You are a jolly good chap. My wife thinks I'm an alcoholic. She thinks I drink too much. Do you know, I work for the Sultan of Brunei. Who do you work for?'

'The Queen.'

He hiccupped and laughed. 'Good answer. Do you smoke? Do you mind if I do? I own nineteen hotels in the area. My Grandmother built all of these hotels. I'm trying to extend my port folio by buying that pub, that one on the corner. But they don't want to sell. I'm a photographer by the way. Yes, I've got a project on the go at the moment. I'm photographing all these hotels that surround this garden. It's a project of mine. You have to have a hobby, don't you, because I'm a bit of an artist. I like you, what's your name? I like you, I don't know why, but you're a jolly good chap.' He rolled himself a fag, which took ages and ages. 'I've lost a lot of money. Oh yes. Lost a fortune. Virtually bankrupt. But I've still got my hotels. This garden used to be a cemetery, did you know that? All the gardens in London used to be cemeteries. This one used to be a cemetery before the war, and then afterwards, it was a private garden, for residents only. Did you know that? Listen, what's your name? When I was about your age I was going out with an actress. I won't tell you who.'

'Was it Charlotte Ramplingg?'

He gassed out an alcoholically vapourous laugh. 'No, Nicole Kidman.' Then he unscrewed a half bottle of brandy he'd discreetly pulled from his pocket. 'I'm joking.'

'Yes.'

He was quiet for a minute. 'I'm a photographer by the way. I've got a project on the go at the moment. I'm taking pictures of all the hotels that surround this garden. But I can't quite get it right, it's not quite right. Tell you what, now that we're friends, I'm going to give you something. I'm going to give you a drawing I did of the garden. As a present. I'm going to bring it in for you tomorrow. I like you, you're surly. A surly fellow, but you're a good chap.' He looked blankly at me. 'You know, you remind me of someone.'

'Who?'

'I . . . don't . . . know.'

'Hmmm.'

Some tourists wandered past, smiling at us, like we were just *so* lucky to be sitting *so* casually, *so* relaxed and without stress and torment, here, here in this viridian idyll.

'He's my boyfriend!' Alan Ashby squeaked at them. 'Do you like my young lover?'

The tourists either didn't hear him or didn't understand what he said. Luckily. I wanted to say something but it was much too much effort. A sharp retort said quickly is beyond my capabilities nowadays. Something like: Have you looked in a mirror in the last twenty years? Something like that. Wait. Have I looked in the mirror recently? Oh, dear God . . .

Alan Ashby took a slurpy swallow of his brandy, careful not to waste any that may have dribbled down his chin. 'I have to be going. Can you help me up?'

'You made your ownn way down, sso I reckon you can make your own way back up. Stand on your own two feet and that.'

Alan Ashby looked at me closely, trying to focus, his breath making me wince. 'I'll bring . . . you . . . that . . . drawing tomorrow.' Then he laughed to himself as he gradually managed to stand up. 'I swear on my wife's life.'

His blue bag clinked and clanked violently as he stepped over one of the bushes, a Cornus I believe it's called, and off he tottered.

Drunks are such bullshitters. Such liars. And like all drunks, Alan Ashby's full of self-pity and lies. They say things and they really mean it. Really believe every wretched word, just so you'll believe it too. How can you not believe them when they say it with such conviction? There's little choice in the matter, it's not really worth

185

arguing or questioning, is it? You can only doubt, that's all. Doubt is your (eventual) only honest response to the chronic band of Jack the Giant Killers. I killed a fly the other day. I didn't mean to, it was an accident. It got caught in the window as I was closing it. But you see, at least I've told you it was only a fly. Alan Ashby is a *photographer*. And not only that, but now the fucker's going to bring me a drawing! Oh, he's really outdone himself this time! He's going to bring *me* a drawing! ME! If I ever see that drawing I'll spit on it and burn the fucker. That fucking bastard. I'm disgusted. The invasion I'm suddenly feeling. What a fucking disgrace. I know, I know, doesn't he know who I *am*? Who I *was*? What I could do! Bring me a fucking drawing of the garden! The garden! Of all the things in the world you could draw, and this fucking garden is the top of his list! This! All of this . . . SHIT!

I can't believe how suddenly furious I am about it. But it's linked to everything that's been going on, that's gone on; and I know you've been waiting, and please, allow me to congratulate you, you've been very patient. But . . . Alan *Ashby*. Who would have thought that this fool, this idiot, could reach the parts that other idiots couldn't reach? I'm pinched, really pinched, and I don't know why . . .

. . . I can't believe it. With ten minutes to go to locking up, the shit kids have come in to play football. I'd already closed the other two gardens, and as I walked round the left side of the hut, I couldn't believe my eyes. There must be twenty of the little fuckers, all running around, hoofing the ball into the shrubs. I don't actually care, but for God's sake, ten minutes! I might have to start herding them out now. It's a good idea. By the time we've exchanged pleasantries, it'll be time.

'Okayy, kidssx, gardenss clozingg now.'

'Hey,' one of the little sportswear brats laughed, 'it's dat trampy dude, man.'

Another council flat inbred shit kid asked, 'Hey, why are you a tramp, man?'

'Okayy, kidssx, gardenss clozingg now.'

Some teenage jailbait prospective young mum giggled, her red

186

football shirt five sizes too big for her gamin frame. 'What. Did. He. *Say*?'

'He's dat drunk tramp dude, man,' a big kid said. 'He's dat tramp wid a job we wuz laffin at. He wuz like so drunk he never even heard uz!'

'Okayy, kidssx, gardenss clozingg now.'

'See! He is like well drunk.'

'Like your muvva, innit?' Council Flat Inbred Shit Kid hissed.

'Don't talk bout my muvva like dat man, it's disrespectful. You disrespectful to my muvva?' And the big kid squared up to Council Flat Inbred Shit Kid, who looked scared.

'Okayy, kidssx,' I urged, half to deflect, walking them slowly towards the middle gates. 'Garden'ss clozingg now.'

'You is drunk, man. Why is you got a job if you is drunk?'

'Tramp! Tramp!' Jailbait sneered, oblivious to the irony.

'I hadd an opahrashunn. My nerrve wass . . . severedd. Come onn kidssx, gardenss clozingg now.'

'I can smell da drink on him, man.'

Jailbait suddenly went all serious. 'He's freakin me out. Let's go, innit.'

I looked at Jailbait, recognising her from a few years ago as a polite young thing that used to ask me questions about the garden. Used to ask me why the sprinkler wasn't on so she and her friends could play in the water. Asked me if it was okay to play football at the top of the garden because it was out of the way. Asked enthusiastically why the flowers had been pulled out. Cheerful, innocent stuff like that. I looked at her and I knew she recognised me too, the me from three years ago; and it was that that freaked her out. My, how we've both changed.

The kids eventually left, continuing to jeer me. Telling me I was a fucking idiot, a drunk, a tramp. I locked the remaining gates, just in time it turned out, because at the last one they decided to run and try and get back in. But I'm not that slow, oh no, not even at my age and in this condition.

# 65

I cannot wait for Bandana to turn up. Not because we're bestest
buddies. No, not that. I'm waiting for Bandana because I'm fucking off as soon as possible. I'm going the very minute Bandana
pokes his head through that gate. You may guess that I'm still ever
so slightly annoyed about yesterday. Well, it's not a big deal, not
really. But when I opened my eyes after falling asleep during half
of Ashby's monologues, I had myself a moment of clarity. All of
a sudden the last few years didn't so much flash before my eyes, as
slowly, agonisingly pass by, highlighted, underlined, bleached red
for danger danger! As I wiped away a tear, and this parade of what
can only be described as disgust faded away, I looked at Alan Ashby, and I looked at myself, sitting there with him as he assumed,
in his drunken haze, that we were bonding. How low can you go?

So I had a little drink, just a little one, for the first time in ages.
You don't believe me, do you? Well, it doesn't matter, I know the
truth. Hmmm, you might know it too. Anyway, I had a drink, so
what? I think I deserved one. Don't normal people have a drink to
relax? To take the edge off?

I know what you're thinking, you're . . . I don't know what you're
thinking. And in a way I don't care. Walk ten whole English yards
in my shoes, I double dare you. You wouldn't, couldn't…Do you
know what it's like to come out of a black-out? To suddenly regain

conscious thought? Yes? No? Maybe? Well, I do. It wasn't pretty, and I don't want to talk about it, but it was just one event that occurred during my three year jackanory sabbatical.

I'm recovering now. I'm not on my uppers anymore. I'm cleaning up my act. My nerve was severed, but I'm getting better; from tomorrow it begins.

And did Alan Ashby bring me this masterful fucking drawing?

Did.

He.

Fuck.

# 66

I'm a bit nervous to be honest. Yes, I'm close to being sick. I'm not sure why, but I felt inclined to act on a whim. So I've come to the British Film Institute for the afternoon. I can't explain why, but my guts are rolling. It's so busy, and there are so many people, that I feel like everyone's staring at me.

This morning, after lying in until about eight, I bought the Saturday papers. For the first time in what feels like years, I casually checked through the Arts Review pages and the film and exhibition listings. I don't usually do anything on a Saturday. Or a Sunday; or any day I suppose, except when I go to work. But anyway, today I saw something advertised and thought I'd check it out, off the cuff, completely against routine. I even walked here! All the way from W14! It took longer than I thought. And it's hot today, very hot, must be in the thirties. Feels it, definitely.

Look at this place! I remember when it was still the National Film Theatre. From Waterloo Bridge it doesn't seem all that different, but close up, the redevelopment, the bars and restaurants, the rebranding! Well, I know it was a while ago, but still . . . I might try Tate Modern next; the next time I get brave.

Truth is, I don't know what I'm doing here. Or *what* to do here. Everyone else seems to be fully aware of what they're doing and where they're going. Whether it's strolling or sitting, laughing and engaging with each other in a dignified way. I don't think I can remember what that feels like; it's difficult to expand on that statement without a little selective confession.

It was about a year ago, a sunny July afternoon. I'd had a little drink, and for some obscure reason found myself watching some sort of Afghanistan dance troupe performing miracles outside the neighbouring Royal Festival Hall. I can't remember what actual day it was; it may have been a weekend, it may not. Anyway, I was feeling very sorry for myself, the events leading to that unknown day having taken their toll. Hey, there's only so much a man can take, you know. When you reach your breaking point and survive, only then can you lecture me on the pitfalls of self-pity and self-loathing. Of inertia and impotence. Yeah.

So, I was really enjoying the Afghanistan dance troupe and their agile ways, drinking economy vodka out of a two litre water bottle. The searing heat was baking my grotty, straggly hair, and the sweat glistened in my beard as I casually glanced over to a group of people sitting nearby. This happy gang of new media new middle class, were laughing, engaging with each other in a way that had become completely alien to me since my self-enforced disconnection from my most civilised of social groups. To be honest, as I sat there staring, I believed, not half believed, really really fully believed, that I was hallucinating, dreaming this scene up. A group of friends, chatting away, basking in the glory of Afghanistan excellence; young children eating ice cream; a toddler giggling at his father's cooing. There's a weird vicariousness about being intoxicated and observing friends and family in that context. It's wishful thinking. Everyone does it.

An hour passed. Maybe less, maybe more. The entertainment changed without me noticing. Some fire-breathing jugglers were now leaping around, drinking turpentine and spitting fire; which made me laugh, I don't know why. Anyway, realising that at least half an hour had elapsed, I burped out a sickly vodkaholic vapour, licked my white, dehydrated lips, and looked around.

Still busy, still populated by twenty-first century gold-plated happiness, I was feeling quite relaxed until I had a look for the gang of new media new middle class. As I squinted at them, sitting where they'd been all along, my one focused eye happened upon the puzzled face of a cheerful looking fellow staring right back at me. Initially, I closed my eye, thinking that I was about to either get a mouthful, or they were all going to suddenly move on. Instead, I sat bolt upright. My eyes burst open, if that's possible, and I stood hurriedly to my feet, wavering momentarily, before somehow managing to shimmy and dodge between the masses. I wasn't running, but I was moving at pace; as much as my fear of discovery would allow. It was no good though. That face. It hadn't been an immediate recognition. It was like a computer photo-fit, scanning twenty to the second through the many horrors I'd encountered in my life.

As I broke through a group of Brazilian school children and tripped down a set of steps, and I really do mean tripped, I heard a shrieking, almost mocking laughter, followed by something I hadn't heard for a long time. My real name. I collapsed at the bottom, out of breath and out of time, with no available escape route. Bring it on, I thought.

A shadow loomed over me, and with the sun behind him, I threw a tired, resigned hand over my eyes.

'OH. MY. GOD!' the silhouette shrieked. 'It is you! JEEEESUS CHRIST! Look at you! Still emptying bins by any chance? Or more accurately: eating out of them?'

I didn't even bother to look up. 'Simon.'

'I can hardly believe it. Look at that beard! It's almost fashionable! I'd heard all about it, your *situation*, but . . . seeing it with my own eyes!'

I shrugged, and said in the most languid fashion possible, 'Can you shhpare any change?'

'You . . . are . . . *joking*? Oh! You *are* joking! Oh yes, you've still got your sense of humour. I can see that from the way you're dressed. You know, I was nearly sick with excitement when I spotted you. I mean, it's *you*.'

'Yess, Simon. It is.'

'Are you shaking? Have you got the shakes! *Classic*! Guess who I'm here with? Go on, guess.'

'I don't care.'

'Oh, I think you will.'

'Oh, I think I won't.'

'Wait a minute. You must have seen them for yourself.'

'Seen what?'

'I can *barely* contain myself!'

'Surprise surprise.'

'Oh no, the surprise is all yours! Surprise surprise! You've never met your . . .'

As he finished that sentence my eyes glazed over and I couldn't swallow. My heart banged and thumped and smashed against my chest. And before I knew it, I was running down Southbank, falling over, scuffing my face, my knees, hands bleeding, nails snapping as I clawed my way back to my feet. I ran all the way to the steps of the bridge. Okay, so it wasn't exactly a marathon, but at least I had escaped Simon Tabernacle and his filthy lies. Hadn't I? No. Because as I lay on the steps regaining my breath, feeling like a dead man, with people politely stepping over me, pleading for God to take me now, I heard a voice. A voice that if I'd been just one more millimetre towards madness, would have convinced me that I'd just died and was in the presence of an angel. An angel of *doom*, but an angel nonetheless.

'It is you.'

'I can't breathe, I can't breathe . . .'

'Are you okay, are you hurt?'

'What do you want?' I said, covering my face. I couldn't let her see. I couldn't let her see what had happened to me; I was too embarrassed.

'I can't stay long. Andrei's going to wonder where I am.'

'How beautiful,' I said. Then I winced, because I meant to say dutiful . . .

'I don't have long. Simon's covering for me.'

'How *dutiful*. Your *other* husband.'

Erica was quiet for a second. 'Look at you.'

'. . .'

'Listen, I'm sorry. I'm sorry about . . . about what I said to you . . .' She knelt down, putting a hand on my arm. 'Come and see me. Come and see *us*. When you're ready.'

'Go away.'

'Did you hear what I said?'

'Go away. Please . . .' And I covered my face again. I could breathe now, quick, deep breaths, but it was punctuated by sniffs, you know the type, the sniffs designed to control something almost uncontrollable.

'I have to go. Simon's waving. I have to go.'

I parted my dirty, bloody fingers, and saw her look at the ground rather than at me as she stepped back before turning and walking away. She hadn't changed, not at all. She still looked the same. Slightly shorter, tidier hair, not so ungroomed, but still . . .

Simon had always been Erica's fag slag hag best friend or whatever the phrase is. He knew everything. And although it irritated me quite a lot at the time, Erica said she needed someone to confide in. Why him? I don't know. Because Tabernacle walked, just like then, right on the edge; certainly whenever our paths crossed. It seems that undying sisterly love for the woman was Simon's only redeeming feature; and that must have been how the pair of them managed to cover up that particular incident. What a fucker. I can't believe I knew him when he was just another talentless pleb.

It was dark by the time I moved from that spot. Several people asked me if I was all right, if I needed an ambulance or anything; but it was only blood on my hands, it would wash off. I felt very sorry for myself. No fucking surprise surprise there. No, that's something that's only recently started to lift. And today, on my return to the exact spot I last saw Erica, I'm turning over a new leaf . . . Wait. Fuck off. A leaf! Leaves can fuck RIGHT OFF.

You see, I'm not an alcoholic. Never have been, not even close. Oh, it turns out I've been a drunk for quite a few years, but it's not the same. I've had a moment of clarity, and now it's finally time for change. Yes, I'm shaking and I'm nervous, but I haven't touched a drop since the shit kids called me a fucking idiot. That's the difference between me and the tramps and the smackheads, the homeless and the prostitutes. They can't stop, they don't want to - but I do; and I have and I will. It's over, it's finally run its course.

I'm drying out.

# 67

That's really interesting. Really quite strange. I'm looking in the mirror right now, on this pleasant Sunday morning, and I'm staring at a clean shaven face. I've cut my hair too. Just trimmed the length out of it; and do you know what I look like?

Like I used to, more or less. Hmm, well, more forehead and less hair, but anyway . . .

I think I'm pretty good at this drying out stuff. Once I put my mind to something I don't mess about. It's like reconnecting with the memory and idea of focus and concentration. Where once upon a time it was used for, say, Life Drawing, now it's for rehabilitation. It's the same really. On. Off. Find. Destroy. Exercise. Statement. Drink. Don't drink. It's all going to be okay because I like this feeling. Yeah, the way my mind is clearing away the sordid debris of the last few years is painful, but it was all my own fault, and so there's no one to blame except myself. That *is* unusual, because people usually just *love* blaming everyone else. Me, I'm taking full responsibility. Make no mistake, it was all my fault. Everything.

When I found out about Erica being pregnant, it wasn't so much that she was pregnant that annoyed me as much as her . . . What annoyed me was . . . She, she hadn't said anything, that's all. Not a word. I was confused. So, obviously I ran through the reasons for her lack even of selective confession, and it seemed to me that Andrei was definitely the proud father. It made the most sense, didn't it? At that time it had to be the case, because what was the alternative? If, and it's a big if, I was the father, then surely she would have told me, and not just let me let her go; surely. I think it turned out we were pretty similar in a lot of ways.

So, I left it. Just let it be. Luckily, I had a spy in the camp, Nick, who, despite all his melodramatic moral reservations, still kept me informed. Nothing specific, but enough for me to feel right in keeping my distance. It all made sense. Erica and Andrei were having a baby and they were happy; why ruin it with an unnecessary enquiry? What would that have achieved? Okay, I know, I know what. But if I was involved somehow then surely she would have said something. Come on. *Come on.*

During this time I started seeing Suzanne, a painter I'd met one night, who I recognised from the Old Blue Peg. She used to work behind the bar, and you know how it is, I like bar girls, they serve me beer. So we started seeing each other and it was good; it was new, and it felt like it was right for me at the time. Why not move on?

Suzanne was funny and interesting, just my type, and she had a nice line. An actual nice line. She was pretty good at drawing, and her paintings were interesting too. Sort of semi-expressionistic abstract symbolism with a feminist slant. I liked her skinny body and her long, choppy chocolate brown hair; and I liked her eyeliner and her legs. I drew those legs. The proportion, the length, the shape they made as she stretched; it was as close to something important as I could get at the time.

We'd been together for a few months, and I was happy with the sort of part-time lover structure of our relationship. It wasn't genetic attraction, but it had been impact attraction; and that was enough for me. Like anyone else, I just needed *someone.*

Suzanne didn't care what I was doing. It didn't matter to her that I was a nobody. She went ahead and rather delightfully reinvented me as a *Park Ranger*, what a promotion! Ha! Oh, dear God. Sorry, let me just wipe away a tear. We talked about art all the time; about maybe sharing a studio - if all I wanted to do was draw, then why didn't I just do that? Good idea. No argument from me.

Everything was going well. Suzanne had been working on a

triptych for a group show about *Sex and the Female Nature* (ha!), and I was working towards clearing the shrubs and bagging up the leaves. But that didn't matter. I had good things going on, and my everyday was unimportant, wasn't it?

I remember the Private View for the *Sex and the Female Nature* show was on a Wednesday night at some bar in Brick Lane. I was late. My hours had just started going up and it was mid March, 19:30 closing time. So this meant that by the time I arrived, the Private View was well under way. Generally, they run from about 18:00 to 21:00. I had about an hour to enjoy.

When I caught up with Suzanne, her eyes were glistening with delight. She was happy with the paintings and the show in general. I didn't really recognise that many people. My circle had changed a bit. This was Suzanne's universe, it was different. I grabbed a beer and wandered around the split level space, evading the drunken, splaying limbs that gestured wildly as contemporary electro disco pop bounced off the work and the walls. You should have seen how sweaty and blotchy these people were. But the truth is, it *was* hot in there. The sheer weight of the haircuts and vintage attire adding to the humid, slightly nauseous atmosphere. Laughter, there's always loud fucking laughter at these things.

Anyway, Suzanne was busy entertaining, enthusiastically chatting to her studio-mates, looking sweaty and blotchy in a rapidly dishevelling original Mary Quant Go-Go dress. I was *tired*. I didn't want to be there. I hate art and I hate Private Views. But my heart was struggling with the conflict, no longer capable of battling myself every single day. That's exactly how I felt, because I was tired. Yeah, but really I was jealous. Despite all the plans, I still wasn't doing anything, not even life drawing - I was too busy, you know, clearing shrubs, bagging leaves, popping blisters on the palm of my drawing hand . . .

. . . Excuse me a minute.

Okay, let's get this over with. So I was standing and, umm, and what happened next? Yeah. That's it, that's right. What happened next was that I was standing there, trying desperately not to look at the work. Standing, watching all this *laughing* and all this mutual confirmation and congratulation. And I was feeling upset. Really upset. Then Suzanne kept flashing me these happy smiles and loving eyes, and there I was, terribly, *terribly* upset. She came over and gave me a big kiss, which I didn't respond to, then asked me if I was okay, and I said, It's over, and walked out the door.

I can't remember what happened after that.

So you know what's coming, you must do, it's sort of obvious. Something really upset me, didn't it? Yeah, well, Erica was there, of course she fucking was. And of course she was like, seven months or something; and all these people were laughing, making a fuss, hands on her tummy, feeling the kicking; the whole fucking lot. I felt like dust or grime, hidden on top of a picture rail. I was there all right, with this maternal celebration going on right in front of me, but not visible. I was paralysed. I felt every kick, every hand on that stomach. And I was shocked by it. It was genetic, a genetic and territorial invasion.

During this extravaganza, I stood, transfixed, unable to approach, and even less able to walk away. At one point, Erica, shiny and full cheeked, looked straight at me, smiling, then spun away with nothing but such a happy-happy face. Not, you know, not the tight face, the one I wanted, the one that says I always ignore you like this, uh-uh, oh no. It was contentment. A face of sheer, undiluted happiness.

I was devastated. It seemed to me at the time that I'd been rendered obsolete. Even if I was involved, it was obvious that it didn't matter. I didn't matter. I no longer had any effect. It was total disconnection.

Then, just when I thought it would never end, they began to drift off. As I was digesting all these feelings of powerlessness, I caught Erica almost look back, so nearly, so nearly look back. I could tell, I could see that she had waited, staggered her exit so she could do it; but didn't. That was what upset me. If only she'd just fucked off. Walked away. Left me with nothing at all, not a single, microscopic fragment of recognition, then I really think I could have dealt with it. Really I do.

She did it to hurt me. And it did.

# 68

You should have seen Bandana's face when I came in. He didn't recognise me! He's never seen me like this, as a human being! He was all polite and formal. And I couldn't help it, I played along, nodding as he explained where things were, and what key to use for this, what lock to use for that; what bins fill up quicker after the lunchtime crowds. I was struggling not to laugh, really, I was straining so much that I thought I might burst. Then he paused, looked at me very carefully for what seemed about twenty minutes, and finally, quietly, muttered, 'Cunt.'

I spent the next hour apologising, but also complimenting Bandana on his professional attitude. If I ever die and someone comes and takes my place, then at least I know they'll be in good hands. Oh, he wasn't laughing at first. But after a while he did see the minor amusement, in him of all people, taking the job that seriously.

He confessed to me that he thought something was up. He'd noticed a change in my demeanour, a seriousness that seemed to suggest I was working something out. Surprisingly, he was pretty supportive about it - my return to some form of accepted civility. Although, he did then ask me if he could have the secret stash of vodka I'd hidden in the tool shed next to the spare petrol cans, and of course, I said he could. Bandana was as happy as Larry. No surprise there; free oblivion is the best oblivion.

I'm not saying I didn't feel terrible during all this. Oh, I was nervous and scared, of course I was. I couldn't wait for Bandana to go actually, couldn't fucking wait. When he did go I closed the door to the hut and cried my eyes out; that's detox, isn't it? Don't need rehab. Just needed to stop. Because, I'm not disgusting and weak like these others. Our dearly departed CONRAN, English Phil and the like, crying empty tears of shame, then refuelling with Special Brew and White Ace. No, they weren't like me before the fall, they were always heading for it. It was a priority for their personalities. For me it was actual events. Events caused my descent into the apocoholic chasm. But events also caused my ascent; and I always knew I would make it back, I always had that knowledge, because I knew it was only pretend.

I have a confession to make. It's about my severed nerve. You see, I sort of played with semantics about that. When I said "severed nerve" I wasn't lying. It's just that I meant my nerve had been severed, or more simply, "I'd lost my nerve." I did have a wisdom tooth pulled out, and it did hurt like a motherfucker; so that's true. But you see, if you redirect, tell it like a story you can believe, you'll believe it.

It's so weird to be sitting here, like this in the mess room, sober and, well, to be honest, twiddling my thumbs. Used to doing something, aren't I? Used to helping the time pass by, and I don't mean reading or doing something constructive. It's so funny to remember the time when it all started. I can isolate the precise period when I upgraded from just drinking occasionally, to just drinking.

The following New Years Eve after Suzanne's Private View, a full eight or nine months later, I was working, even on the last day of what had been a spectacular year. Of course, I was loosening up for the festivities later that night. And I'd not long had that wisdom tooth out, so I was drinking to sedate the pain. Well, sedating all pain really. Leading up to that time I'd gradually seen less and less of Nick. I think it was difficult because Jane and Erica had bonded over the maternity stuff, and Nick was too close; I respected that. Still, for about ten years I'd spent every New Years Eve with Nick and Jane. We'd gone on holiday. We'd stayed in. They'd come over.

My ex-wife even cooked a medieval feast one year! Every December 31st we'd spend the chimes together in a huddle, bringing in the New Year. But not that year. That year, despite my attempts at organising a catch up, or at least, some sort of polite interaction, I'd been ummed and arred at. Noncommittal. Can you imagine what I made of that? It didn't bother me. I had loads of other things to do, loads of offers. Well, Special Brew, K cider, and stale mince pies with CONRAN at the Cabaret Project, but still . . .

It's fair to say I'd become a bit of a liability in social terms. Drinking at work and turning up to things half hammered. Falling asleep or falling over before Nick had even had his third pint; you know, that sort of thing. At first he was okay about it. We didn't talk about the why, we didn't need to, and we were good at that bit; but when it became the norm and not the exception, well, you don't need that sort of hassle, do you?

I finished work at 16:30 and fell into the nearest pub. Which I was then thrown out of. I wandered, I think, to the off-licence, bought a bottle of something wet and retch inducing, and sat waiting for a bus to the North. North London. I missed quite a few, through chatting really. To myself, to other people at the bus stop; there was no rush. I had nearly all night, didn't I?

I remember it struck me that I should sober up a bit before knocking on the door. Nick wouldn't like me to turn up drunk, even though everyone else would be. Of course there was the small matter that I was uninvited, but what's a little gatecrashing between friends. Or enemies. So I waited for about an hour across the road, sitting on some bins. There was music, flashing lights, guests arriving, departing; coming back with more booze; that sort of thing. Looked good.

Eventually, I stumbled over, feeling very pleased with myself and my sober exterior. As I approached Nick's gate, some people joined me there. I can't remember who, but they knew me, hadn't seen me for ages, and I smiled, confident that I could get in now I was with company.

Jane answered the door, saw me, almost hid her horror, and welcomed us in. She specifically asked me how I was while leading me over to Nick, who tried hard to give Jane some secret looks. But failed miserably. I didn't mind. I wasn't staying long, places to be, benches to sit on. That's what I promised, hamming it up for effect. Funny thing was, I didn't really feel drunk at all. I felt sober, a really strange clarity; it was a pure, crystallised, sobriety.

Nick still seemed on edge, even when I asked for an orange juice. He needn't have worried. I was bored by the company, his included. I made an excuse and went to the toilet, spending quite a long time relieving myself. Then, while looking in the mirror, I rather sadly reflected on everything, accepting what an idiot I was.

It may have been winter but I was wearing a tight, washed out, slightly dirty, brown polo shirt. My arms had scratches and yellow bruises all over them, and my fingers were trembling as I turned the tap on to wash my hands. I just. Felt. Defeated. Nothing to live for. Nothing to die for. I had a look in the bathroom cabinet and found only cotton wool earbud cleaners and toothpaste. And a new toothbrush - which I stole.

There was a knock at the door and the handle turned. Another knock. A shrieked request to hurry up. I took one final accusing look at myself, and indulged in the hopeless, selfish awareness that I had just considered ruining everyone's New Years Eve. How pathetic did I feel? Very. I decided to leave the party. So, I walked out the bathroom and headed for the stairs. I was stopped on the way by some bird I used to know, who was obviously stark staring mad or drunk, because she didn't seem to notice what a complete fucking shambles I was. Anyway, about halfway down, I sighed, a terrible, terrible sigh.

Looking up at me was Erica. I pinched the bridge of my nose, rubbed my eyes, then rolled them to the side, and was momentarily distracted by one of Nick's black and white photographs hanging on the wall; one of me jumping down some stairs in a derelict house we found in Kings Cross only a few years earlier. History nearly repeated itself. Instead, I turned back to Erica, glanced at the glamour puss brunette she was talking to, then stepped past some revellers as I descended.

'Happy New Year,' I said.

'Yeah.'

I breathed out, but away, so she couldn't smell my breath if it stunk. I really wished I'd used that toothbrush, I can tell you.

'You're looking slim,' I said. 'Tiny, in fact. That's a lovely dress.'

'Thanks,' Erica replied, pouting involuntarily. Perhaps even mournfully.

'Andrei babysitting tonight?'

Erica's friend vacated the area.

'This isn't the place,' Erica said.

'The place for what?'

'I'm not talking to you when you're like this.'

My eyes glazed over. 'Talking to me when I'm like . . . *Talking* to me?' I didn't understand the statement. Either of them. 'Talking to me? About what?'

'Look at you.'

'Do you know, when my sister had a baby, she went mental. How have you been?'

Erica bit her lip. 'I don't want to talk to you. Not now.' And then she nervously folded her arms. Her eyes searching for rescue.

My mouth flinched the word "When?" but it was only as I swallowed a burp that I realised I hadn't said it out loud. 'When?' I repeated. 'Why do we need to talk? There's nothing to talk about, is there?'

She seemed tired as she said this, 'I hate you so much.'

'That's a relief. Moderate dislike is so . . . so . . .' I couldn't think of anything.

We stood scowling at each other for a second. I said something. She said something. I can't remember what exactly. Probably something important. Then Erica looked right at me, her eyes scanning every single crease, scratch, blemish, wrinkle on my face, eventually whispering to me, that hate, thick in her voice.

'*You disgust me.*'

And she really meant it. I was so shocked by her honesty that I didn't notice Andrei approach us on the stairs, followed by Nick and Jane. I ignored the aggressive waffle spilling from Andrei's mouth, and ignored Nick's attempts to reason with me, suggesting that I leave. I couldn't take my eyes off Erica, standing there, her face on fire, unrelenting.

She looked *so* beautiful.

Andrei grabbed me by the neck and dragged me to the door. As he tried to throw me out I caught his wrist and pulled him down to the ground. We wrestled on the path and lawn for a second before he managed to overpower and straddle me. He hit me right in the jaw, on that side, the wisdom tooth side, lower left. And it hurt, really really hurt. Then after each punch and slap, he hissed in my ear, 'My wife. My son.' On. Off. On. Off.

Eventually, Nick caught Andrei's fist, and then, with some help from other, *caring* people, lifted him off me. As I leant up on my elbow, checking my nose to see if it was broken, I saw that Erica was still giving me the glare of hate, and even uttering the cliché words, 'Stop it, stop it. It's not worth it. That's enough.'

I sat up and called out, 'Andrei! Hey, Andrei! A simple and polite hello would have sufficed, because violence . . .' And I couldn't think of anything else to say, my head hurt.

Jane knelt down and handed me a tissue for all the blood. 'You just never learn, do you?' Then she went back inside to what was left of the party.

Fireworks started to go off. The whole sky lit up. And in every house except the one in front of me, there was cheering and singing and celebration. After a few minutes of pinched reflection and self-pity, I struggled to my feet and walked the long walk into Camden. I high-fived everyone I met on the way, declining offers of help, and laughed off inquiries as to my beaten and bruised condition. I told them all, very cheerfully, 'Don't worry, it's only a scratch. It's only . . . a scratch.'

## 69

I don't know what was wrong with Bandana when I came in, but he was really edgy, nervous, pensive even. Weird. I sent him away as soon as I could, because to be honest, the vibe he was giving out was driving me a bit mad. He was sort of, like, in a daze. I don't know, strange . . . And he hasn't done any work today. Oh, he blamed it on not having any petrol or two stroke, but come on, you only have to remember to ask the supervisor when you phone up in the morning. I'll leave a note to remind him. There's absolutely no way I'm coming in on Friday with all the gardens in a fucking state just because his mind, what there is of it, is too distracted to do something. *Anything.* Even at my worst, and I don't really want to talk about it, even then, at least I did the bare minimum. I'm sure of it.

The only problem with not drinking the pain away anymore, is that instead of reinforcing my biased version of any number of chosen traumas, I now have to honestly face up to them. And part of this required confrontation is *reconnection.* So guess what? Having spent so long hiding in a self-confirming fog, I now have no idea how to do it. In this day and age of multimedia, multi-format communication, I'm finding that a simple phone call is absolutely terrifying me; that *simple* phone call would be presumptuous, wouldn't it? And a blind text would be too informal, sort of casually invasive perhaps. Hmmm, what about smoke signals? Or carrier pigeon? An aeroplane with one of those banners? See? No options. None at all. Even *thinking* of contacting Nick is scary. I mean, the last time I remember seeing him was at that fabulous New Years Eve party; and I do mean the last time I *remember* seeing him. I feel like I need to deflect actually, yeah, I think I'm going to go for a wander. It's close enough to closing time now anyway.

. . . Oh, that was horrid. I just saw the street give birth to its latest prostitute. I was sitting down at _____ Gardens, patiently waiting to lock up the gates. I tidied up the rubbish that had been left all around the benches - crushed cans of Polish imported beer, those free shitty newspapers you get outside Tube stations, and closed up. I was the only person in there at that time of night, and despite feeling an unseasonably cold chill, it was nice to have the garden to myself. Peaceful. Just right for the sort of reflection I needed to put myself through. I dragged my weary feet to _____ Square, quickly checked that no one was sitting or hiding in there, and locked the two gates. One of the gates doesn't close properly. The slidey bit doesn't catch, so we have to use a chain. It's fiddly to run the chain around and through the bars . . . Anyway, I locked it and started to make my way back to the main garden.

In front of me, actually, in my way a bit, was a tall bird and a very short bloke. She was wearing a pair of those fashionably skinny-fit black jeans, and a pair of flat silver shoes, with a nondescript black eighties style top; she looked a bit like Mel and Kim. Well, one of them, obviously. He was somewhat less fashionably attired in what can only be described as a Ratso Rizzo outfit. You know, like Dustin Hoffman in *Midnight Cowboy*.

And incredibly, he did have the face of a rat.

Despite my best intentions to completely ignore them, I couldn't. The bloke had his arm around her, holding her tightly around the waist, sort of leading her along. She was slightly hunched, not cowering, but like she was ill or something. I heard him softly reassuring her, but still assertively walking towards the main street, busy at this time of night with tourists and the local shite life. I couldn't hang about, I needed to lock up my best and last garden. So I accelerated slightly, and unfortunately for me, glanced at them as I overtook.

It wasn't much, but I still wish I hadn't heard it. I looked over as I sped past and was caught cold by the thick, choking unease in her voice.

'I've never done this before,' she spluttered, disorientated. 'I don't know what to do. I don't know how to do this.'

'Don't worry,' Rat Face cooed. 'You'll be *just fine, babe. Just fine.*'

And as I walked by she looked straight at me. And God forgive us all . . . I swear the look in her eyes said, "Help me. Please." But I didn't. I looked down at the ground and kept going, desperately attempting to ignore the lingering image of her tragic and beautiful tear-filled eyes, pleading with me to interfere. How could I? Why would I? It's none of my business.

What's it got to do with me? WHAT HAS IT GOT TO DO WITH ME? Is it my responsibility? Is it? Even if I managed to rescue her this time, that little fucker would only hang around and wait for the next opportunity. It's the way it works. I've seen the crows stalk the black birds in exactly the same way. Even after I've chased them off, even though the crows know that I'm the king of the jungle, the cunts display an arrogant knowingness that I'm not always about, won't always be around to save Mister and Mrs Blackbird and the little ones. They just know. They always fucking come back.

So, what does it have to do with me? Nothing. Not my problem. Not my fault if she's in over her head. I've seen that glazed and defused look before - it's crack. How you going to pay me back, babe? *How you going to pay daddy back?* Oh no, uh-uh, there's no reason to interfere in something which has absolutely nothing to do with me. No reason at all. None whatsoever.

# 70

I met Nick for a coffee yesterday. He wasn't particularly keen at first. In fairness, as I've only been dry for just under a week, even I thought that this might be a step too far. I have to say that I immediately regretted calling him. And when my back started to ache, not through excessive manual labour, but through stress, I knew I'd made a mistake. It's a different sort of pain, isn't it? It isn't physical, because it's more internal than that, an unshakeable, unstretchable tightness across the shoulder blades; and for the first time since the shit kids called me a fucking idiot, I nearly had a drink. Oh, it was close, so close. The ache was very real at that moment, I can tell you. And it was during that moment that I realised something else as well: I've lost confidence. It's true, I'm *timid*. Or contrite. I'm not sure which.

Nick was late, which made me feel a bit paranoid. We'd decided to meet up at a cafe in Camden. I'd been waiting for about an hour when he eventually turned up. I was very patient. I had no idea what I was going to say. What I could say? I mean, how do you reintroduce yourself to someone you've known for years and years? What would you say? I'm back? Remember me? It's been a long time?

And so, after fifty seven minutes of fearful contemplation, I said, 'Hey.'

Nick sat down and ordered a coffee. 'You've got a fucking cheek.'

'How you been? You and Jane?'

'Good. We're good.' Nick had put on weight. His face was thicker and his guts now showed through his fancy jumper. He looked older. His hair was specked with more grey than I remembered, but he smelt clean, recently showered; I'm not used to talking to people like that.

I moved my empty mug from my left hand to my right. 'Been busy?'

'Yeah.'

'You still living in Chalk Farm?'

'Yeah.'

'Do you fancy a pint?'

'You're a fucking idiot.'

'I know.'

He leaned back. 'So how long you been dry then?'

'About a week.'

'A week?'

'Yeah.'

'Is that a real week or a drunk's week?'

'A real week.'

'That's not that long a time really.'

I looked at the table. 'No.'

'You look thin. Bastard.'

'Thanks. Liquid diet.'

He took a sip of his coffee. 'What have you been up to?'

Nervous, I smiled, 'Can't remember.'

'What is it you want?' Nick said, in a small, casual, almost disinterested voice.

'Just . . .' I watched Nick swallow the last of his coffee then check his phone. 'I don't know. I just needed to . . .' But it felt like it was too late, and I'd lost confidence in our friendship. The time that had passed, the events, I couldn't ignore my gut feeling that it had been a mistake to expect anything; even some nostalgic courtesy.

Nick checked his phone again. 'I don't know what to say.'

'Hmm.'

He shrugged. 'I suppose I always knew you'd straighten yourself out eventually. It's a shame. I've never had a tramp for a friend before.'

I sniffed indignantly. 'Tramps don't have jobs.'

'Idiot.'

'It's true.'

'Why didn't you let me help you?'

'. . . When?'

Nick opened his mouth but couldn't say anything. Then he ordered another coffee for himself and one for me. 'A week?' he said slyly, as the waitress brought our coffee over. 'Only a week?'

'Yeah.'

'Are you in a programme or something?'

'No, nothing like that. It's been a slow burn but I've never had an addictive personality. I just stopped. After various traumas, of course.'

'Of course.' He looked at his phone. Again.

'Somewhere you need to be?'

'Waiting for a text.'

'Right.'

'A work thing.'

'Yeah.'

'You still in the park?'

'Garden.'

'What's the difference?'

'Clue's in the words.'

He smiled. 'You must be recovering. Last time I saw you, you were lost for words.'

'New Years?'

Nick laughed. 'Yes. New Years.'

Then he stopped himself from elaborating, I could tell, and of course I wanted to know exactly what he was going to say, but . . .

I let out a long, tired breath. 'Look, I want to, well, I suppose, what I want to say is that I'm sorry. For anything I did or said during the last few years. At first it was like a joke, a game I was playing where I was the only one who knew the rules. Or could break the rules. I know what I can be like, could be like, at the best of times. And I'm sorry if I upset anyone. Jane, you, anyone else. After a while I didn't know how to stop. It all got out of hand. And I think it turns out I wasn't as in control of events as I thought I was.'

I took a sip of my barely lukewarm coffee. As I looked up from the table, Nick appeared at the door. I watched as he paused, nose against the glass, scanning the cafe. Then he saw me and walked in. He didn't smile or anything as he sat down opposite.

Confident, after the rehearsal, I said, 'Hey.'

'I don't have long,' he murmured, checking his phone. 'I've got to be somewhere. What is it?'

'How have you been? You and Jane?'

He shook his head and shrugged, already exasperated. 'I've really got stuff to do.'

'Sorry. Sorry, I forgot. How are you and Alison?'

'Fine.' He gave me eye contact for the first time. 'You're looking better.'

'Thanks. You've put on weight.'

'Fuck off. What do you want?'

'I want to see Erica.'

'Why?'

'. . .'

'Why don't you just phone her?' he said, curtly.

'I need to know she'll see me.'

'All this time you've had. All the times she tried, I tried, and suddenly you're interested? You're a fucking disgrace.'

'Was a disgrace. Was.'

'A shave and a haircut doesn't mean you're not an arsehole anymore.'

'Will you ask her?'

'No. I won't.'

I let out a long, tearful breath. 'Look, I want to, well, I suppose that what I want to say is that I'm sorry. For anything I did or said during the last few years. At first it was like a joke, a game I was playing where I was the only one who knew the rules. Or could break the rules. I know what I was like, could be like, at the best of times. And I'm sorry if I upset anyone, you, Alison, anyone else. After a while I didn't know how to stop, it all got out of hand. I think it turns out I wasn't as in control of everything as I thought I was.'

'They're settled now,' he said, in a small, quiet voice.

'I have to see her. I have to tell her I'm sorry . . .'

211

'I don't think she cares anymore.'

'Please.'

'It's not that easy.'

'I can't contact her, Nick. It's impossible. I can't do it by myself.'

He rapped his fingers on the table. 'Look, I'll think about it. I'll have to get back to you.' And off he went, his chair screeching sharply on the floor as he stood, leaving me to finish my mug of cold coffee.

I don't think that went too badly. Not *exactly* according to script but . . . Fuck though, what an idiot. I'd forgotten Nick and Jane had split up.

# 71

Three weeks is a long time. I'm feeling much better about things now. It's surprising how easy it's been to dry out. Oh, I know I've been eating a lot of cakes, cheesecake in particular, but do you know what? Cakes are good aren't they! I really like these super sharp cheesecakes from a local patisserie I've been frequenting. Lemon sharp and tangy. Mmmm, fantastic.

I can't believe I forgot Nick and Jane had split up. Let me see, New Years Eve . . . Then when? I don't remember. I think I went round about eight or nine months later (not long after the Royal Festival Hall fiasco), and Alison, introducing herself, opened the door to Nick's house and made the mistake of letting me in; something like that. When I woke up from passing out in the bathroom, Nick was sitting there, watching me. I did shout at him. I remember that much. It was the look in his eyes, the shake of his head that annoyed me. Did he think I didn't know? Didn't know what was happening to me; how far off the scale I was falling; a dead note?

That spat resulted in our You Can (finally, definitely) Fuck Off mutual agreement. As I left, I said to a bemused Alison, But you're not *Jane*? You're too fat! Then fell out the door. I'd forgotten, hadn't I? Between coming in and passing out I'd completely forgotten who she was. I have a memory like an extremely shattered mirror that I'm never going to piece together. It's only when I catch a fragment, a momentary reflection, that it comes back. Poor Alison. She wasn't fat, but I suppose I wanted to make a point about something; I don't know what, I might have to wait a long time for that revelation . . .

I don't know why Nick and Jane split up. I think she was having an affair. That's approaching thirty for you, the reassessment we all go through; perhaps it's just part of being an adult. I may have just made that bit up. Anyway, it's been three weeks since I saw Nick and I haven't heard back yet. That's not so long, is it? Hmm, yes, it is. Okay, well, I'll have to wait and accept whatever comes my way, because I had my chance, it's not up to me anymore.

I've said my hi-hi-hi's to Bandana, and sent the increasingly vacant fellow home. He still has an air of preoccupation about him. I haven't asked about it, perhaps I would have before, I don't know. I'm trying to distance myself from those days of feigned interest. I wonder if he saw my note?

That fucker. Bandana's left me with no petrol. Again. That's nearly every week he lets it run out without getting his supervisor to bring some more. Every week! *And* I remind him about it. It's not a big deal. It's just that now I have to get my supervisor to bring me some, and he's a little bit casual. He promises, but never remembers, and so I have to chase it up, and well, it's inconvenient, that's all. Not a big deal. Not really. Whatever.

That's not true. It is a big deal. I think it's because I'm still in avoiding mode. I've been avoiding people since my return to civilisation. It's difficult to explain, but some people sort of look like they want to ask me what happened; almost morbidly fascinated by my resurrection. As if now that I'm sober and sensible again, I'll want to tell them all about it. Not me. Uh-uh! Selective confession still wins!

But I still see it in their eyes. My supervisor, the Irish Fairy, the police, the locals, shop keepers, traffic wardens, bin men - they all give me the same look. Like now I'm normal again, back to the old me, we could chat as if the last few years never happened. But there's still that old curiosity, a crackling undercurrent in their eyes. You don't ask the afflicted at the time *what's happened to you*, do you? You don't remind them who they used to be when they're traumatised. Just as you wouldn't remind them how fucked they were when they're not; it's not worth it, and it's not your place. We all have our problems, but they rarely spill into the everyday. We swallow it and pretend it's all right even though it's obvious what's happening. No one really wants to know about it at the time. But afterwards, when you're over it . . . When it's easier to walk away from because it's solved. We're all interested then, aren't we?

You see, for me, I was only interested in things as they were happening. Drunks, smackheads, prostitutes, fairies - I was fascinated by the daily diet of trauma, conflict or friction. I didn't want to know about the reason, the history, the why they did it; it was irrelevant. And so it is with my former glory. I won't be sharing any information with any of these people. It's none of their business. That cycle has ended and another has begun.

Would they really want to know that I was happier being miserable? What if it was the devastation that made me feel alive? No past, no future. Only the present in glorious Technicolor (or High Definition, obviously; it's not medieval times for goodness sake). Only the present to think about. No mortgage, no debts, no responsibility, no two point four . . . Nothing. A tutor told me once, that by inhibiting myself, concentrating on one thing, I was actually freer to do my work. At the time I thought it was bollocks. But think about it. When you have all the time in the world to do whatever you want, you end up doing nothing. Limit your horizons and everything is possible. Trust me, it's true. I've seen it. Life doesn't have to be so difficult, you only have to limit your ambitions and expectations; it's easy.

I think the bins need emptying.

# 72

Bandana looked scared shitless when he came in to work today. He was somehow managing to exhibit even more nervous energy than usual. He wouldn't say, couldn't tell me what was making him so jumpy, and he seemed suspicious of any polite enquiry. Then he was barely off the phone, constantly checking, looking left and right over his shoulders; it was quite a show. I have to say that after a while my feigned interest petered out, mostly because I have a busy weekend ahead of me.

Nick texted me yesterday. A simple message that said: "Erica will call you." I didn't ask when. I simply replied with a thank you - easier that way. Losing confidence in a friendship is amazing. It's like there's no way back, and usually it's the opposite, you forgive everything; that's the unconditional contract. Ah well, it doesn't matter. I don't deserve anything else anyway. Stage one was complete and it only took three and a half weeks! How long would Erica take to make that call? Days, weeks, months, years?

Minutes. About an hour later my phone went. I was surprised because it hadn't gone off for ages. I barely recognised the ring-tone - it was still that Berlin brothel music from *Smiley's People*. I was pottering about over at _____ Square, edging, mowing and blowing, sweating in the late summer sunshine, when it vibrated in my pocket. The number came up as unknown, but as the sleazy tune sang out, my guts twisted sharply and boomed; not so unknown by DNA then.

It was a short conversation. Some polite enquiry. A slightly reluctant tone. But generally quite positive, and, this sounds funny, but there was a definite air of the adult about it. We agreed in principal to meet up for a coffee on Sunday. To have a chat, but with no promises, plans might change. I'm not really sure what that meant because I just want to apologise, have a slice of cheesecake and move on. I mean, I know it won't quite work out like that but . . .

So I think I'll hang about for another half an hour, and then make my way home. I have the rest of today and all of tomorrow to rehearse a whole load of stuff that I'll never get round to saying. If I'm clever, I won't bother. I'll just chill out and wait and see what happens when we meet up.

# 73

Shhh, shhhh, I'm waiting for Erica. She's late, of course. And I'm far too contrite to be annoyed or irritated. I'm not even thinking of texting or phoning to see where she is. Oh no, there's no fear of that. Because secretly, and not-so-secretly, I'm hoping she won't turn up. The relief I'll feel if it turns out she isn't going to come. I can feel it already, a happiness spreading all over my body, reaching the parts that other feelings can't reach. I really like this idea now, convincing myself she won't bother; saving us both the trouble.

Get this. I'm sitting on a bench in Regents Park. A park! Her sense of irony (or horror) is commendable. It's quite a nice day though, and it's strange to be sitting in a park as a civilian - not that I feel like a *professional* in the field or anything, but someone really ought to clear the leaves out of the shrubs . . .

I know it's not really warm enough today, but I really feel like buying an ice cream . . . Actually, I think I'll wait for cake at the cafe. I'm not sure why but I'm very into cake at the moment. Except carrot cake. I don't like that. Danish, cream, chocolate, anything lemony and sour; the sharper the better - I like all those sort of cakes. I don't mind doughnuts but prefer eclairs. I bought a bakewell tart the other day. It was like eating 1977 or something. Mmm, that and treacle tart. I made a bread and butter pudding last week. I left the crusts on, and it's better, lending the pudding a sweet crunchy texture to contrast with the soggy body. I might make a trifle next. One of those posh ones with mascarpone *fuck*.

Shhh, shhhh, Erica has just walked up to me, dressed sedately in skinny black jeans, a thick vintage looking dark chocolate and cream cardigan, and a fluffy autumnal scarf. Her blonde hair still quite wild, but shorter than I remember.

'Hi,' she said in a deliberately neutral tone.

'All right?' I replied, carefully.

'Where do you want to go for a coffee?'

'I'd like to go for *a* coffee in *a* cafe.'

Erica inhaled sharply, clenching her teeth and breathing out as she said, 'Where?'

I tried extra hard to sound friendly this time. 'You picked the venue, I thought you'd know somewhere?'

'The park has one,' she said, pointing vaguely in the cafe's direction.

'We'll go there then?'

'Okay.'

We walked silently to the cafe, her eyes fixed to the ground. I don't know why but I felt weirdly confident; which must have just been deflection or something. As we ordered, and I did linger at the cakes but couldn't decide which to have, we didn't really say anything, just cursory, phatic inquiries regarding the coffees. How many sugars and so on. I had a latte and Erica had a cappuccino. I was getting quite distracted by the cakes, actually. Not because they looked nice, but because they looked disgusting. Gaudy and over-decorated. I made sure I paid for the coffees, and then we carried our own to a table by the window, overlooking the park.

The latte was almost cold by the time I sat down.

Erica leant on her elbows and looked pensively into her cappuccino. 'So, how have you been?'

I thought about it first. Then I said, 'Spectacular.'

'Spectacular arsehole.'

'Supersonic arsehole, actually.'

She didn't allow herself a smile. 'So. Not drinking anymore?

'No.'

'Why?'

I laughed. 'Work/life balance?'

Erica was quiet. I thought she was trying not to laugh, but her eyes had moistened ever so slightly; and not in a happy way. She hadn't really looked at me yet, still hadn't met my eye.

'I'm sorry I took so long to contact you,' she eventually said.

'You have nothing to apologise for.'

'Perhaps I do.'

'That's not why I wanted to see you.'

'Okay.'

I breathed in, choosing my next words carefully. 'How have *you* been?'

'Good, I've been really good. Busy.'

'Painting?'

'Yes.'

'Painting what?'

'Are you interested?'

'Yes.'

'Really?'

'Really.'

Erica sat back, relaxing slightly. She cleared her throat, then seemed to change her mind about what she was going to say.

'Oh, you know, same motifs. Familiar thematic exploration. How did you put it that time?'

'Regurgitation. Nostalgic regurgitation.' I barely managed to curb a giggle.

'It's not funny.'

'What isn't?'

'Anything.'

'*Anything?*'

She finally looked at me directly, a steely eyed, unflinching assessment. 'So why now?'

'Start with the worst first?'

'I'm just the first of many, am I?'

'Not in that way. You know what I mean.'

'I don't think so.'

'Yes you do.'

She stirred her cappuccino. 'So I'm the worst?'

'Worst treated.'

'Oh, right.'

'Well, that's that sorted out . . .'

She sniffed. 'Idiot.'

I shifted in my seat. 'Look, I told Nick that I just needed to see you so I could say sorry. I just want to apologise for, well, if I say *everything*, then that's everything covered, isn't it?'

'And . . . what?'

I smiled at her, I couldn't help it. 'That's it?'

Erica picked up her teaspoon, then put it down again. 'It's a bit . . . insubstantial.'

I bit my cheek then looked at my cold latte. 'What else have you been up to?'

'What do you mean?'

'Anything else . . . anything . . . any other news, gossip?'

She sighed. 'I remember sometimes you used to be really direct. A sort of bizarre contrast to that awkward, difficult and evasive side you had. I remember you told me once that if I wanted to know something, then why didn't I just ask. It was like, whenever it was something important, you didn't want to read between the lines. I think it's because you delighted in making me lay myself bare.'

'That's a bit provocative.'

'Stop it. Don't talk to me like that.'

'Sorry.'

'I'd forgotten what it was like. Talking to you.'

'I know. I'm sorry.'

'It's been nearly three years.'

'I know.'

She turned away towards the window, her face coldly illuminated by the late afternoon sun. 'I don't want to be here. I don't want to talk to you.'

'I know. I understand.'

'I should go.'

'Yes.'

'Stop it, stop being like this.'

'Stop being like what? I don't have anything else to be like, it's just the way it is. I don't know what to ask. I don't know what to say. Everything is wrong, I can't . . .'

'Can't what?'

'I just can't.'

'Yes, you can.'

'But I don't know what to say.'

'You had plenty to say when I told you I'd leave Andrei.'

My eyes flushed. I couldn't speak for about twenty seconds. Nothing wanted to come out, and I had no control over my tongue. My brain knew what I wanted to say, but I couldn't quite form the words; because my nerve was severed. Erica knew it. She could feel my contrition, my weakness; and her confidence grew from that. It was true, I *had* forced her to lay herself bare (on several occasions), and it had been for sport, a request by my stupid id, superego or whatever.

Today, it was my turn.

Erica interrupted the silence.

'I told you I loved you, and that I'd leave Andrei.'

'You didn't tell me you were pregnant.'

'I was angry. I was angry with you. You hurt me. I told you I loved you and you just laughed. Do you know how that made me feel? Have you any idea what it took for me to say that to you? And then you just . . .' She looked away.

'And then I told you I loved you too. And then you didn't tell me you were pregnant.'

She flashed a look at me but was calm as she spoke. Not that it was rehearsed or anything, more that it was just the truth, an honesty I was unfamiliar with. 'How could I? After you fucked that life model? Do you know how that made me feel?'

'You were married, Erica. We were having an affair. And you know what my situation was. I had nothing. I still have nothing.'

'It didn't matter.'

'It mattered to me.'

'What did?' she said, annoyed, or becoming annoyed; I couldn't tell which. 'What mattered to you? The fact that you had *nothing?* Nothing at all?'

'You know what I mean.'

Erica shook her head. 'No, I don't. You need to tell me. I need to know why.'

'Why what?'

'. . . Why you didn't . . .'

'That isn't what this is about.'

'It is. I need to know. *I want to know*. You don't have a choice anymore. These are my rules, I'm in charge. You don't have the right to ask for anything other than my forgiveness after everything you put me . . . Put *us* through. And I do, I do have the right to know why you did it, why you . . .'

But Erica stopped herself from finishing that sentence, a sentence that she really needed to say and I didn't want to hear. Instead, her face blazed crimson as she stood up and walked out. I didn't move. My first instinct was to stay exactly where I was. But I forced myself to jump up and follow her outside. She was moving quickly and I had to chase her, faster than walking pace to catch up.

I touched her on the arm.

'Erica, wait. Please. Come on. I'm sorry.'

I wasn't expecting it. I mean, obviously in a way I was, but not just then. As she turned she slapped me really hard in the face, catching my eye with her finger. It really hurt, I really felt it, and my eye was really stinging. She'd slapped me before, but not like that. I was pretty shocked to be honest, and I started laughing.

'My eye! Why the *eye*, Erica?'

'You're such a faker . . .'

'No I'm not. Look, tears.'

'Fuck off.'

'Is that a general fuck off or . . .'

'What are you doing? What do you want?'

'I want to see my son. With my good eye.'

'You can't. You're not his father.'

'Yeah, I remember. Andrei's his father, you told me. But he's *my* son.'

She looked at me fiercely, swallowing a sob. 'You're too late, this is all too late.'

'Why is it, why is it too late?'

'Because you seem to think this is all about you. And it's not. This isn't just about your story. This is about my story, mine and my baby's. You didn't want to be part of it, you didn't want us. And now, now you come here expecting us to reconnect? And don't start laughing. I remember all your disconnection reconnection bullshit.'

Erica was upset now. I could tell this wasn't exactly how it was supposed to go, for either of us. It was strange, three years, all the time that had passed, and yet in some ways it was just like it had always been: tense, difficult, passionate. You can't fool genetic attraction; even time can't dull that. As she started to cry, I wanted to hold her, but I couldn't. I wanted to, but I knew she would push me away. My story wanted to believe that. Her story? I don't know. She was right. I hadn't thought about what had actually happened to her during the last three years. I assumed I knew, arrogantly reinventing her narrative to suit and embellish my own.

She stood in front of me, tightly gripping her arms.

'Erica.'

'Go away, just . . .'

'Tell me.'

She wiped her nose. 'Tell you what?'

'Tell me your story.'

# 74

Look at these leaves. That fucker hasn't done them again. Not even touched them. I don't know why I'm so irritated by Bandana these days, it's not like he's changed or anything. He's still the same as before, snorting, sniffing, whistling. Oh yes, he's taken to whistling now. No particular tune, just a noise, a phatic melody. He snorts, sniffs, clears his throat, bulges his eyes, and now finishes on a little whistle. It used to charm me in a strange way. Used to. I suppose I'm just not sedated anymore.

Unsurprisingly, Bandana wasn't clearing the leaves or even emptying the bins when I arrived at the mess room. He was sitting down, scribbling quite frenetically on the shift timetable sheet; really scoring the paper, going right through to the dirty Formica surface beneath.

'Hey,' I said, wearily.

Bandana jumped at first, but relaxed when he saw it was only me. Then he leaned forward, rocking gently as he admired his rabid mark making. 'I just sold a gun,' he said.

I put my bag down and checked the fridge for milk. 'Hmm?'

Bandana bulged his eyes, sniffed, and then cleared his throat. 'Just sold a gun. I found a gun a little while ago, can't go into it, it was for protection. And then this dude comes up to the hut this morning and he knocks and I answered. Anyway, we start talking and he says he was waiting for someone, that he has some business to attend to, and I said, joking, "Do you need a gun?" And he looked at me like a gift just dropped in his fucking lap. And he goes, "Maybe." So I said "I have a gun if he needs it, for a price." Well, I never thought the fuck would actually buy it from me. Man, he was awesome. He goes to me, "Is this the *rental* price?" Like probably because he's seen that shitty fucking *Layer Cake* or something, and I said, "No, that's the price for you to have it." I have to tell you, I needed the money, really, but I can't go into it, debts need paying. Anyway, this square says to me, "What do I do with it?" And I say, "Anything you want. It's fucking loaded so be careful." And he says, "No, what do I do with it afterwards?" and I say, "Anything you like. Throw it in the Thames, obviously." So he goes to the bank and I wasn't thinking because I'd asked for a hundred, which is too much for a dirty piece, but he wouldn't have known, would he? And I wasn't thinking because obviously he probably had a daily limit of two fifty or something. Anyway, this dude comes back, which surprised me actually, and he gave me my money, and I hand over the piece, and show him the safety and tell him never to come back here ever again. "We can never meet again" I say to him, and he goes, "We never will." But I was sort of suspicious suddenly . . . But then, as I say, I really needed the money . . .' And Bandana showed me the hundred, already crumpled up in his filthy, cut covered hand.

'Did you ask the supervisor for petrol?'

'Oh! I am so sorry! I completely forgot! I'll phone now . . .'

'I'm phoning in anyway. I'll ask.'

'Sorry.'

'It's just petrol.'

'No it isn't. I've let you down.'

'Don't worry.'

'I'm sorry.'

'It's fine. It's okay.'

No petrol today means no petrol until tomorrow. The supervisor, if we're lucky, will probably get round to dropping some off in the afternoon. And that means it will be Wednesday morning before Bandana has even bothered to pretend to do any work. I'm not that fussed really, honestly, it's true. The thing is, at this rate I'll be left with a lot of catch up to do next week; and I have a lot on my mind at the moment.

I listened to Erica's story. It wasn't that bad to be honest. People live in loveless marriages and relationships all the time. Nothing new in that. There's a lot worse to endure . . .

So I listened to Erica's story. It was surprising how easy it all seemed, the familiarity, the reconnection - three years didn't feel that long. She was different though, less feisty, not so carefree; motherhood having stolen that away from her. She told me about Andrei and how he didn't take her seriously as an artist. It made her feel worthless, she said. A trophy wife that should be grateful to be with such a high achiever. But he had taken her for granted, even before they were married. I asked her why she married him then, and she didn't really know. Love, I suppose, she said. Career choice, I thought. She couldn't fool me, she loved having the good look-ing, intelligent, charismatic husband, with his successful fingers in various pies. It made them a super-couple. She was glamorous and part of the art scene, he was published and becoming famous; it's not that difficult to understand.

At first, of course, it was *like a dream come true*. And while it was all shiny and sparkly, he seemed interested in her. But it didn't take long before his fidelity came into question and his confidence was seen as arrogance. Erica was lonely. And, she repeated this quite often, that he doesn't, that's right, *doesn't* take her seriously as an artist. I just listened. Erica was quite tearful. I think she needed someone to talk to, to get it off her chest; and who better than me, a professional in the field? *I am such a good listener.* Oh yes I am, ask any of the muggers-the murderers-the buggers-the burglars . . .

I listened for a long time actually, and I felt quite bad at some points, not guilty exactly, but close. She talked about herself, *a lot*, but I didn't mind. I liked it because she spoke to me in a normal way, like I was a human being; and it had been quite a while since that had been the case; not from her, other people.

I think the funniest part was her insistence that she had things to apologise for. I mean, *you* know how it is, but come on, she doesn't have that much to apologise for, does she? Erica regretted telling me that Andrei was the father. She had wanted to hurt me, a verbal slap that Andrei physically inflicted, you remember when, at that New Years Eve party, the one where I met Erica on the stairs - I said something, she said something, Andrei gave me a moderate beating. I didn't bother mentioning what Andrei hissed as he punched and slapped me. And I didn't get the impression she thinks he knows; but that exchange, the direct reference he spat at me . . .

All this eventually led to the boy. Erica hadn't brought any photographs with her; which I thought was pretty understandable really. She said that when he was born he had blond curly hair, but it had darkened and straightened out over the last year or so. And he's really funny apparently, with a wicked look in his eye. It was hard for her to tell me these things, which was odd, because usually parents can and will go on and on and on about their little cherubs for ages and ages and ages.

Nothing Erica had ever done or said to me before hurt as much as that conversation. As I looked at her, I imagined our boy in my arms, wriggling, laughing, his wicked eye met by my own . . . Tickling him, sitting him on my shoulders, throwing him in the air; my heart content as I held him tightly against me, knowing he's safe . . .

We ended on a hug, and I won't lie, it was a difficult moment. But we recovered and left it open, for a period of reflection, to get our heads around what it all meant.

Erica told me the boy's name, and it's nice, sort of Russian like his . . . It's nice, a good name. I like it.

# 75

Bandana didn't come in to work today. When I arrived at 13:00, all the bins were overflowing and litter was scattered everywhere. The gates were open though, in all three gardens, but none of the bins had been emptied. When I opened the hut there was no physical evidence Bandana had been in at all; recently he's been leaving a tidy pile of doodles and rantings on the table. Once, I found one with what looked like weird alien hieroglyphics on it. Another time there were all these drawings of devils and angels fucking each other. They were really badly drawn, you know, in a completely un-informed understanding of anatomy and composition sort of way.

Anyway, I wasn't happy because it meant that I might have to do the bins myself - and that would mean emptying them in front of the dwindling lunchtime lingerers. Not so many now we're into September, but some of the office folk are still popping in, grabbing the last chance to eat their ciabattas and drink their take-out cappuccinos in the cool afternoon sunshine.

So I decided to leave it. I'm not emptying bins in front of any-one. What if Turkish Delight sees me? She still comes in, her and her mate. And it would be just my luck that she'd come in as I'm getting milkshake dregs all over my work boots or something. Oh no, Turkish Delight doesn't need to see that. I call her Turkish Delight because when I first saw her she was wearing a shiny purple summer dress, her dark hair tumbling around her neck; her thick, wet, pouty lips, full of eastern promise. I quite like it when women look like cakes or confectionary . . . Does that make me sexist? Anyway, what if Turkish Delight saw me? Or Pin-up Girl. Or even Pretty But Slightly Squashed Face Girl; what if they saw me? *Emptying bins*? I'm not used to doing it. Bandana's let me down. He's upset me greatly and he's not even here.

I rang the supervisor, and he told me he'd opened up and that Bandana hadn't even bothered to phone in sick. Apparently, my boss tried to get hold of him but his phone was off. Very strange - although not altogether unsurprising considering the company Bandana keeps. That dirty, filthy, crumpled up hundred he showed me yesterday, must have burned a crack shaped hole in his heart last night.

It's going to be a slow day, I can feel it. I'm off tomorrow and Thursday, and I can't wait. I'm fed up being here now, in this job. At least it's 20:00 closing. *Love* the hours going down, just fucking love it.

That hasn't always been the case, oh no, I used to love being here, gave me somewhere to be, didn't it? A sanctuary, a disgusting, debauched, degenerate paradise. Its sallow community of reprobates gathering under the all embracing cloak of the London Planes. Me included, it turns out. I'm bored of all this now. Time for a mug of tea and a cake; only six and a half hours left to go . . .

# 76

Oh, the shit kids are in.

With just twenty minutes until closing, they've slithered in, riding their bikes and their scooters; screeching and wailing. The tinny whine of mobile telephone music penetrating the evening calm. They haven't been in for ages and ages, or I've not taken any notice - don't care which. You know, I think it's a rather good idea to close the other gardens now . . .

. . . Hmm. Well, I strolled round the other two gardens, and fortunately they were empty. It's true to say that I was actually praying the shit kids had gone by the time I returned to my best ever haven. But alas, as per usual, God must have been busy or hearing a different song, because the kids were still there, kicking a football into and at everything. I checked my watch and decided it would be in my best interests to start shepherding them out a little bit early. Oh, there'd be complaints, from them, from some blokes drinking cheap vodka partially hidden in paper bags, but so what? What's a few extra minutes early to them?

I sped past a pair of love birds sitting on a bench and said, firmly, 'Garden's closing now.' To which they looked at me with such total bemusement, I knew I'd have to tell them again on the way back, and probably have to jangle my keys at them as well. It wasn't a good start. So I strode on up to the centre gates. I gave the blokes drinking their bottles of vodka out of paper bags the thumbs up, smiling, as I told them the same thing. They laughed drunkenly but started to shift themselves. I nodded confidently to myself: at least the drunks understand plain English . . .

As I approached the shit kids, with dread in my throat and my stomach spinning and booming, they did a really weird thing. Three of them ran away. They just pegged it, ran off as fast as they could. The two remaining little cherubs, minded by Jailbait, picked up their bikes and started to walk towards the gate. Jailbait looked at me. I said, 'Garden's closing now.' She said, 'What time is it, please?' And I said, 'About three minutes to eight.' And she said, 'Thank you.' She was looking at me really closely throughout this polite exchange, and I felt strangely embarrassed. She never took her eyes off me, and I didn't know where to look.

'Are you better now?' she said, softly.

I had to think about it. I wasn't sure if I'd heard her right. 'Yes. Yes I am.'

'Is it all right if we play football in here tomorrow? If we stay up this end?'

'Yes. Yes, it's fine.'

The two with the bikes had stopped just outside the gate. Jailbait joined them, and then all three silently watched me as I locked up.

'Goodnight, Mister Park Keeper,' they said.

'Goodnight,' I replied quietly.

The drunks were gone but had left their empty vodka bottles very neatly by the bin. Good drunks. I locked the centre gates and made my way down to the love birds, reminding them that the garden was closing. They giggled, and then, not taking that much notice of me, kissed each other before strolling past me and out the last gate, hand in hand.

# 77

Bandana's left. He's never coming back. He phoned in and said he was never coming back. Never. Ever. Returning. How much notice do you have to give for a job like this? A telephone call, that's all. Just a telephone call . . .

My favourite Ratboy monkey was sitting in the hut when I came in. He'd been covering Bandana's shift for the last two days and was very agitated about the kids playing football in the garden. Oh well. He was very pleased to see me though. He shadow boxed and sparred with me, and I had to hit him quite hard on the arm to get him to stop. Now I remember why I was so disappointed when I didn't have to work with him any more. Luckily, after I gave him his dead arm to go along with his dead head, he went off to his own garden for his own shift. He was counting the money - two and a half extra days buys a lot of Mars bars and Coca Cola . . .

It's cold today, and quiet. The garden's pretty much empty. Except for Mister Physicist. Do you know what, I've seen him nearly every day since that first time down _____ Square. Everywhere I go he's there, sitting in one of the gardens; sitting outside one of the pubs; or just wandering the streets. Mister Physicist doesn't seem to be doing much physicisting. Every time I see him I mutter under my breath, Misssster Physicist. Like that. Misssster Physicist. I don't care if he hears me or not, in fact, I hope he has. I hope it throws some sort of random variable into his calculations - although if I say it every time then it's not so random, actually it's . . . and . . . well . . .

I had a quiet Wednesday off. Yeah, didn't really get up to much. Pottered about. Did the shopping. Bought some cake. Kicked my heels. Sat around. Went to bed early; that sort of thing.

Then Erica phoned me yesterday. I'd just finished my lunch. A crumbed ham and watercress sandwich on brown bread, with organic mayonnaise, thickly sliced vine tomato, and seasoned with cracked black pepper and sea salt. I was reading the paper when she phoned, and it was a brief conversation. I didn't say much. I just had to listen and abide by her rules. They weren't really rules, more like casual requests . . . Anyway, I'm meeting Erica on Monday after work in Hyde Park, near the water fountains on the Bayswater Road side. I finish at 14:30 and I'm meeting them, yes, *them*, at 15:00. It's just around the corner, so I'll be there in plenty of time. It's literally just a few minutes walk away.

# 78

Look at the time. I love it when night falls and the evenings draw in, the garden ninja silent. It's easy this time of year to kick people out. They don't want to argue. It's cold and it's dark; and we're all afraid of the dark, aren't we? There are lamps at the top of each of the four gates in my best ever shadowy paradise. These lamps are designed to provide a point of comfort on your way out, a feeling of security for the night ahead. If they worked. Oh yes, of the four just one works, one of the two centre lamps . . . The streetlights that surround the garden provide only cursory illumination. If I were a child, the shadows cast by the Mahonias would scare me as they rustled and shook in the breeze; a sinister phalanx of razor-sharp moonlit sentries.

I haven't done much pruning this year. It's quite overgrown at the far end of the garden, the east end. It's not as bad as it was, but sometimes the kids or the prostitutes or the smackheads still sit there, vacantly staring down at the hole where their hearts should be. It's an enclosed space, a blind spot from the busy streets and the police. I only go down there to close up. I always leave the bins until the safety of the morning. There's no other reason to go down that end. Just open, and then close.

I feel quite relaxed. Strangely content. I thought I'd be more nervous about Monday but I'm not. I've waited all this time, all these years, knowing in my heart of hearts the truth about Erica. How I felt about her then. How I feel about her now. And then there's the boy . . .

It's time to close up.

# 79

The other gardens were empty and virtually litter free, but look at this, I can see loads of rubbish around the benches as I wander up to the east end of my favourite garden. Fuck it, I'll tidy it up in the morning. Oh wait, someone's sitting on one of the benches. Just get this geezer out, lock the other gates, and I'm done.

'Garden's closing now, mate. If you'd like to make your way.'

'What?'

'Garden's closing now. If you would like to start making your way, thank you.'

'What time does it shut?'

'Right now. I'm closing right now. This gate first and then the others. So if you'd like to start making your way.'

'What time does it shut?'

'Right now. I'm closing right now.'

'Yeah, I heard you. And what time does it shut?'

'Right now,' I repeated, tossing a couple of empty beer cans in a bin as the geezer eventually rose to his feet.

'You don't recognise me?' he said, quietly.

'No,' I replied, not looking at him. 'And I've been here nearly all day and you just need to leave, because the garden is closing now, thank you.'

'Is the front gate still open?'

I sighed. 'Yes. Yes it is.'

'I'll go out that way then.'

'Fine.'

I marched down and locked the centre gates. Then I stood by the front gate, waiting. My new best ever friend ambled along, ignoring me as I jangled the chain, taking his time. These fucking new media new middle class types.

He paused by the hut.

'Do you live here?'

'No. Garden's shut, mate. I need to go home.'

'To your wife?'

'Sorry?'

'Are you in a rush? To get home to your wife?'

'What's it got to do with you?'

'Just a question.'

'Uh-huh. I need to close up.' I couldn't see his face, it was obscured by the shadow falling from the Indian Horse Chestnut.

'Close it,' he said.

'Sorry?'

'Close it.'

'I'm not allowed to lock people in. You just need to leave.' And I shrugged my shoulders, hands out, as close to a *please* as I felt inclined to offer.

'No. We need to have a chat.'

A car passed and its headlights flashed across the hut and over my new best fiend's face. I turned and locked the gate.

'Recognise me now?' he said.

# 80

The hut has two chairs. One by the table (my throne), and another next to the electric radiator, sort of just in front of the sink unit. I don't get many visitors. Don't really invite guests round.

Andrei sat quietly, assessing his surroundings. He seemed quite interested in it - the certificates of excellence for showing a pride in London by the cultivation of flowers and shrubs; the police information cards; pictures of dancers. I waited. Or rather, he was making me wait. So I didn't bother offering a mug of tea or anything; I had no reason to be that accommodating.

Andrei had changed. The last time I saw him he had a dark mop of shiny hair, a grown up art scene style. Now he had a kind of trendy crew cut. His hair was specked with grey, and his hair-line was quite receded. Oh, he still had his sharp features, but they were partly hidden by a pair of expensive looking charcoal half rim glasses with no branding on the sides; probably a pair of Alain Mikli or something. He was wearing a sort of posh donkey jacket and a pair of sharp black trousers. He seemed quite relaxed, thoughtful and calm. But he never directly looked at me as he eyed the wooden, cobwebbed interior; glancing beyond, to the side, at the dirty floor.

After a while, perhaps twenty minutes or so, I cleared my throat, about to say something. But I stopped. I didn't really know what to say. All I knew was that when the conversation started, there was a good chance it would be difficult. Yeah. So I waited for Andrei to begin.

And eventually, he looked up at me.

'I like your hut,' he smiled.

'Thanks.'

'I popped by the other day, but you weren't in.'

'That's a shame.'

Andrei paused, then said, 'Yeah, it was. Are those your certificates of excellence?'

'No.'

'No, they wouldn't be would they. I wonder what level of excellence you need to achieve to work in a job like this?'

'You'd be surprised how difficult opening and closing a gate is. Look at tonight. Look at the people skills one needs.'

'Yeah, I noticed. Very professional.' Andrei snorted and let out a quiet laugh. 'Did Erica ever come here?'

'No.'

'She's missed out. It's lovely.'

Casually, I said, 'How did you know where I was?'

Casually, he replied, 'There's this modern invention called the internet. I put your name in, and eventually there was a link to your company and a list of gardens. Your name was on that list. It was a different garden, dated from a few years ago, but it was a starting point.'

'Well done, Sherlock.'

'I couldn't exactly ask Erica, could I?'

'I don't know. Couldn't you?'

Exhaling, he said, 'No. No I couldn't. Not at all.'

'So, Andrei. What do you want?'

'I don't know. I'm not sure. What do you want? What is it *you* want?'

'I think you'll find I asked first.'

'I think you'll find I answered.'

'That's not an answer. That's deflection.'

'Yeah, you're right, it is.'

For some reason I straightened out my combats. 'Well, as much as I've enjoyed our little chat, if you have nothing else to say . . .'

'You see,' he said sharply, 'that's the thing. I think it's more about

240

what you have to say. If *you* have anything else to say. To me.'

I pretended to think for a second. 'No, I don't think I do.'

'How much do you get paid? For a job like this?'

'Oh, I get paid in love, Andrei.'

'Can't be much. Unskilled labour. Low maintenance, low pay. Bread line. Barely enough to live on I'd guess. Even for a single man living on his own in a derelict or something.'

'What's your point?'

'You know what I'm getting at.'

'I don't know what you're getting at. Perhaps you should just tell me.'

Andrei paused, stuck his tongue in his cheek, then said nonchalantly, 'I saw you on Sunday.'

'Where?'

'Where do you think?'

I shook my head. 'I don't know.'

'With Erica. In Regents Park.'

'You followed her?'

He nodded. 'Yeah.'

I scratched my chin, thinking it through. 'I see.'

'I wonder if you really do?'

'This exchange is nearly as tedious as one of your novels, Andrei.'

Andrei pulled his jacket tight, folded his arms and leant back. 'Which one?'

'Any of them, they're all the same.'

He gave me a wry smile. 'You're right.'

'Did I mention the I need to go home bit?' I said, sort of shaking my thumb behind me.

Andrei sat forward, looking at the floor. He rubbed his head, pulled his nose, then scratched his ear. 'She'd been agitated for a few weeks. Distant. More distant than usual. I couldn't quite put my finger on it. She was distracted. Not working, not even going to her studio. Nothing. I didn't ask her what the problem was, you know how it is, that creative blank we all go through - I put it down to that. Oh wait, I'm sorry, I forgot. You're retired, aren't you? Well anyway, I wasn't overly worried about it, and to be honest, the way it works between us these days . . .'

'You're rambling, Andrei.'

'Yeah, I suppose I am.'

'If you just said what you actually wanted to say . . .'

He glared at me. 'You're right, you're so right. I didn't think I'd find it so difficult, so hard to just . . . I don't think I realised how important all this was to me until now. With you sitting there, me sitting here.'

'What's your point?'

'The point is, I knew you wouldn't just stay away. Stay out of our lives.'

'It was just coffee, Andrei.'

He spoke quietly. 'It wasn't just fucking coffee.'

'You're right. It was a latte.'

'Was it good?'

'I've had worse.'

'The latte, I mean.'

'That's just lazy.'

'Really.'

'You may have lost your hair but you haven't lost your sense of humour, Andrei. Unfortunately, it's misplaced on this occasion.'

'Oh? So it's not a laughing matter? Suddenly no place for jokes? That's unlike you.'

I shrugged. 'Fair enough.'

Andrei chewed his lip, distracted by his own train of thought. 'We'd been having difficulties, I admit it. But things had evened out. It was better. We started liking each other again. Loving each other again. I'm sure of it.'

'Is this leading somewhere or are you just trying to bore me to death?'

'I thought something had been going on, but it didn't matter, it was quid pro quo. I'm not that jealous. I'm not a jealous man. We'd had our problems, and I'm no saint, I've fucked other women. But it was only that, just fucking. An ego trip. It was a way of feeling invincible. Testing emotions and testing things out. Even so, I suppose I did deliberately upset her at times, trying to provoke her. I suppose I wanted to feel something . . . I was trying to get her to tell me, to tell me she was fucking someone else, and she never did. I just wanted that *knowledge*. And she kept her secret, she never told me. But it wasn't the only secret she had, was it?'

242

'. . .'

'Don't look at me like that. Do you really think that fucking idiot could keep his mouth shut? You probably know better than I do that she has a soft spot for him, like a brother or something. I fucking hate the talentless cunt.'

I took a deep breath. 'Do you want a cup of tea?'

Ignoring that, he carried on. 'So then I knew about you and Erica, of course I did. And she'd been good, so careful, I never ever smelt you on her. She was surprisingly adept in that deception too.'

'Andrei . . .'

'Stop using my name.'

'. . . Okay.'

'I didn't care what she'd been doing. That she'd been fucking you. I couldn't really blame her for looking for something else. I mean, I could but . . . The problem was later. Afterwards. I can't explain it. I was happy. I was happy to be a *family*. I'd had my troubles, if you know what I mean, that modern masculine malaise - a shallow pool.' He laughed. 'A family. I loved that idea. And then later . . . At first I ignored what was blindingly obvious. I didn't want to consider anything other than the fact that I had a family now. But then Simon couldn't keep his fucking mouth shut. The thinly disguised references. Oh doesn't he look like his father, he'd say, and Erica's eyes would burn right through him and he'd giggle, apologising. But it was like they were celebrating it, celebrating their lies.' Andrei sniffed, and then was quiet.

I waited. I'm good at listening. And waiting.

He pointed at me, shaking his finger, speaking in a low voice. 'She's happy. Yeah, this week, since Sunday, she's been happy. She saw you, and it made her *happy*. Look at you, look at all of this.' He shook his head, not believing it.

'Andr . . . Listen, I just wanted to . . .'

Andrei took his glasses off, put them carefully into a case, and then put the case into his pocket, tapping it afterwards. 'If Erica had . . . If she'd just told me that she'd met up with you, then that would have been all right. I wouldn't have liked it, but it would have been okay.'

I sighed, not out of boredom but out of sympathy. Really.

I said, 'Look, what happened between me and Erica, it was a long time ago. A lifetime ago. Things have changed. I've changed . . . It's . . .'

Andrei's eyes blackened suddenly, and a wetness washed over them. 'I asked her where she'd been,' he said. 'I asked her what she'd been up to, and she laughed and gave me the coldest kiss. A *perfunctory* kiss. Do you know what that means?'

'Yes.'

He narrowed his eyes. 'Not just what the word means.'

'I know what you're talking about.'

'I hadn't felt that kiss for years, but I recognised it straight away. Do you know what she did later? I watched her sit and look at our son, stroking his face as he slept. She's done it before, a million times, but this time . . . This time it was whole. Do you know what I mean? It was *whole*.'

'. . .'

'I knew one day you'd come back. You'd come back and she'd want you. I knew that.'

Blinking, I said, 'I . . . I'm not sure that's true. And it's not just about her.'

Andrei nodded quickly. 'My boy.'

'Andrei . . .'

He was very calm as he said this. 'You fucked my wife, but you can't have my boy.'

I frowned. 'I haven't said . . .'

'You've said enough.'

'I haven't said anything.'

He nodded his head. 'You're right. Not words. Actions. You fucked my wife, but you can't have my boy.'

'Yeah,' I sighed, slightly irritated. 'You've already said that.'

Ignoring me, he continued, 'Actually, you can *have* my wife. But you can't have my boy . . .'

'Andrei . . .'

'Do you know what this means?'

'I don't know. Surprise me. What does it mean?'

He shrugged. 'It means *the end*.'

Tired, I stood up and walked towards the mess room door. I looked out at the Indian Horse Chestnut, leaned against the door frame and shook my head. The end. What a drama queen. There's no such thing as the end. There's always tomorrow. It doesn't matter what happens today. There's always another fucking drama just around the corner. I let out a deep breath. The trees were swaying and the leaves were falling like snow. That never ends either. Every. Single. Day is exactly the same. The end? What an idiot. I turned to Andrei and

I was laughing so much, so hard, that at first I didn't realise. There was a noise, a sound like wind whistling through a tunnel. Then I realised it wasn't a sound at all, it was a feeling - Andrei had shot me, in the stomach, like Van Gogh or something. I didn't fall backwards, but I did waver.

When I turned and saw him holding that gun, well, he looked *so serious*. It was so funny I nearly choked laughing. He was talking at me and giving me this look, like, "Now you'll take me seriously!" No. Now I *won't* take you seriously! Oh, how I roared, how I bellowed. My eyes full of tears, unable to restrain myself - the gun, the shallow pool, firing blanks; the absurdity of it all.

But then I stopped laughing.

I looked carefully at Andrei, surprised by him, his conviction. What the fuck was he doing with a gun? Where'd he get it? I could probably have got him a better deal from Bandana if only he'd asked . . .

Andrei looked shocked. I don't think he thought it would be like this, I mean, I was silent, silent like a ninja. He grabbed my collar, screaming something right in my face, and if I could have I would have giggled, but I was feeling a bit faint. He pushed me, yeah, that's right, actually pushed me! And I fell into the shrubs beside the Indian Horse Chestnut. I swallowed hard and blinked. That night sky, the London smog, I don't know, it was like seeing it for the first time despite the fact that it was close to the last.

The sky was so dark, almost black, like a crimson and viridian mix; pulsing, throbbing, and so, so vibrant. I'm not sure, but I think I heard Andrei yelp; and then he stormed off, jumping over the railings. The idiot even caught his trouser leg on one of the spikes and nearly fell. He was in a hurry all right.

Me? No hurry. I can't explain why but . . . having the chance to reflect . . . My life didn't really flash before my eyes. It was more like on a carousel, like a slide show. Me at three, happy on a seaside holiday with my mum and dad. Me at fourteen, smiling, having just lost my virginity with the seventeen year old girlfriend of a cousin at a wedding. Me at twenty, at art college, depressed and sad; but serious and committed. Probably the last time I was actually really committed to anything . . .

And now, here I am at thirty seven, lying under the Indian Horse Chestnut, imagining my son in my arms, his wicked eye meeting my own . . . Tickling him, throwing him in the air, sitting him on my shoulders. My heart content as I hold him tightly against me.

Knowing he's safe.

## The End